FRAGMENTS OF THE HEART

By Ally McGuire

2023

BUTTERWORTH BOOKS

Butterworth Books is a different breed of publishing house. It's a home for Indies, for independent authors who take great pride in their work and produce top quality books for readers who deserve the best. Professional editing, professional cover design, professional proof reading, professional book production—you get the idea. As Individual as the Indie authors we're proud to work with, we're Butterworths and we're *different*.

Authors currently publishing with us:

E.V. Bancroft
Valden Bush
Addison M Conley
Jo Fletcher
Helena Harte
Lee Haven
Karen Klyne
AJ Mason
Ally McGuire
James Merrick
Robyn Nyx
Simon Smalley
Brey Willows

For more information visit www.butterworthbooks.co.uk

CATALOGING INFORMATION
ISBN: 978-1-915009-48-7
CREDITS
Editor: Nicci Robinson
Cover Design: Nicci Robinson
Production Design: Global Wordsmiths

Acknowledgements

A book is a team effort, and I'm so grateful to have a great team around me. Nicci Robinson, my editor; you are always so great at pointing out the things that create a better story. Thank you for your patience and guidance. Margaret Burris, my proofreader, has such an amazing eye for the little things that can make or break a book. And to each and every ARC reader, thank you for taking the time to read and review. It makes all the difference to my nerves when a book is about to come out. And to the readers who take this heart's journey and always look for a happy ending? I see you.

Dedication

To my wife,
who would always take the leap with me.

CHAPTER ONE

THERE WAS NOTHING QUITE as sensual as tropical heat. As Kelly Pierce wiped the sweat from her brow, she grinned at Marta, the short, sturdy bar worker who'd provided more than enough heat of her own. Brazil had its fair share of women loving women, even though they moved in more clandestine circles. For Kelly, that only added to the allure. Hot, sweaty sex in dark alleys or in the backs of work vehicles transporting artifacts always made these trips even better.

Marta tilted her head toward the stairs, the question clear in her eyes, and Kelly held up her finger when her phone rang.

"Unfuckingbelievable." Jack's exuberance could probably be heard in lower parts of South America. "You fucking found it."

Kelly sipped her beer and relaxed in the chair with one leg slightly shorter than the rest. She liked the imbalance and sat there every night. Flaws were always more interesting than perfection. "So you won't be firing me then?"

"I'd ask you to marry me just so I could bask in your brilliance if your British sarcasm wouldn't flay me alive within twenty minutes." Jack Franklin, director of the British National Archaeological Society, sounded very much like he might drop to his knees in front of her.

"I still don't understand why they chose an American for your job. Surely someone with more understanding of what actual history is should be in the post?"

"Fuck off. The finds you've made are going to make you the star of the convention in the spring. What the hell made you move the dig twenty miles north?"

Kelly inhaled the smell of barbacoa and waved at a few colleagues who entered, all of them clearly still high on the success of the dig. They made their way to the bar, and she nodded again at Marta, who was clearly still waiting for Kelly's attention. But she served the newcomers with the same friendly flare she served everyone.

"That's where the anthropology part of my specialty comes in, Jack. I *talked* to people. Remember what that's like?" She laughed when he grunted. "I spent some time with the local tribes, and we got around to discussing ruins buried in the forest. We spent all that time looking for something along a shoreline that wasn't a shoreline five hundred years ago. A couple of locals showed me the ruins, and I knew that's what we'd been looking for. So I went back and moved the dig crew."

"Well, it's fucking genius that you did. Funding for it will last a full two years, so hopefully we'll build on what you found." He cleared his throat. "I know you like to have some time off between digs..."

She sighed. "I don't *like* to have time off. I need it. I miss my flat in London and good tea. What do you want?"

"It's the data set you've submitted. It's enormous, Kelly, and without context, it isn't going to make a lot of sense." His tone grew cautious, meaning he knew he was in for an argument.

"Every single piece is geotagged. What do you mean, there's no context?" She looked at Marta, who leaned on the bar, her well-defined muscles pushing at the sleeves of her white T-shirt. Kelly should just hang up and go enjoy what Marta had on offer.

"I want you to sit with the Descriptive Statistics Officer who will be cataloging everything."

Kelly held the phone away from her and frowned at it like it had turned into something strange, like a courgette. "Why is someone in America cataloging British finds from a dig in Brazil?"

"Because she's known for being the best at what she does. She's fast, intelligent, and runs a team capable of handling the workload you've deposited in our laps."

Kelly drained the rest of her beer and held the bottle up toward Marta, who gave a brief nod. "And you're telling me we don't have capable, intelligent teams in the UK? Where we understand archeology in a way the Americans never will? That's absurd."

"Obviously we have capable people here, and I'm going to ignore you harping on about Americans and our pitfalls. The issue is workload. The drought—"

Kelly huffed. "The drought showed up thousands of sites we didn't even know were there. I'm aware."

"Then you're also aware that our teams here are stretched to capacity as they try to get to every site possible before it disappears again, and all that data means the numbers nerds are buried and wouldn't get to your data batch for at least a few years, which may affect future funding bids. Please?"

She hated when Jack was nice. He was much easier to say no to when he was being a wanker. "DC or New York?" At least she could have some fun with hot city women.

He hesitated. "Oklahoma."

She hung up.

Marta touched the ice-cold beer bottle to her temple and drew it down along her jaw. "All good?"

Kelly stood and took the bottle, then grasped Marta's hand. "It will be." She led them upstairs and put Okla-bloody-homa out of her mind. Tonight was about seeing how much stamina Marta had and how many positions they could test it in. Tomorrow, she'd deal with the future before she immersed herself in the past.

***

Kelly stretched and breathed in the already humid morning air. Monkeys swung from the tree tops, silent shadows watching the slow, carefully moving humans below them. They always made Kelly vaguely uncomfortable, with their knowing eyes and human-like behavior. Like she was being judged and found wanting.

"Kel!"

She turned and jumped lightly into the fifty-foot rectangle dug four feet into the earth. She moved carefully around huge tree roots, watching closely in case one turned out not to be a tree root but rather a snake of a size more suited to prehistoric times than modern Brazil. But then, this part of the rainforest was damn near prehistoric. Hence, the remains of the settlement long thought to be a fairy tale in most corners of academia.

She knelt next to Antonio and looked at the arrowhead in his hands. It was yet another piece of the area's history slowly revealing itself. If she had to guess, she'd say that the tribes still in existence were distant relations of the neolithic people who'd once inhabited this densely forested paradise. She squeezed his shoulder and watched as he photographed it in the place where he'd found it, including the geotag and number so it could be added to the catalogue.

As she made her way around the rest of the site, much of which still had to be excavated, she thought about Jack's request. There were few things she hated more than statistics. Cauliflower, which looked too much like little wasted brains, and tofu, which was a lot like eating emaciated sponges, were top of the list. Then came statistics and statisticians. Dry and drier.

But...Jack didn't ask for much, and he cut her a hell of a lot of slack when it came to her digs. And somehow, he'd managed to find money for expeditions that wouldn't have stood a cat in hell's chance of getting funding from any other agency. He didn't say it, but she owed him.

The rest of the day went the same as the other days had gone. The team found artifact after artifact, and they laid them out on long tarps under huge awnings while others worked on digging out the remains of buildings, hacking away at the jungle that had consumed them. At the end of the day, members from all three of the local tribes came to see what had been found, and over cups of beer they discussed the use and possible nature of the more obscure findings, and their knowledge proved invaluable when there were things Kelly and her crew would have known nothing about, knowledge passed on through generations.

Before the sun went down, she headed to her trailer. They'd learned quickly that the night prowlers weren't to be messed with here, and most of the team retired before dark. The eerie cries of the danger cats mixed with other night animals who sang a song of death for anything too weak to fight back. She dreamed of a woman who moved with stealth and blended in with the colors of the forest, a woman who drew her in and kept her from leaving, but she went willingly, knowing there was nothing behind her worth holding onto.

The next morning, pushing aside the strange and slightly disturbing dream, she took a Jeep and went into the city. Once she was at the bar, she took her usual place and called Jack. It was lunchtime there, but Jack was obsessively attached to his phone and would answer, day or night, meal time or no. It was a fixation she couldn't understand and didn't want to. Her digs often took her to places left behind by modernity, where she had no signal of any kind. She liked it that way. She could immerse herself in the world without people expecting her to give up her time and energy for the mundane.

"'Lo?" Jack mumbled around what was likely something unhealthy.

"I'll go to Oklahoma, though I'm not even certain where that is. Isn't it called the dirt canteen or something?"

He burped. "Dust bowl. And that was during a drought a hundred years ago. It's actually quite green now. Nice people. Neighborly."

"Nosy and bothersome, you mean." She tapped at the scratched, worn table, remembering a night she and Marta had enjoyed using it in an entirely different way once the crowds had gone. "How long are you thinking I'll be there?"

"As long as it takes for the stats person to feel like they've got a handle on the data, so they can begin to do what they do with it." He burped again, this time accompanied by a gurgling sound. "I appreciate it, Kel. The government is really on our ass about international cooperation, given the way our digs cross borders and we're moving artifacts around."

"Yeah, I get it. I'm not doing it for them though. I'm doing it because you'll be a pain in my arse if I don't, and I need you to be the money guy who makes me look good." She wouldn't, of course, tell him that she appreciated everything he did. He could read between the lines if he wanted to.

"Always good to know you love me the way I love you. If only I could find a woman to warm the cockles of my heart the way you do." He laughed at his joke.

"I shan't be warming the cockles of your anything. Go back to eating your slop."

She hung up and looked at the worn, scarred wood of the old beams. Places like this fed her soul. Real people living real lives in places that whispered their histories through the people who passed through them. Leaving this for Midwest America left her feeling hollow.

With a sigh she pushed away from the table. She'd do what was necessary. She always did. People were examples of their culture, and she'd find the same thing in middle America. And then it would be off to the next dig in the next country. For now, she'd drink in all Brazil had left to give and make it part of her. She was nothing if not a compilation of the places she'd been and the people she'd enjoyed. Occasionally, she wondered who she'd be if it weren't for that, but she pushed that thought aside. Life was for what next, not what if.

CHAPTER TWO

"I WISH YOU WOULDN'T do that. You know how it irritates me." Shawn Scott nudged the dirty workout shoes with the crumpled socks stuffed into them off their sides and under the desk opposite. "And not wearing shoes at work is unprofessional."

In response, Bree propped her feet on her desk and wiggled her brightly painted toes. "And you know how much I long to be a professional who is taken seriously in our oh-so-serious environment."

Shawn gave a last look at the shoes, which weren't lined up properly but were nearly out of sight enough for her to ignore them, and turned back to her computer. "You're a heathen more suited to the stage than to statistics."

"And you're a crotchety ninety-year-old stuck in a thirty-something year old body that should really be put to better use, given how much time you spend on it. We all have our shit."

Shawn flinched at the language, which she knew Bree enjoyed using mostly just to get under her skin, but also because swearing was second nature to her. "My body is used exactly the way it should be, thank you. I keep it healthy and strong, so I'm fit and well in my old age."

Bree popped open a soda and wiggled her eyebrows. "What good is living to an old age if you're so busy worrying about everything that you don't really live?"

Shawn shook her head, irritation rising. "That socially constructed notion is nonsense. I don't have to take risks or be loose with my health in order to have a full life." She'd never understood the need for external validation or the desire for groups of friends who drank to excess and shared dramatic stories of heartbreak and ambition. It required too much energy and far too much interpersonal contact.

"Okay, grouchy. We're a little sensitive today, aren't we?" Bree took her feet from the desk and craned to look at Shawn's computer. "What has your panties in a twist?"

Shawn frowned. "I don't wear panties. And what I'm wearing isn't twisted." She rubbed her hand over the back of her head, a nervous habit she'd never been able to shed. Hair sifted through her fingers, a reminder that she needed to get it cut tomorrow, when the only stylist she trusted would be on duty. She hated when it touched her collar. "We got a request from the UK. A British-funded dig in Brazil—"

"The Pedra Furada dig?" Bree's eyes widened.

"Why do you insist on interrupting me?" Shawn ignored Bree's eye roll. "Yes, the Pedra Furada dig. They've uncovered nearly fifty new sites aside from the eight hundred already found and have brought in dig teams from all over South America and Europe. The amount of data they've already sent in is immense and because the UK is currently stretched, they've requested our help to get the data entered as quickly as possible for funding reasons. Brazil itself doesn't have the computational technology to get through it the way we do." She didn't mind the bit of pride that seeped into her voice. She'd worked darn hard to build the team she directed, and the fact that it had an international reputation meant she'd succeeded in her desire to be the best. Of course, you were only the best if you kept succeeding, so she couldn't allow their standards to slip even one iota.

Bree turned to her computer and brought up the work schedule, then clicked on the Furada file. Images flew past as she scanned them, and Shawn knew her photographic memory would be processing the information as quickly as a computer.

Bree practically vibrated with excitement as she exclaimed over the beauty of this item or that one. "How amazing to be part of something like that. Can you imagine? Digging in the dirt or exploring caves and finding stories from an ancient culture?"

"You'd have to be willing to fly. And get dirty." Shawn knew she'd hit a button when Bree didn't respond, but she didn't apologize. Sometimes the only way to get Bree to focus was to remind her of the foibles that kept her from engaging in the world the way she said she wanted to but never did.

They worked in silence until break time, and Shawn pulled her lunch from the bottom drawer of her desk. Fortunately, the salad section hadn't moved over onto the fruit the way it had yesterday. Each part of her meal was perfectly compartmentalized in its own little square, and it gave her mild satisfaction that each flavor would be its own.

Bree stood and stretched, then picked up her patchwork design purse. "I'm eating downstairs with a few people from research, if you want to come along."

Shawn glanced up from her tomato sandwich. "Thanks for the offer."

Bree gave her a quick smile, slid on sandals and left, leaving the door cracked slightly per Shawn's desire. She hated closed doors and not knowing what was happening on the other side of them. It was the one thing Bree never teased her about.

Her phone rang, and she waited until the second ring to answer. "Shawn Scott."

"Hello, Ms. Scott." Carolyn Peter's voice was melodic and husky, a good quality for someone running a serious institution.

"Ms. Peter. How can I help you?" Shawn ignored the flutter of embarrassment and desire that always came over her when talking to Carolyn. It used to be far worse, but she'd managed to put their brief and awkward fling behind her. Mostly.

"Have you read the email regarding the Pedra Furada dig data?"

She had, of course. She always read every email the moment it came in and tried to respond to them as quickly as possible. "I did."

"You didn't reply?"

Shawn scanned the email. "It didn't require one. There was plenty of information along with the request from the UK. No questions were asked so I didn't feel the need to respond." She hesitated. "Should I have done so?"

Carolyn paused for only a second. "You're right. It was an oversight on my part. I should have included something to the effect asking if you'd be willing to take on this particular project, given the turnover parameters."

Shawn waited.

"That's the question, Shawn. Are you willing to take on this project and do it in the time table requested, so they can maintain their funding?"

"We can do that, yes." Relieved that the question had been clearly stated, Shawn could now engage. "Are they looking for pure statistics or descriptive modeling based on the statistics?"

"Good. I'm glad you feel you're able to handle it. And they've been specific about needing descriptive modeling." Carolyn's hesitation was longer this time. "Shawn, there's an extra element to this project which is unusual, but we feel it's necessary. The director at the dig site will be joining you and your team to—"

Shawn felt a little dread begin to rise. "We don't need any outside influence." She winced. "Sorry for interrupting. But that would color our findings."

"In this case, Shawn, we need you to be flexible. She's an anthropological archeologist, so her input would be invaluable with regard to your descriptive findings, as it *is* descriptive findings we're after."

Shawn wasn't sure how to respond. Gut instinct told her to fight it, to stick to her guns and say no one should interfere with their analysis of the statistics. But she had a feeling Carolyn wasn't asking so much as politely letting her know what was going to happen. And surely with a background like that, the person in charge would understand the brevity and logic necessary when compiling the data. Perhaps, then, it would be okay.

"When is this person arriving?"

"She'll be here next week." The relief in Carolyn's voice was obvious. "I understand she's the one responsible for finding the new dig site, which was long thought to be a myth. I imagine you'll have plenty to talk about."

Somehow, Shawn doubted that. She rarely had much to talk to anyone about, as she rarely understood their need for undeserved validation or their desire to talk about things without meaning.

"So..." Carolyn said and once again seemed to hesitate. "Have you had any more luck with the dating site?"

Shawn sighed. This lack of division between work and personal information was part of why she and Carolyn hadn't worked out. One of the many reasons, really. "The last time I went online, someone connected with me, and I had hope until she called herself a Swifty and started talking about a concert she'd been to where everyone had erupted into song. I don't know what a Swifty is, nor do I think a hundred people without pitch would be a good time."

Carolyn laughed, and it made Shawn smile a little. She was fully aware of how awkward and offbeat she was with the rest of the world, and Carolyn understood that, even if they didn't have a romantic connection.

"No, I can't imagine you'd like that at all. There's someone out there for both of us. We'll find them eventually." There was genuine hope in her tone.

"I'm perfectly at home with my cat. No one moves my things or insists on watching or doing things that bore me, and I don't have to consider anyone else when I want to spend the night reading a research article or discussing policy with people in other countries." Although it was true, Shawn knew how it sounded to someone who was desperate to find their soulmate and who regularly wanted to go out with friends.

"Okay, well, there's someone out there for me then." Carolyn's smile was obvious in her voice. "I'll email further details about our guest when I have them."

The conversation clearly over, Shawn hung up without saying anything else. The social niceties reserved for life weren't necessary in her brief discussions on the job. They took up time better used for work.

She didn't look up from her notes when Bree came in, her usual buoyancy back in place. Shawn plugged in numbers from items found at an archeological dig in Egypt, taking the time to note the similarities and differences found in nearby sites, and made notes according to those numbers, including what the lifestyle had likely been like, what they'd likely eaten, and the average lifespan of a society with those elements at play. The developing picture was interesting as it related to the neighboring site, which seemed more rudimentary in its progression.

Bree picked up one of Shawn's perfectly placed pencils and drummed it on the desk, startling her from her focus. She plucked the pencil from Bree's fingertips and put it back in line with the others.

"It's five-thirty. I'm going home." There were smudges under Bree's eyes, and she blinked hard behind her big glasses.

"Are you okay?" Shawn asked, looking her over.

"Just tired. Staring at a screen all day is starting to give me a headache. I probably need to get my prescription checked." She tapped at her glasses. "See you tomorrow."

Shawn nodded and leaned back to stretch. Hours had flown past with her hunched over the desk, and she could feel it in her muscles. Following Bree's lead, she shut down her computer and gathered her things into the correct pouches of her backpack, and then headed out. The building was already mostly empty, which made sense. Few people felt the need to work past five on a Friday night, or any night, really. She got into her electric SUV and checked the power. There was plenty for her purposes.

She headed to the gym and was relieved at how few cars

were in the parking lot. No one liked to work out on a Friday night either. That was a particular relief in the locker room. Her short hair, compact body, and strong jawline often meant that she was mistaken for a guy, and she'd had no end of disgruntled and shocked looks from women who thought there was a man in the locker room. Like a guy wouldn't know he was in the wrong place. The connection between short hair and masculinity was a sociological phenomenon she greatly disliked.

She pushed the oft-considered issue away and went into the cardio area. She'd start with the rowing machine, and then move on to the treadmill before she hit the weights. As she rowed, she thought of her conversations throughout the day and became more restless. No, she wasn't what people considered normal. No, she didn't have the social graces that most other people learned from birth. But she was damn good at her job, and she was someone who would always be honest with people. Granted, that could be part of the problem.

She moved to the treadmill. *Why can't anyone like me for who I am?* She cranked up the speed and ran faster and harder, trying to outrun the constant feeling of not being enough.

CHAPTER THREE

THE PLANE HAD BEEN circling for fifteen minutes, and Kelly rubbed at her temples. Flying never bothered her, but there came a point when the pressure built and erupted into a headache. When the plane touched down, she was up and out of her seat the second the seatbelt sign was turned off. She slung her backpack over her shoulder and waited impatiently for the others ahead of her in first class to do the same. As soon as she got into the cool air of the airport, she breathed a little more easily. The view from twenty thousand feet had shown long, beige flat land punctuated by occasional hills. Oklahoma City grew out of the ground like a tumor of cement and glass. Huge modern cities weighed her down if she spent too much time in them. London, too, even though it would always be her home.

After grabbing her suitcase, she stepped out into mild humidity and was surrounded by the American Midwestern twang. With a sigh, she headed to the car rental place where she'd reserved a pickup truck she felt was suited to this environment. A lesbian in a pickup was the ultimate in the American gay scene, right?

She entered the address of the house Jack had secured for her into the GPS and followed it to a rural piece of utterly American scenery. Ranch style houses with immaculate yards and flags flying out front went on for long, wide street after long, wide street. The house she pulled up in front of was the same. Single story, spread out, with large windows on every side. Flowers looked like they were desperately trying to avoid death in large, brightly painted planters beneath the windows.

It was a million miles away from the trailer she'd been in for the last six months and nothing like Marta's apartment with all its character, but it would do for the short time she hoped to be there.

She pulled her suitcase from the truck bed and was heading toward the door when she heard someone call out. She turned to see an older man with gray hair leaning on the fence.

"Pardon?" she said, wishing like hell she'd gotten in without being noticed.

"I said, you must be my new temporary neighbor." He tilted his head toward the house. "It's a rental, and people seem to come and go all the time. Met some nice folks over the years. Some not so nice too, who didn't belong around here."

Kelly sighed. Normally she'd challenge a statement like that, but she really wanted a shower and a nap. "Well, hopefully I won't be here long either."

"Name's Buck," he said, clearly looking her over.

"Kelly. If you'll excuse me, I've had a terribly long flight."

"You're from London?" He clearly didn't care about her desire to get clean.

"I am." She edged toward the door, not wishing to be rude but hoping he'd take the hint.

"Well, you should come over for a drink later and tell me about it. I'll invite Greg and Sarah, over on the other side of you, too."

God, Americans and their insistent friendliness. "Thank you. I'll take you up on that another time, perhaps. Today I'm really too tired to be sociable."

He looked only briefly disappointed. "Sure, no problem. You get some rest, and we'll set up something for another day." Once again, he looked her over. "Mighty nice to meet you, Kelly."

She gave a brief smile and let herself in after getting the keys from the lockbox beside the door. Once in, she closed her eyes and breathed deeply. This was temporary. She had men look at her like that no matter where in the world she went, and this was no different. Maybe they even had interesting stories to share. She had to remain open-minded. Shutting yourself off meant shutting off potential avenues of knowledge.

Little pep talk over, she walked through the house and found it pleasant enough. Three bedrooms, three bathrooms, and a large, open plan kitchen and living room. It was more space than she'd had to herself in probably the last three years. She dropped her suitcase onto the guest room bed, dug around until she found something to sleep in, then took a long, hot shower.

But when she dropped into the comfortable bed, her mind decided it wasn't quite time to sleep. She remembered Marta's almost tearful gaze as they'd spent their last night together. It had been a given that it wouldn't be anything serious, since Kelly would be moving on, but emotions were tricky things and couldn't be relied on to stay in their cages. That was always the risk of hooking up with someone when she was on a dig. But it was a risk she was willing to take, since spending lonely nights on her own didn't appeal to her in the least. Marta had said she hoped Kelly would keep in touch, but they both knew it wouldn't happen. Life wasn't about looking back, at least not when it came to living it. She did enough looking back with digs. It didn't mean she wanted to miss out on any experiences here and now.

Finally, she drifted off thinking about the job ahead. God, she hoped the person would be someone interesting to work with for however long this took.

***

At the millionth stoplight in five miles, Kelly seriously considered calling Jack and telling him to stuff it. Reacquainting herself with city life after a dig was always a chore and took plenty of time, but usually she was back in London or in a city she found exciting. Oklahoma was exceedingly fond of long, irritating stoplights and low, flat terrain occupied by very large buildings that blocked out the sky. She'd woken with her typical re-entry headache still in place, and the coffee at the little café around the corner had surely been made from the gravel and dirt in the parking lot. The only good thing about her morning was the cowgirl she'd seen getting out of a truck in front of some kind of barn shop. The woman's torn jeans and cowboy hat were the stuff of American romances. Or erotica, anyway. It was the first bright spot since she'd landed.

She pulled into the underground lot of the Oklahoma Archeological Center and gave her name to the guy at the guard booth, who called someone and then lifted the barrier. She wasn't surprised to see the gun at his side, but as someone who'd grown up in the UK, guns still bothered her, no matter where in the world she was. And given their prevalence here even for the common person, it made her yearn for her place in London even more.

She parked and grinned a little at the plethora of trucks surrounding hers, and then took the elevator to reception. Two people sat at the desk, both looking far too perky for eight thirty in the morning.

"Hi, I'm Kelly Pierce," she said, glancing between them. "I'm here to see Shawn Scott."

The brunette with her hair pulled into a severe ponytail nodded and picked up the phone, and the guy with a military-type cut handed her a badge. "You'll need to wear this today, and if you come back, we'll get you an official staff badge."

"If I come back?" Kelly smiled and leaned on the desk. "Do many people go running off?"

"They do when they work with Scott," the brunette mumbled, and then louder, said, "If you'll take that elevator there, we'll send you on up. Once you have your staff badge, you'll use it to get around the building."

Kelly sighed and did as instructed. Not a great start.

When she got off the elevator she looked around, but no one was there to meet her. She shoved her hands in her pockets and began to meander down the hallway. Desks were arranged in typical Big Brother style, back-to-back and side-to-side, with little dividers between them to give a semblance of privacy. Along the wall were offices with floor-to-ceiling glass windows, providing no privacy whatsoever for the goldfish worker inside.

All of them were empty.

She kept going, wondering if she'd been sent to the wrong floor, when she heard someone speaking. She followed the sound until she reached a large conference room, filled with people listening to someone at the front. Kelly stepped in and leaned against the back wall to listen. When she saw who was speaking, her heart sped up a little.

The dapper butch at the front held the room's attention with clear authority. She made little eye contact, her attention mostly on the photos appearing on the huge screen at the front. She was on the short side and had a muscular, stocky body that Kelly decided she'd like to see in action. *Naked.* Her eyes were a pretty summer green, and when she looked at Kelly, she ran her hand over the back of her short hair, a sexy move if Kelly had ever seen one.

"Because of the scale of the project, we're requesting that everyone be available for input. If you need assistance or if you're in the middle of a project, let me know so we can reallocate it to someone else." She motioned to the screen. "Statistics first, remember. No descriptive analysis until all the data is finished."

"Don't you have to have a sense of the description in order to add to the statistics?" Kelly asked loudly enough to be heard from the back and grinned at the speaker, who immediately frowned at her.

"That's not how things are done here." Her tone was final, and she dismissed Kelly as she looked around the room. "Any questions, any uncertainties, come see me. The amount of data means it could become overwhelming, and we don't want any mistakes."

She walked away from the podium, apparently done with the lecture, and everyone else began to leave as well, evidently used to the person's abruptness. She stopped one person walking past. "Can you point me to Shawn Scott, please?"

The person's eyebrow went up a little. "You were just listening to her. And if you want a little piece of advice, don't interrupt her. She really hates that."

Kelly nodded, and the person scurried past with a quick look in Shawn's direction. So she'd be working with a hard-ass, eh? A cute, hard-ass butch who didn't like being interrupted or challenged. Perfect. This was going to be way more fun than she'd anticipated.

She waited until Shawn came her way and smiled. "Hi. I'm Kelly Pierce."

"You're late. The meeting started at eight, and you got here at eight thirty-two."

Kelly leaned against the doorway again, blocking Shawn's way out. "Then I was actually half an hour early, since I was told to be here at nine."

"Then you were twenty-eight minutes early, not a half hour." Shawn frowned and ran her hand over the back of her head again. "But you should have been here at eight." She edged forward like she wanted to leave, but Kelly didn't move.

"This isn't a nine-to-five job then?" Kelly would happily have this little hard ass on the back foot right from the beginning. She wasn't about to be pushed around or talked down to.

"It is, usually, but because of the Pedra Furada project we asked everyone to come in early today in order to get a jump on the logistics." She edged forward again. "Can I get through, please?"

Kelly moved aside and waved her past. "Of course." When Shawn strode past her and didn't say anything, Kelly shrugged and followed. Shawn seemed surprised when she turned around to find Kelly still behind her as she entered her office.

"Can I help you with something?" Shawn asked, setting a file down so it was perfectly aligned with the edge of the desk.

"Well, since I was told I'd be working with you, I suppose you need to get me set up so I can do so. Unless you've changed your mind, in which case I'll be on the next flight to London." Kelly took in the sparse elements of the desk, the pencils lined up, not a paper or paperclip out of place. People's personal spaces said a lot about them. This only confirmed her initial impression that Shawn would be fun to mess with.

"It isn't about what I want. I've been told this is necessary. I personally think that you being here could skew our findings, but so be it." She looked past Kelly as though uncertain what to do next.

"Hi!"

Kelly turned to see the antithesis of Shawn breeze through the door. She had a pink tint to her long hair and was delightfully barefoot.

"You must be Kelly Pierce. I'm so excited to meet you. I've read all about the dig and your discoveries, and I'm so envious of all you've accomplished. I wish I could have been there when someone made that first find. Was it incredible? How many people did you talk to? How hot is it there? I bet it must have felt like you were melting—"

"Bree."

Shawn's tone brooked no argument and stopped the woman named Bree in her tracks. She looked chagrined and deflated, and Kelly instantly wanted to protect her. She held out her hand. "I think you and I are going to be lifelong friends. Nice to meet you."

As suddenly as she'd deflated, she picked up again. "I'd love that, and I can't wait to hear all about it." Bree looked past Kelly to Shawn and gave her what looked very much like a "take that" kind of look.

Shawn shook her head, her jaw working. "Kelly Pierce, this is Bree McIntosh. She's our assistant statistics manager and despite her voluble nature is an incredible asset to science."

Bree sat on her desk, her eyes wide. "Shawn Scott. You've never said anything that nice to or about me in the decade I've known you."

"It wasn't nice. It was accurate." Shawn turned to Kelly. "We can set you up at a desk down the hall—"

"How will I work beside you from a desk down the hall?" Kelly asked, giving Bree a little wink that made her press her lips together to keep from laughing.

"Working with me doesn't literally mean working at my side." She looked at Bree. "Does it?"

Kelly noted the little bit of vulnerability in her tone and the way Bree seemed to soften.

"Technically, I think Carolyn wants you to go through the primary sets of data with Kelly at your side so you can do the statistics and descriptive analysis at the same time because of the tight turnaround specs. That means that Kelly needs to be beside you as you go through the data, so she can provide you with extra details for description. If she worked down the hall, then you'd do the statistics first and she could do the description separately into another file, but that would take a lot more time, and you wouldn't have control over what she entered with regard to the different artifacts." Bree never looked away from Shawn's unswerving eye contact.

Fascinated by the nature of the exchange if not the content, Kelly took in their body language, their words, their positioning in the office. This was a hierarchy where the boss wasn't entirely certain what the rules were, and her assistant was there to sharpen the lines for her. She looked between them in the ensuing silence, waiting for the next move.

"I don't want to move to another office," Shawn finally said and picked up a pencil she began to slide through her fingers.

Bree nodded like she understood. "You don't need to. We just need to bring in an extra chair so she can sit beside you."

Shawn sighed and did that hand through the hair thing again. "Fine." She turned to Kelly. "I get here at eight forty-five every morning so I'm ready to begin at nine exactly. If you aren't here on time, I'll start without you."

Kelly gave a mock salute. "I'll be here, don't worry. But I'll start tomorrow to give you time to adjust to my being in your space." She looked at Bree. "Where can I get a good cup of coffee? This tastes like pig's swill."

Bree hooked her arm through Kelly's. "Come on. I'll show you around and give you the lowdown on the local foodie scene."

"Bree."

Bree turned around.

"Shoes." Shawn looked pointedly at her bare feet.

Bree grinned and wiggled her toes. "I won't enter any zones where it will matter." She blew Shawn a kiss. "Back soon."

They walked out, and Kelly heard something muttered behind them but couldn't make it out. "That's the kind of welcome I haven't had in a while," she said as Bree led them to the elevator.

"Mine or Shawn's?" she asked with a smile.

"Both." Kelly grinned down at her. She wasn't Kelly's type, but she was cute and sweet. And she clearly knew her way around Shawn.

"Shawn is..." Bree tapped her lips with her finger. "Extraordinary. She's got a mind like you've never known, but that also means she doesn't deal with the everyday world the way most people do. When you get used to it, and to her, you'll see she's a marshmallow under that steel trap outer layer."

Even with the little she'd seen, Kelly had a feeling that was true. But getting past that kind of outer layer was going to take some effort.

Good thing she'd never been afraid of a little hard work.

CHAPTER FOUR

SHAWN MOVED HER PENCILS horizontal and then vertical, then diagonal and back again, starting over as her thoughts whirled like a tornado. Contrary to popular belief, she liked working with people. Socializing, no, but she found working with intelligent, competent people who asked the right questions and challenged themselves and their colleagues to be refreshing. Often, she'd find herself mulling over those conversations at the gym or while she was eating dinner.

Technically, that meant she should find working with Kelly Pierce a good thing. Someone who had deep knowledge and could provide context should be a boon to the project.

But she was way too...too...*everything* for it to work.

She was beautiful in a way Shawn had never come across. Her long, wavy brown hair was highlighted naturally so it looked like dark and milk chocolate flowing together. Her brown eyes were full of light and laughter, and Shawn had a feeling she'd been messing with her, even though they'd only just met. She was tall and trim, the kind of body that was used to physically intense work. Her accent was sexy as hell too and added to the overall package.

Not one of these things should have been what Shawn noticed about someone she had to work with. But not only had she noticed, she also couldn't stop thinking about her. Not that a woman like Kelly would take a second glance at someone like Shawn. Heck, she couldn't even get a good date in Oklahoma, let alone with someone who travelled the world and clearly navigated it far better than Shawn ever could.

What was she thinking? You didn't date co-workers. It was in the policy she'd written herself. Dating in the workplace created drama, and drama meant mistakes as well as wasted work time. The whole line of thinking was nonsense, and she needed to get focused.

Bree swept back into the office and flopped into her chair. "Isn't she something?"

"She was late, and she seems like she has the same respect for professionalism that you do." She wanted to say, *yes, yes she's something*. But that wasn't going to happen.

"Well, then we'll all get along just fine." Bree pushed the back of Shawn's chair with her foot, moving it so Shawn was facing her. "You okay?"

After ten years of working together, Bree knew Shawn probably better than she knew herself, and Shawn knew what she was asking. "I'll be fine. I'm glad she said she'd come back tomorrow though. I'll need to adjust my thinking so I don't fight having to do the statistics and descriptive entries at the same time. I know that, and I'll be okay by the time she gets here tomorrow."

Bree nodded. "Good. You can call me tonight to talk it through if you need to."

It wasn't a question, so Shawn didn't respond. She returned to her work and focused on getting her current project done so she had a clear desk to work on in the morning. Still, throughout the day her discomfort with the situation grew and so too did her irritation. By lunchtime she was nearly pounding on the keys as she input the descriptive correlations on the statistics she'd already produced.

"Okay." Bree tugged at her chair, rolling her away from her desk.

"Okay, what?" Shawn tried to jerk her chair back to her desk. "I'm in the middle of something."

"You're in the middle of breaking your keyboard. Get your lunch. We're going outside."

Shawn frowned. "I eat my lunch at my desk."

"Today you're eating outside with me. Come on, keyboard basher."

With a frustrated sigh, Shawn yanked open her desk drawer to pull out her lunch and then slammed it closed again. She followed Bree downstairs and out the back door to the courtyard, where Bree straddled a bench and opened her My Little Pony lunchbox.

Shawn sat normally and placed her lunch on her knees. A breeze slid over her, and her shoulders began to drop incrementally. By the time she reached her side of carrots, her jaw had unclenched, and she stopped frowning.

"Thank you," she said, moving on to her pieces of apple. "I don't know why you put up with me when no one else does."

Bree briefly squeezed her knee. "You have an entire team of people who love working for you."

"It isn't the same as the way you put up with me though, is it?" Shawn glanced at her and gave her a small smile. "They work with me, and I'm glad. But you get me. Thank you."

Bree waved a breadstick covered in hummus at her. "You're welcome. Talk to me about what has you stressed out."

Shawn continued to eat her apple as she considered the question. "I like the way we do things. Our methodology works. We do the numbers, and from the numbers we develop theories about the people attached to those items attached to the numbers. There's a direct correlation. It's comfortable and logical, and it makes sense."

"And?" Bree prompted when Shawn got quiet.

"And the way they want us to do the Furada project isn't what we've built our reputation on. It feels haphazard. What if we input the data and descriptors together, only to find out that if we'd waited, we'd have found different data that changed the descriptors? We'll have to start all over again."

Bree nodded thoughtfully, obviously taking Shawn's concern seriously. "I see your point. And you're right; that's how we usually do things because there's a process that works."

Shawn breathed a little easier. She wasn't wrong to be worried about it.

"But."

Shawn looked up. "But what?"

"But the Furada dig isn't new. We already have a massive data set as well as descriptive analysis of hundreds of sites, so we aren't building something from scratch. We're balancing that against an enormous project already well-established. That means the new data and descriptors will be part of that set, so correlations have already been made. Basically, we're just matching new information with details we already have and using Kelly's insight to expand on it."

Shawn tilted her face toward the sun. "How did I not consider that?"

"Because Ms. Hottie UK tilted your world this morning." Bree laughed. "I've never seen you so flustered."

Shawn shook her head but didn't say anything. She didn't lie or even obfuscate, so she couldn't respond.

"Aside from Hottie UK," Bree said, her tone serious, "this is work you know and love. If you can be open to her insights, I bet you'll have some damn good conversations."

Challenging conversations were good, as long as people didn't get emotional about them, and they usually did. But Kelly Pierce was a scientist, so she must be used to being challenged, right? "I tell myself it will be fine and then I get irritated again."

"That's life." Bree snapped her lunch box shut. "You feel it a little more intensely than other people do, I think, but that just makes you more awesome."

Shawn stood and breathed in deeply again. "It doesn't always feel that way." Bree was the only person in the world she could be completely herself with, and that meant exposing the million little wounds in her soul inflicted by not quite fitting in all her life.

"I know, boss." Bree bumped her with her shoulder and held the door open for her.

FRAGMENTS OF THE HEART

Shawn was glad she didn't follow that up with platitudes or unsubstantiated nonsense about the world needing all types of people. She'd had enough of that for a lifetime.

They went back to work, and she settled into her routine more easily, and when the day was done, she felt good about finishing the project so she could start the new one tomorrow. As she turned out the office lights, she couldn't help but feel like tomorrow might be the start of a lot of new things.

When she walked out of the gym an hour later, she felt better after the long pep talk she'd given herself throughout the session. She felt so good, she might actually splurge and get herself pizza tonight.

The feeling disintegrated like ancient bone exposed to sunlight when she saw someone leaning against her car. Someone tall, with long hair and a smile that did funny things to Shawn's stomach.

"Hello there." Kelly didn't shift as Shawn moved toward her. "Hope you don't mind me ambushing you, but Bree mentioned that you work out every night, and she happened to mention that this was your gym. She also happened to mention what kind of car you drive." She grinned and rolled her eyes. "I took the hint."

"Hint?" Shawn shifted her gym bag on her shoulder. "How is sharing all my personal information with you a hint?"

"I'm pretty sure she wanted me to come chat with you. If not tonight, then another night."

"Why?" Shawn asked. "We'll be working together every day."

Kelly's smile seemed to be saying something Shawn couldn't parse. "That's true. But that will be work talk, and I'd like to talk to you as a person. Get to know you."

Shawn shifted her bag to the other shoulder, but that wasn't comfortable, so she shifted it back. "Why?"

"Why do I want to get to know you?" Kelly asked. "Because we might be working together for some time, and I always find work is better when you make an effort to really understand the people you're spending time with. Don't you?"

Shawn wanted to get into her car and drive away from this conversation that was quickly confusing her. "No. I think a strict divide between professional and personal means that no one gets distracted by discussing things that aren't work-related." Shawn took a chance and looked into Kelly's eyes, and her knees went disturbingly weak.

"I see." Kelly shrugged a little and shoved her hands in her pockets as she moved away from Shawn's car. "I guess I'll see you tomorrow then." She gave Shawn a brief smile and turned away.

"Pizza."

Kelly stopped and turned around. "Sorry?"

"No need to be sorry. I said pizza." Shawn ran her hand over her neck, trying to find the words. "I was going to get pizza."

Kelly waited, her head tilted to the side, her gaze fixed on Shawn.

"So...if you want pizza." If Shawn swore, she would have sworn quite loudly at herself. "You could come. For pizza."

"I'm sorry, was it pizza you were going to have?" Kelly laughed when Shawn gave her a puzzled look. "I'd love some pizza. I'll follow you."

Shawn opened her door, threw in her gym bag, and got in without another word. Her hands were shaking and her insides felt like wind-blown Jell-O. What was she doing? Bree would tell her to keep going, to be herself, and that it was good to let people in. But that was the kind of person Bree was. Shawn looked in her rear-view mirror and saw Kelly's truck pull up behind her. Fortunately, she couldn't see her well because of the angle of the setting sun.

She drove slowly and considered driving right past the pizza place and losing Kelly in traffic, but that would be rude. It was just pizza, not a romantic dinner for two. She could do this.

Shawn parked and waited for Kelly to join her at the front door. She opened it for her and inhaled a light, citrusy scent as she walked past. And then she was assaulted by the noise of about thirty kids in baseball uniforms as they celebrated something or other at the various tables. This had been a terrible idea.

Kelly tapped her shoulder. "It's a little loud in here for any kind of conversation. Is there a park or something nearby we could take our food to?"

Relief almost made her dizzy. "It's one point eight miles away."

Kelly nodded, then ordered herself a small everything pizza to go. Shawn grimaced at the thought and ordered a cheese and pepperoni for herself. They waited in awkward silence since it was far too noisy to say much of anything. There was a mirrored door opposite them, and Shawn watched Kelly in the reflection as she looked around, seeming to take it all in. She even smiled at some of the kids' antics, and more than a couple parents gave her a second look. Did she even notice? If she did, Shawn couldn't tell.

Kelly stepped up to get her pizza when her number was called, and a guy moved to her side. Shawn frowned when he was too close to Kelly, and when he held out a piece of paper insistently, she nearly said something loud enough to be heard. But Kelly took it and shoved it in her pocket with a gracious smile, and the guy walked away looking proud of himself.

Shawn grabbed her pizza box and hurried outside. The open air helped with the agitation, a little.

"Everything okay?" Kelly asked, appearing beside her.

"Follow me to the park, if you still want to." Shawn got in and drove off, and she wasn't sure if she was glad or not that Kelly was behind her. What did she care if Kelly got people's phone numbers? It wasn't any of her business, and this was exactly the reason it was important to keep the personal and professional separate.

She pulled up at the park and headed toward a picnic table situated almost exactly between two trees. Kelly took the bench opposite her, and they began to eat.

"Did something upset you back there?" Kelly asked after her first bite.

Shawn picked at a slice of peperoni, moving it so it was a better distance from the other piece. "You took that guy's phone number. But you don't even know him."

"You've never given your number to a person you want to go on a date with?" Kelly asked.

Shawn looked up. "Why would I want to go on a date with a woman I don't know?" She wasn't sure how to interpret Kelly's expression.

"Because that's how you get to know someone. You like the way they look, there's something indefinable, maybe, that you find attractive. So you give them your number, or you get theirs, and you meet up to see if you could develop something more."

Shawn scoffed and shook her head in disbelief. "That's likely part of why fifty percent of marriages end in divorce. People should take the time to get to know each other before they bother to go on a date. That way, they know if they're wasting each other's time before they spend more effort on something doomed to fail."

Kelly chewed slowly, her brow furrowed. "That's a very pragmatic way to look at relationships. What about the spark? That something that makes you want to take a woman home and do the dirty?"

"The dirty?" Shawn tried to ignore the way the word sounded extra sexual in Kelly's accent.

"The kind of intensity that means you don't even make it to the bedroom. That fission that makes you want to get out of your clothes as fast as you can."

"That makes it all about sex. Not dating."

"Dating leads to sex though. Doesn't it?"

Why on earth were they talking about this most intimate subject? "Why do you eat pizza with everything on it? All those flavors mashed together means you can't taste them individually."

"A change in topic. Okay, I can go with that. I like the explosion of all the flavors on my tongue. I like having everything, all at once. I'm not one for moderation." She grinned, her eyebrow raised as she took a big bite of pizza.

Shawn had a disconcerting feeling they weren't really talking about pizza but rather they'd somehow returned to the previous discussion about sex. She didn't know how to respond, so she didn't.

"Why don't you want to work with me?" Kelly asked after a moment of silence.

"I didn't say that." Shawn was certain she hadn't voiced it out loud.

"I'm pretty good at reading people, so you didn't have to say it. And if I'm honest, I'm not crazy about the project either." Kelly crumpled her napkin, threw it in the box, and pushed it away.

Shawn pulled the empty box over, took out the napkin, and set it aside. "You're not?" Why did that feel disappointing? Shouldn't she be glad that Kelly felt the same way?

"I'm not an office person. I'm an out-in-the-world person. I appreciate the numbers side of things only as far as they relate to where I've found the objects. What I'm really interested in is people."

Shawn took her time to think that over, and it was nice that Kelly didn't seem to mind the silence. "So you don't want to do this project because you'll be stuck inside. And you're not interested in statistics."

"It's a simplification, but yes. That's pretty much it. However, as I said, I like people, and I like getting to know them. And you and Bree seem like interesting people with interesting stories, so I'm looking forward to getting to know you." Kelly glanced at the napkin and box but didn't say anything.

"I..." Shawn faltered, once again unsure how to respond. "I like numbers. They're easy. They make sense. If you have so many artifacts of one kind, that means a certain percentage of the people were likely of a type. That type likely means they were of a certain culture, and so on. It's logical." She shrugged and placed her napkin with Kelly's, then put her pizza box on top of the other. "People aren't like that though. They don't make sense. They're always changing their minds or getting emotional about things they can't or won't change." She didn't go on to explain how difficult she found that and how often it had made her the victim of harassment, ridicule, and even violence.

"You're right." Kelly shrugged, looking thoughtful. "People are complicated. Sometimes that can be really beautiful, and sometimes it can be confusing and awful. We are the stories we create, and sometimes those are nightmares instead of dreams."

Shawn got up and dropped their pizza boxes and napkins in the garbage can. It was good to step away for a second, to get distance from Kelly and her gentle understanding, and the nice way she phrased things. Most people weren't so kind or eloquent.

Shawn went back to the bench but didn't sit down. "I should get home."

Kelly nodded and walked beside her to the parking lot. "Thank you for inviting me to eat with you. Sharing meals is one of my favorite things to do when I travel. There's something intimate about it."

Shawn swallowed. She hadn't meant it to be intimate at all, but she had to admit that it felt that way. "Sure. No problem."

Kelly opened her truck door but stopped before she got in. "Oh—and that number I took? Sometimes it's just easier to say thank you and then bin it than it is to get into a discussion about the fact that he's got entirely the wrong body parts to light my fire." She winked, got in the truck, and drove off with a wave.

Shawn sat on the curb beside her car. Kelly was a lesbian too. She dropped her head into her hands and groaned softly. How was she supposed to work beside someone so...so...everything?

CHAPTER FIVE

KELLY SAT AT THE table by the window of Expresso Presso, the coffee place Bree had recommended near the office. The coffee wasn't bad; it was just rather bland. It had the notion of a coffee bean but not quite the actual thing. She'd have to keep searching. Hopefully Bree's coffee tastes weren't the norm.

She watched the customers coming and going, most clearly on their way to a job of some sort, given their suits and sensible shoes. She'd managed to find her least fucked-up jeans and a black long-sleeved V-neck, but it was as far as she was willing to go. She'd slept poorly and needed a good caffeine fix before shutting herself in an office for the day. And for the foreseeable days.

But that was made a little more bearable by the enigma that was Shawn. She was hot, and Kelly was almost positive she had no idea how attractive she was. Her beautiful eyes were expressive and clearly showed her way of being in the world, which was to say, she wasn't quite part of it. Kelly always found people who viewed the world through their own special lens fascinating, and when you added a hot body, extreme intelligence, and more than a little vulnerability, it was a hell of a package.

And Kelly was fairly certain she was single, given their brief but interesting discussion about dating. Or, non-dating, as Kelly had started to think of it. While they may not have much time together before Kelly left again, she might be able to show Shawn the value of getting to know someone in a more intimate, less direct way.

She glanced at her watch and headed across the street. Being early meant she wouldn't set Shawn on edge right from the start, and she had a feeling this was going to be like stumbling through the dark in search of a flashlight. She'd get there, eventually, but would probably stub her toe a few times along the way.

She got her employee badge from the pair at the front, whom she'd started to think of as Office Barbie and Ken, and then headed up to the main floor along with plenty of other office types. What she wouldn't give to be heading out to a dig site instead of into an office to sit in front of a computer.

Shawn looked up. "You're here early."

It was a statement, not a question, but Kelly shrugged. "What can I say? You made an impression on me." She took the new chair beside Shawn's desk and rocked back in it. "And I want you to like me."

Shawn frowned but didn't say anything. She sipped from a bright purple mug emblazoned with *I am smarter than you, really.*

"I don't doubt that for a second." Kelly nodded toward the mug.

Shawn winced and set it down. "Bree got it for me, and I like the color. But I don't like people thinking I'd be that condescending."

Kelly had a distinct feeling that Shawn's kind of blunt honesty felt condescending to most people, but that was because most people weren't so genuine. "I don't doubt that either."

Shawn gave a small nod, and a little smile touched her lips. "We should get started."

"Okay, boss. How should we do this?"

Shawn's head shot up. "I'm not your boss."

Kelly wasn't sure why that created such a swift reaction. "Just a turn of phrase. I know we're co-workers. Don't worry."

Shawn blew out a breath and pulled up the file of artifacts. "I thought about this all night. I think I should log the statistics on each item, and then you can give me some pertinent facts about the item, which we'll tag so it goes with other items."

Kelly scooted the chair forward, the wheels hardly making a sound on the thick carpet. "Sounds simple enough. I'll follow your lead."

She saw Shawn swallow and noticed the way her fingers were

trembling slightly. Should she say anything? No. It was better to fall into a groove, and if it continued, then she'd say something. It was going to be a long, hard trial if she couldn't get Shawn to relax.

The artifact they started with was the first item found when they'd switched to the new site. Only four inches long, it didn't look like much. But when they'd found it, the place had gone crazy.

Shawn punched in the GPS coordinates and filled in an extensive spreadsheet that sent Kelly cross-eyed within minutes. "I'm glad I don't have to do that for every item I find while I'm out in the field. It would drive me wappy."

"And I wouldn't have a job." Shawn smiled a little but didn't take her eyes off the computer and the data she was entering at the speed of light.

Kelly waited in the silence, which soon grew tiresome. "So—"

"Please don't interrupt me when I'm in the middle of input." Shawn's tone wasn't sharp, but her authority was clear.

Kelly sighed and leaned back in the chair. To be fair, it wasn't long before Shawn looked up.

"Pertinent data with regard to piece 1, location BZ602?"

Kelly studied the artifact on the screen. "I'd been speaking to the Yanomami, the local tribe in the area, and after they got to know me, we really began to share aspects of our lives and cultures. That was when a couple of children offered to show me the secret place where ancestors still lived." Kelly could still feel that thrill of anticipation when they set off. "We walked for about an hour—"

"I don't like to interrupt people, but what does this have to do with artifact 1?" Shawn stared at her, frown lines deep.

"You don't want to know how it was found?" Kelly asked. "Most people in our field are interested."

Shawn shook her head, her fingers still poised over the keyboard. "We don't have time for stories. I need facts pertinent only to the item itself so we can move forward to the next."

"What a dry way to look at history. What are we if not our stories?" When she saw Shawn about to object, Kelly held up her hand. "Okay. You'll have to bear with me, because that's not usually how I operate, but I'll do my best." Seeing that Shawn was mollified, Kelly looked again at the artifact. "That's a Sorocaban knife, related to the dig at BZ509. But there are minor differences, like the length of the hilt. That was found later at BZ529. This indicates a time divide that means BZ602 was likely an earlier settlement." There was so much more she could say—that the sweltering heat and jungle had made it feel like the ancestors were surrounding them. That the natives had been hesitant to move anything at all until they saw evidence of the culture and Kelly had talked about the importance of the world remembering the stories of the people who lived there.

Shawn's fingers flew over the keyboard and data sheets from the other digs Kelly mentioned showed up, were tagged with the new site find, along with keywords, and then with a paragraph almost word for word what Kelly had said.

"That's impressive," Kelly said.

"Thank you. We worked hard as a team to get the system in place." Shawn brought up the next photograph and started the process again.

Kelly groaned inwardly. This was going to be a long, drawn-out way to do things. Maybe she could find a local gay bar and enjoy some company who would be interested in relieving the tedium. Flirting with Shawn was fun, but someone so buttoned-up wasn't likely open to the kind of night sports Kelly was looking for.

"Kelly?" Shawn asked, her gaze penetrating.

"Sorry." Kelly looked at the next item and provided the necessary details. And on it went until twelve thirty, when Shawn stopped typing in the middle of a sentence.

"Lunch time." She opened her bottom drawer and pulled out a plastic container. She opened it and revealed compartments dedicated to a sandwich, carrot sticks, a tiny salad, and what looked like a brownie, though it wasn't much more than a bite.

Kelly hadn't even considered bringing her lunch, not that she wanted to continue to sit in the office. "I need some air. Where is Bree, by the way?"

"She said it would be best if you and I began working together without her there to distract us, so we could settle into a routine." Shawn glanced at her lunch and back at Kelly, like she was just waiting for Kelly to go so she could eat.

"I don't suppose you want to bring your lunch with you and join me in the cafeteria?" Kelly put her hands on her lower back and did a small backbend. It felt good, and she didn't miss the way Shawn blinked rapidly as Kelly's breasts pushed forward against her top.

Shawn didn't say anything. She just put the lid on the plastic container and stood.

"Excellent." Kelly turned and led the way, grinning to herself. She'd expected that to take a lot longer.

They got to the cafeteria, and Kelly motioned to a table by a large window. "How about that one? I'll join you once I've got my food."

Shawn set off, and Kelly watched as she made her way through the room. Her slacks fit her small, solid butt just right. A few people said hello and Shawn responded in kind, but she looked tense as she sat at the table. Kelly turned to peruse the options at the food stations and was reminded what American food meant. She opted for a grilled cheese and fries, and decided she'd definitely follow Shawn's example and bring a lunch from now on. And she'd find whatever passed for ethnic food in Oklahoma City too.

She sat across from Shawn, who looked at her meal. "I was thinking about how different this must be for you."

Kelly speared a fry with her fork. "How so?"

"You spend most of your time outdoors. You talk to people about all kinds of things. You eat things other than bread and melted cheese." Shawn nodded at Kelly's plate.

"You're right." Kelly pulled apart the sandwich and was a little dismayed that the cheese split instead of coming apart in melty gooeyness. "But you wouldn't believe how popular bread and melted cheese is in a lot of countries."

Shawn nodded but didn't say anything more.

"Can I ask you something personal?" Kelly asked after they'd both been eating for a while.

Shawn looked up warily. "I guess."

"Do you think about the stories behind the artifacts? About the people and how they lived?"

Shawn looked a little relieved, probably that the question was work-related and not about the fact that she ate all of one item before she moved on to the next. "I like the connections. Like earlier, when you said item 1 was connected to items at BZ509 and BZ529. The way that one artifact connects the three areas over time and distance is interesting, and it shows us changes in their lifestyles."

Kelly waited, but nothing else was forthcoming. "But what about the people? Do you picture them using the tools, in communities or alone? Do you see them sitting around a campfire and sharing a meal and stories? Does that knife represent who they were as souls on this big rock in the universe?"

Shawn stared at her for a long moment, her eyes seeming to look first into one of Kelly's eyes, then the other. What was she searching for, Kelly wondered? And why look into one eye instead of both at the same time? At some point, she'd ask. If she did so now, she ran the risk of Shawn becoming self-conscious and not looking at her at all.

"That would be conjecture, imagination. We don't know that they did those things. We can't know what they talked about, and the soul is an existential concept best left out of science."

Kelly took that in. How odd to document lives and not give them any consideration. They couldn't possibly approach their work any differently. But before she could respond, Bree bounced over and pulled up a chair to sit with them.

"How is it going?" she asked. "Isn't their grilled cheese fab? I love it."

That gave Kelly her answer about Bree's level of culinary expectation, and she hoped that someone, somewhere would have good coffee. "I think it's going well." She looked at Shawn. "What do you think?"

Shawn nodded slowly as she ate a carrot stick. "I thought you'd be harder to work with, and I'm glad you figured out how to provide the data without the extraneous details."

"The extraneous details are part of what make us human." Kelly couldn't help but state what was, to her, an important point.

Bree jumped in when it looked like Shawn was about to argue. "I'm glad you worked it out. I knew you would." She opened a children's lunchbox featuring horses with multicolored manes and pulled out a juice box. "I'd love to hear about some of your travels. Like the dig you did in Russia. That must have been crazy."

Shawn continued to watch them attentively, and Kelly felt a little like an animal being studied in a lab. "Why don't we have dinner tonight and chat about it?"

Bree's eyes grew wide. "That would be amazing. Really?"

Kelly laughed. "Why not? Would that be so strange?"

Bree looked around the cafeteria. "We don't tend to go out together as a group very much."

Kelly didn't miss the tone of sadness in Bree's voice. "Well, I'm all about getting to know people. I'll choose the place and meet you there at seven." She looked at Shawn. "Will you come too?"

Shawn looked from Bree to Kelly. "I don't know," she finally said.

"Okay, well, I'll text you the time and place, and if you can make it, that would be great." Kelly gave her a warm smile, hoping to convey that she'd be safe and welcome. "I'd really like to get to know you outside of work."

Shawn swallowed hard and looked at her brownie, the last thing left in her container. "Why?"

"Because you're interesting. You're intelligent, hardworking, handsome, and we share an interest in a field that means we'll have plenty to talk about. Even if we do see things rather differently."

"I'm handsome?" Shawn looked genuinely surprised. Then she closed the container and stood. "I need to get back to the office." She hurried off, leaving Bree and Kelly behind.

When she was gone, Bree burst out laughing. "You've got her all twisted up."

Kelly grinned, but her heart ached at the idea that Shawn didn't know how special she was. No one should feel that out of sync with the world. "It's good to get people out of their comfort zone. Now, tell me about yourself."

Bree launched into some of her background, and Kelly kept an eye on the clock. When it was time to head back to the office, she had a plan brewing in the back of her mind. Somehow, she was going to let Shawn Scott know she was something special. If that was the only good thing to come out of this assignment, so be it. It would be worth it.

CHAPTER SIX

SHAWN GRUNTED AS SHE forced the bench press bar up and back into place. Sweat trailed down her temples and her tank top stuck to the bench.

Why did Kelly say those things? She lifted the bar again, bringing it slowly to her chest and back up. More confounding was that she seemed to really mean them. Sure, Shawn knew she was intelligent—that was a fact that couldn't be disputed. But the other things? *Handsome.* Her arms trembled as she settled the bar in the holder again.

Her music dimmed as a notification chimed, and she checked it as she sat up.

Would you meet me for a drink at the following address? Bree is busy and can't make dinner, and I'd like company. Kelly.

Shawn stared at the text until someone's presence felt too close. She looked up.

"Are you still using that?" A guy with a tank top that might as well be two long flaps of material, since the arm holes were so low, looked disgruntled.

"I'm done." Shawn grabbed her water bottle and towel and headed to the mats to stretch. She laid the phone beside her and continued to stare at the message as she worked through her poses. Kelly had said all those nice things and now she was asking her to go for a drink. Shawn picked up her phone.

Okay.

She sent it and had a feeling she should send more, but that would be small talk. She'd given her answer, but the dictates of social conversation meant she should say something else. She hovered over the keyboard.

See you there at six.

That was better. A little extra, plus the clarification of time that meant she could still shower and feel confident in her appearance when she got there. She continued to ponder the situation as she got ready, barely noticing the usual sideways glances and looks of distaste, thanks to the thoughts whirling in her head. Kelly was so incredibly beautiful and spending the day working with her had been surprisingly easy after her initial need to set boundaries. In truth, Shawn had been impressed with her knowledge and recall, and her input had saved Shawn an inordinate amount of time trying to connect the new pieces with those already catalogued. Bree had eventually joined them, and they'd entered into a system where Bree would get the details for one item while Shawn was inputting the numerical data for another, and then Shawn would take over asking Kelly questions while Bree moved on to the next piece. It had worked better than Shawn could have dreamed, and they'd gone through a surprising amount in a short time.

But Kelly wasn't asking Shawn to go for a drink so they could talk about work. She wasn't so inept not to know that much. So what did she want to talk about? Shawn had shared personal things with her already. Would they be sharing additional things? Unusually, Shawn found herself wanting to know more about Kelly, about what she liked and disliked, about the places she'd been. They were things Shawn didn't usually care about, since people in her world were so transitory, but there was something different with Kelly.

She left the gym, punched the address into the GPS, and headed to an area she hadn't been to in a long time. The bar, Blue Chili, had the usual array of trucks out front but didn't appear too busy, much to her relief. A long, deep breath helped steady her before she got out. She could do this.

She took the wide wooden steps two at a time and pulled open the door. She waited a moment for her eyes to adjust then looked around. Kelly raised her glass from across the room, and Shawn forced herself to walk normally instead of hurrying over the way she wanted to.

"Good session at the gym?" Kelly asked and blatantly looked Shawn over.

"I always enjoy working out. It's good for my mental health." Shawn slid onto a barstool, then off it again. "I'll go get a drink. Do you need another?"

Kelly shook her head and raised her hand. "He'll come take our order. No need to go to the bar."

"Oh." Shawn slipped back onto the barstool and folded her hands on the table, then took them off again and rubbed them on her thighs. "What made you choose this place?"

"I did a Google search for best quiet bars for conversation and it won, hands down." Kelly looked around. "It feels both deliciously American as well as a little lower key than usual."

Shawn looked around. There was an old-fashioned jukebox against one wall, cowboy hats hanging here and there, and memorabilia from the Thunder and Oilers in prominent positions. She'd been surrounded by this type of thing all her life and had never considered how an outsider would view it.

"It's strange how rarely we stop to analyze our own cultures when we spend so much time analyzing the cultures of other countries." Shawn finally looked back at Kelly's warm brown eyes.

"That's very true. I find that I notice it far more when I'm away for long periods of time. I come home and London wraps me up in a warm, citified hug and gives me strong tea and good biscuits."

"Biscuits?" Shawn frowned. "I thought those were distinctly American."

Kelly laughed, a sweet, open sound that made Shawn's stomach flip. "You'd call them cookies, I think. Not the big dough things you have."

Shawn felt her cheeks flush and was grateful for the waiter's interruption. "Water with lemon for me, thanks."

Kelly ordered another beer.

"You're not driving?" Shawn asked.

"I ordered an Uber so I wouldn't have to worry about it, nor about finding my way back." Kelly drank down the last of the beer in the bottle already in front of her. "Water with lemon?"

"I'm not much of a soda drinker. I like iced tea, but I usually brew it myself so it isn't too strong or too weak." The waiter brought over their drinks, and Shawn wondered just how inferior she seemed to other people Kelly must know. "Not very exciting, I know."

Kelly scoffed. "Please. Understanding what you like and how you like it is always sexier than doing what other people do just to fit in."

Shawn swallowed hard. "You think so?"

Kelly's gaze held the kind of promises meant for dim lighting and sensual music. "I do."

"Well, well. Look what the rat dragged back to its nest."

Shawn froze, and the blood rushed to her chest as freezing anxiety immediately gripped her. It was a voice she knew all too well. She didn't turn toward him and didn't look away from Kelly, whose gaze moved from Shawn to the speaker.

"And whom might you be, with your inelegant use of metaphor?" Kelly asked.

Shawn flinched. It was best not to antagonize him. But she couldn't bring herself to speak a single word.

"Me? Why, I'm hurt, Shawn. You haven't told your new friend about your big brother?" He put his elbows on the table and rested his chin in his hands. "I'm Jonah. And I promise you, sweet lady, I can show you a far better time than my perverted little sister ever could." He reached out and took Kelly's hand in his. "Why don't you let me buy you a drink?"

Kelly slid her hand out of his, though she clearly had to tug a little. Shawn wanted to stand up. She wanted to punch him. She wanted to jump in front of Kelly and protect her. But fear kept her rooted to her seat.

Kelly winked at her, then moved off her barstool. "Forgive me, but Neanderthals with more dick than sense have never been my style." She looked him over, disdain clear. "Though perhaps I give you too much credit in that arena as well. Truly, it would be best for all of us if you made your way elsewhere, preferably back to the swamp from which you emerged."

His face turned an odd shade of red-purple and his jaw set. His eyes, always hard and mean, grew cruel. He grabbed Kelly's wrist. "I think maybe you and I should have a talk in private about manners."

What happened next, Shawn wasn't entirely sure. One second, Kelly was calmly facing her brute of a brother and the next, Kelly had shifted and Jonah was flat on his back, gasping for air.

"I can assume we don't like this one, yes?" Kelly leaned over and whispered to Shawn.

"Um...no. We don't." Shawn looked from Jonah to Kelly, and the strangest feeling of elation began to wash over her.

"Excellent news." Kelly turned back to Jonah and placed her Converse on his wrist, shifting so her weight was on it.

"Fucking bitch," he wheezed.

"What a banal response. But what else do we expect from a 'crusty batch of nature, the owner of not one good quality?'" Kelly nodded to the two guys from behind the bar who'd come over and were watching with amusement. She moved her foot off Jonah's wrist, and the guys pulled him to his feet.

Jonah shrugged them off and walked toward the door with them behind him. Shawn looked over her shoulder, finally unfrozen. He glared back at her, but no other insults were forthcoming.

The door closed behind him, and Kelly slid back onto her seat.

The bartenders came over. "Sorry about that. We get them in here occasionally, but watching you handle it made our day."

Kelly grinned and touched her beer bottle to Shawn's water glass. "To getting rid of the filth of the day."

Shawn grinned back, relief and awe replacing her anxiety and fear. "How did you learn to do that?"

"When you're a woman traveling to remote places and you're in charge of a whole lot of men, you learn the value of knowing self-defense as well as you know how to brush your teeth. As a femme, men seem to feel particularly invested in helping me understand how their penises make them somehow more qualified, or more able, in some way. It's always important I disabuse them of whatever puerile notions come into their little underdeveloped brains." Her smile faltered. "I'm sorry though. Growing up with someone like that must have been awful."

Shawn sipped her water. Honesty was the only way forward. "I'm one of five kids. The third, and the therapist said I had classic middle-child syndrome."

"Therapist?" Kelly's tone was gentle, not pushy.

"The family is deeply religious. Church every Sunday, prayer gatherings, multiple kids to show God how good they are at procreating. They even gave us all religious-based names to make it even more obvious. Mine means gift from God." Shawn shrugged, the pain of talking about her childhood muted a little under Kelly's show of strength. That had caused a whole bevy of other feelings Shawn would need to sort out later. "When it became clear I wasn't like them, that I moved through the world in my own way, they started sending me to doctors. When my brother caught me kissing a girl behind the bleachers in high school, they..." Shawn sucked in a breath and picked at a loose bit of wood in the table. "They sent me to a conversion camp."

"Fucking hell. Bastards." Kelly's tone held the kind of contempt Shawn had always felt.

"Yeah. I ran away from the camp and stayed with a friend from high school, someone who had gay parents. They hid me and helped me get emancipated so I could legally live on my own. But I stayed with them until I was eighteen anyway." Those had been the best years of her young life. "They saved me."

"My god. I thought you were amazing before. Now I think you

might be a hotter, butch version of Captain America."

Shawn looked up, glad for the change in subject, and filing away the compliment for later inspection. "You like comics?"

"I love the movies. I never had time for the actual comic books when I was a kid, but as an adult, I've seen nearly every film." She took Shawn's hand in hers. "I'm sorry you went through all that. I think your parents and brother are wankers of the highest order."

"Did you insult Jonah using Shakespeare?" Shawn turned Kelly's words over in her head. "You did! I'm not even that nerdy."

Kelly laughed. "Who better to insult people than the bard?" She stood up, pulling Shawn with her. "Come on. I haven't seen the latest Marvel movie, and it's playing just down the street. Go with me."

Shawn hesitated. "It's a work night."

"As so many nights are in our world. Why work to the exclusion of enjoying life too?" Kelly squeezed her hand. "Please?"

Shawn sighed. "You're extremely difficult to say no to, even though I should."

"Excellent." Kelly led the way out of the bar. "You're buying the popcorn."

Shawn couldn't answer. She should have said movie popcorn had way too much butter and salt. But all she could focus on was the way Kelly's skinny jeans fit her perfect butt, and the way they tapered down gorgeous, long legs. Her tank top was just short enough to show occasional flashes of her lower back, which appeared to have a tattoo that Shawn was almost desperate to see.

Outside, they went to Shawn's car, and she opened her door for her. Kelly smiled and lightly touched her cheek. "Manners maketh man, eh?"

Shawn melted a little under Kelly's gentle touch, and as she made her way around to the driver's side, she wondered just how much trouble she was in.

CHAPTER SEVEN

KELLY STRETCHED, LETTING THE morning sunlight warm her skin. When she was on a dig, she generally had no choice but to sleep in clothing, since she was often in a tent or some other kind of temporary shelter, and she wasn't about to get caught naked when a grizzly or some such thing wandered into camp in search of a snack.

But in her own space, it was all about skin covered in nothing but air. She rose and padded to the kitchen, still stretching, when movement caught her eye.

Shawn hastily turned away from the living room window. She held her arms out to her sides. "I brought coffee," she called out loudly enough for Kelly to hear.

Tempted though she was to open the door in her altogether, it might very well have given Shawn a heart attack. How much had she seen before Kelly saw her move? She grinned. "Just let me throw something on."

She laughed a little as she put on sweats and a T-shirt. But when she opened the door, her coffee sat in the middle of the doormat, and there was no Shawn to be seen. "Damn," she murmured and picked it up, then closed the door behind her. Just then, her phone pinged with a message.

"Sorry. Late for work. Had to go."

Kelly sipped, grinning at the lame excuse. It was only half past seven. After the movie last night, Kelly had insisted they stop for a milkshake to discuss it. They'd enjoyed a long talk about new space discoveries and the plausibility of humans with superpowers. She'd enjoyed her peanut butter milkshake and cajoled Shawn into trying it. She'd admitted, quite begrudgingly, that it was good. She still only drank water though.

When she'd dropped Kelly off at her house, there'd been a moment...a beautiful, tension-filled moment where she'd considered leaning in and taking the kiss she was certain Shawn would have offered. But it was too soon, and she couldn't be sure whether or not Shawn was the fall-in-love-immediately type of lesbian or the kind that could be a little more fluid about how things went. She had a feeling she knew the answer. So Kelly had thanked her for a lovely evening, gone inside, and made quick use of her vibrator.

No problem. The coffee is great, thank you. See you shortly. Sorry you didn't stay.

She took her time getting ready, adding a bit of mascara to highlight her eyes and brushing her hair 'til it shined. She didn't bother with make-up in the field. No one cared a damn what she looked like there, but she liked the way Shawn looked at her here. Like she was simultaneously about to worship her and run a million miles in utter terror. It was adorable, and talking to her last night when her guard was down and she was so animated had not only been fun but had also been damn sexy. And she hadn't been in the least intimidated by Kelly's show of force when it came to her twat of a brother. Perfect.

It was rare to come across someone so genuine, someone without an agenda or who played games of some sort. Sure, her colleagues were great for the most part, but everyone wanted to be the one to make a big find or to get that next big position in the department. Even Kelly had played that game to get where she was.

But Shawn genuinely didn't care. She loved the work for its own sake and taking credit didn't matter as long as the work itself was solid. It was refreshing and also a little daunting. Kelly had no doubt she could make Shawn feel good and draw her out of her shell some, but what then? She'd go back to London and resume her wanderlust life, and Shawn would remain here in the walnut shell she called home. Maybe it was a mistake to pursue her after all.

Spirit dampened by that thought, she set off for the office and entered Shawn's space right on time. Shawn barely glanced up, but the red tint to her cheeks told Kelly what she needed to know.

She perched on the edge of the desk and sipped her coffee. Shawn's eyes flicked to her butt and then away again, her cheeks growing even redder.

"So, how long were you peeping outside my window?" Kelly lowered her voice and leaned down enough that her hair swept over Shawn's fingers on the keyboard. She couldn't help herself.

"I..." Shawn's jaw worked but nothing came out. "I came up the stairs right when you came out of the back, and the sun was just right..."

"Shawn Scott. You didn't answer the question." Kelly moved off the desk and onto the chair beside Shawn's desk. "Were you there long enough to see anything you liked?"

Shawn swallowed and pushed away from the desk. Her focus remained on anything but Kelly. "Yes," she finally whispered. "You've got an incredibly proportionate body. Everything is very... symmetrical."

Bree breezed in and stopped short as she took them in. "Okay. What's going on?"

Kelly grinned and sipped her coffee, waiting for Shawn to respond. She'd let her take the lead on this one.

"Nothing. Work. Working. We're working." Shawn ran her hand through her hair, leaving it tousled. "We were about to start."

Bree raised her eyebrows at Kelly, who just gave a slight shrug. If Shawn didn't want to say anything, she wouldn't force the issue. There was no need to.

Shawn moved back to her desk. "Item 202." Her furious typing filled the air.

Bree shook her head and got settled at her desk, and the same procedure as the day before resumed. In truth, Kelly didn't find it nearly as boring as she'd thought she would. Going through the finds again brought about a little thrill of excitement similar to the moment when they'd found them and describing the connections to other items out loud helped not only to cement them in her mind, but also to make it so other potentially longer-range connections became clear.

At lunch, sitting outside with Bree and Shawn, she said as much. Shawn's nose wrinkled. "You're a long chronology theorist."

Kelly took a bite of her sandwich and let Shawn stew on that for a moment. "I believe in facts, just like you do. But I know there are *facts* that don't support our idea that humans have only been here for fourteen thousand years. Two years ago, there were finds in the Beringian glacier melt that indicated it's closer to twenty thousand years. What else are we going to find in the ice?"

Shawn snapped her container closed, her brow furrowed. "But those finds haven't been substantiated yet. So all we have to go on right now are the facts in front of us. Long theory is just an idea without any facts to back it up."

Kelly tilted her face to the sun, pretending not to notice the rapt attention Bree was paying to the conversation. Her silence meant she was reading between the lines, if Kelly had to take a bet on it. "Haven't you ever known something on a gut level? Something unproven but still compelling?" She opened her eyes and looked at Shawn. "Like there's something pulling you toward it, almost magnetically, that can't be explained but is most certainly in existence?"

Shawn's mouth opened, then closed. Her breathing was a little faster, and she brushed her hand through her hair and looked away. "Eventually those moments can be explained too, with enough analysis and introspection." She flinched. "I mean, analysis and objective research."

"Of course." Kelly gave her a lopsided grin and a wink.

Shawn turned and left without a word, hurrying inside and down the hallway out of sight.

"Okay, spill." Bree turned to face Kelly. "You've got to tell me what's going on. The tension is so *tense*."

Kelly laughed. "For someone with an IQ over 200, your lack of verbal pretense is beautiful." She shook her head and gathered her lunch debris. "But you work with Shawn, so it needs to be Shawn who tells you things. I wouldn't want to divulge anything she isn't comfortable with."

Bree shoved her half-eaten food into her lunch box but didn't take her eyes from Kelly. "Is it that juicy?" She looked toward the door and frowned slightly. "Is she okay?"

Kelly's heart warmed at Bree's obvious concern. "No, it isn't actually that juicy, and nothing untoward has occurred, I promise. If I had to guess, I'd say she's discombobulated, that's all."

Bree immediately lightened again. "Oh, good. I can handle discombobulation." She hooked her arm through Kelly's as they walked back inside. "You've made it under her skin in record time. It's nice that she likes you so much."

Kelly wasn't sure "like" was the right word. She was fairly certain that Shawn wanted some sexy time with her—that she was, at the very least, attracted to her. But it was equally likely that the attraction and ease between them was ramping up her anxiety. How to combat that?

She mulled the question over throughout the afternoon as they continued to work, and the tension abated in the face of numbers and descriptions.

"I'd like to have a little get together at my place tomorrow." Kelly twisted and turned to release the knots in her back. "You two, obviously, and anyone else you think I should meet who isn't a total doorknob. Perhaps a few people from the queer science community?"

Bree looked ecstatic, and Shawn looked flummoxed.

"You should definitely get to know some of our team here. And there's a local group online, and I know a few of them. We get together sometimes. I can get in touch, if you want?" Bree was already throwing things into her handbag. "What time do you want us there? And what can we bring?"

"I'm not—" Shawn looked between them.

"Yes, you are." Bree turned, her hands on her hips. "You're most definitely going, or I will make intentional, irrational mistakes in my entries next week."

Shawn looked horrified. "That's blackmail. And unprofessional."

Bree held up her hand and then turned to Kelly. "We'll be there."

"Let's say around six, and bring whatever it is you like to drink. I'll handle the food." Kelly stretched her hands toward the ceiling, her T-shirt lifting to let the cool air touch her stomach, and she could swear that she heard Shawn whimper. But when she looked, Shawn's back was turned. "See you tomorrow."

She headed out, looking forward to the weekend she'd been dreading. Going out on her own was no problem, and she'd easily find a playmate at one of the surprising number of gay bars in the city, but she wanted connection, not a passing fancy. The thought that had come to her was that Shawn would be more comfortable if there was someone she knew there as well. She'd been fine for the movie, but as Kelly gently pulled down more walls, she'd probably freeze up. This way, she could work on the mortar of more than just her backstory and get to the actual bricks of what made her the person she was today.

And if she happened to stick around after the other party guests left? Well, they'd see where it led. Although Shawn was sensitive, Kelly needed to remember she was also an adult with her own mind, who would be free to enjoy their flirtation or not, depending on her desire.

***

Kelly smoothed the simple white summer dress over her hips for the millionth time. The thin material was loose, which was perfect for the humidity, and the deep plunge allowed for plenty of cleavage. She forgot sometimes how nice it was to free up her inner femme, who so rarely got to come out these days. The food she'd ordered would be here about half an hour after the guests arrived. She wasn't nervous about meeting new people. That was something she loved no matter where in the world she was. If anything, she was nervous about whether or not Shawn would like the dress she was wearing.

The doorbell rang, and she opened it to find two people she'd never met standing there. Both androgenous types, both in plaid shirts and work boots.

"Um, hi. I'm Chris. This is Sue. Bree told us to come over?"

Kelly held out her hand. "Absolutely. Come on in. I'm Kelly, your host."

The conversation was easy. It started with small talk, of course, but it wasn't long before Kelly had found out where they worked and was quizzing them on *why* they did what they did. People's motivations for choosing their profession were almost always interesting and said a lot about them. They'd been sitting at the table chatting for about fifteen minutes before the doorbell rang again. She opened it to find Bree and Shawn standing there with two other women and one guy behind them. Shawn met her eyes, and then her gaze shifted lower. She reached out to grasp the doorframe and looked at the porch, her eyes wide, her knuckles white.

Perfect.

Bree smiled brightly, but Kelly could see the slight tension in it.

"Hey, you made it." Kelly waved them in and gave Bree's shoulder a light squeeze. She had a feeling she knew the source of her tension. "Come on in and get a drink."

Introductions were made all around, and the group was quickly engaged. Bree tilted her head, and Kelly led the way toward the kitchen.

Once there, Bree dramatically draped herself over the kitchen island. "You have no idea."

Kelly laughed, pulled a beer from the fridge, and handed it to her. "Not to the extent you do. I imagine seeing me naked didn't help the situation."

Bree shot up from her half prone position on the island. "I'm sorry. What now?"

Kelly winced. "I figured she'd tell you, and I've already had two drinks. I shouldn't have said anything." She went on to explain the innocent, and pretty funny, situation. She wondered, though, if Shawn had said anything about the incident with her brother. Did Bree even know about that part of her history? If it hadn't been for his arrival, Kelly was unlikely to have been let into that particular part of Shawn's life, of that she was certain. The doorbell rang again, but she assumed someone else would answer it.

Bree's hands were over her mouth, and her eyes were wide. "Well, that certainly explains why I practically had to drag her here by her hair. I was so frustrated I nearly gave up." She began to laugh, and soon she was wiping tears from her eyes. "Oh, what I would have given to see her face in that moment." She gathered herself and sighed. "Now that I know, I can cut her some slack. We'd better get back in there before we find that she's left the cookies she brought on the doorstep and run off."

In fact, Shawn was on the couch beside a woman who seemed to be doing all the talking. When Kelly met Shawn's gaze, she looked relieved. She said something to the woman, who looked a little nonplussed, and made her way to Kelly.

"You look like a sunbeam in the middle of a cave. All I can see is you." Shawn said it simply, with no artifice, no flirtation. Like it was a fact she needed to share.

Kelly took her hand. "Thank you. That's a beautiful compliment."

Shawn grinned a little and ran her hand through her hair. "There are a lot of people here. Why would you want people you don't know in your house?"

Kelly linked her arm through Shawn's and guided her toward the kitchen. Even with the height difference, it felt nice to walk with her this way. "How else would I get to know a wide array of people I won't come across in my day-to-day work with you?"

"Why would you want to?" Shawn's bicep bunched under Kelly's arm, and she gave that cute little grin when Kelly looked at her to see if she'd done it on purpose.

"People are fascinating. The way they interact, the way they don't interact." Kelly positioned them in the kitchen so they could see through to the living room. "For instance. Look at that pair by the door. What do you see?"

"That he thinks yellow looks good with green. He looks like a plant." Shawn tilted her head slightly. "And her skirt is see-through enough that you can see she's wearing some kind of tight shorts underneath it."

Kelly squinted and then laughed. "Both of those things are true. She's wearing a body shaper of some sort if I had to guess. But they're surface level observations. Notice the way she's turned slightly away from him and looks around whenever he looks away. But his body is turned fully toward her."

Shawn watched, and her frown grew deeper. "And you're making assumptions about their thought processes and behavior based on their body language. But how do you know you're right?"

"Because behavioral analysis is a science too, based on facts developed through observation and research." She squeezed Shawn's bicep. "I'll bet you a peanut butter cookie that within the next two minutes, she walks away to talk to someone else, and he stands around not knowing what to do with himself."

Shawn looked at her. "Do you have any peanut butter cookies?"

"No. But Bree told me you do. So we'll bet with yours."

Shawn narrowed her eyes. "So if I win, I get to eat my own cookies. And if you win, then you get to eat my cookies?"

Kelly looked at Shawn's lips and then into her eyes. "Unless you have something better to bet with?"

Shawn blinked and looked away. "I think you may have won anyway."

Sure enough, the situation was exactly as Kelly had called it. Plant man leaned against the doorframe, clearly trying not to look deflated. Tight shorts woman had started talking to Bree. "Right. Break out the cookies."

Shawn shook her head and opened the plastic container. "I made them with cane sugar and pure peanut butter. No preservatives, and the sugar is more natural so it's easier to digest and work off than the chemical option."

Well, that didn't sound terribly appetizing, but Kelly moaned a little when she took a bite. "These are gorgeous."

Shawn's gaze was firmly fixed on Kelly's mouth, and she swallowed hard.

"Forgive the intrusion, but I'm pretty sure you didn't invite a bunch of people here just to put the moves on the boss." Bree stood in the kitchen doorway, grinning as she looked between them.

"I..." Shawn looked between them, but nothing else came out.

Kelly swallowed her bite of cookie. "You're absolutely right, Bree. My sincerest apologies for being so rude." She finished her cookie and took the box of them from Shawn. "Away we go." She hooked her arm once again through Shawn's and headed back to the living room.

"What are you doing?" Shawn murmured, her eyes down. "I only came to see you."

"And now you're going to see so much more of me."

Shawn's head snapped up, her eyes wide.

"While it's good to know where your mind is at, handsome, I meant you get to see me in action with other people. And that means you get to practice some behavioral science. Instead of worrying about what to say and do, analyze. Notice body language. Notice what gets said or glossed over. We'll compare notes over a beer when everyone is gone."

Before Shawn could respond, Kelly held out the box of cookies to a group of people chatting. "You simply must try the cookies that

Shawn made. I feel certain she stole God's recipe."

As predicted, the cookies were a hit and compliments abounded. Although Shawn clearly had no idea how to handle them, Kelly could tell she was taking the challenge seriously. A few times she actually looked like she was studying animals in a cage, and Kelly would whisper something in her ear that made her choke on her drink.

It was so much fun.

And she was actually enjoying getting to know the other people. More than one commented on how they were glad to see Shawn out and about, and she just gave an awkward smile in response. But as she relaxed, Kelly got to see a slightly different side of her, as did the people around them, if their reactions were anything to go by.

"Your daughter had surgery last year. Is she okay now?" Shawn asked one woman, who looked bewildered.

"Wow. I didn't know you knew about that. Yes, she's much better. The tumor was removed, and she's a regular teenager driving me crazy now." She lightly touched Shawn's arm. "Thank you for asking."

And then came other tidbits of information Shawn knew about people. Their partner's job promotions, their mother's illness, their trip to the Caymans. Soon it became obvious that she knew at least a little something about everyone.

Kelly had dropped back, content to listen as Shawn spoke with a couple about their upcoming research trip to Norway, and Bree moved up beside her.

"For someone who avoids people, she seems to know an awful lot about them." Kelly looked sideways at Bree.

"I've been able to talk her into one or two gatherings in the time I've known her, but I've never seen her this relaxed." Bree's affection was clear in her smile. "I hope it doesn't take too much out of her later."

"But if she isn't close to people, how does she know all these things?" She smiled when Shawn glanced over her shoulder as though looking for Kelly. When she spotted her and smiled back, she seemed to relax again and returned to her conversation.

"She listens." Bree thanked someone who put another drink in her hand. "She doesn't always know what to do with the information or why it matters, but she always listens to what people have to say." She took a sip of her drink, looking thoughtful. "She doesn't have a lot of time for what she considers inanities, but she has lots of time for more serious stuff and the things that matter to people, even though she may not get *why* they matter to people."

Kelly turned to talk to a few people who came over but found she didn't want to wander too far from Shawn. Not because Shawn couldn't handle things on her own—that clearly wasn't the case—but because she simply wanted to be near her. The new insights into Shawn's personality made her even more intriguing. And god, did she look hot tonight in her loose, low-slung jeans and black button-down shirt. Kelly wanted to run her hands through Shawn's short hair and tug on that silver belt buckle polished to a shine. Perhaps she should stop drinking...

Eventually people started to leave, and it wasn't long before it was just Bree, Shawn, and Kelly left.

Bree looked around, and there were dark circles under her eyes. "Yikes. It looks like you had a frat party over, not a bunch of scientists. I'll help you clean up." She started to push herself from the couch.

"Nope." Kelly held up her phone. "I've called you an Uber. You can pick up your car whenever. You're clearly too tired to drive."

Bree flopped back onto the couch. "Shawn, can we keep her? Can we?"

Shawn grinned and rolled her head to the side to look at Kelly. "I don't think you can keep people. Did you order me one too?"

"Should I?" Kelly's question hung in the air, and she held Shawn's gaze.

A car honking broke the silence, and Bree practically flew off

FRAGMENTS OF THE HEART

the couch. "Thank goodness. I can't handle the tension. See you later!" The door closed behind her.

Shawn took Kelly by surprise as she shifted toward her. Her hand slid beneath Kelly's hair to grasp the back of her neck, and she pulled her in for a deep, slow kiss.

Kelly melted into a puddle of desire.

Shawn broke the kiss and rested her forehead against Kelly's. "I hope that was okay. I've wanted to do it all night. Since pizza night actually. Maybe since you walked into my office."

Kelly kissed her back, her hands on Shawn's thighs, which flexed under them. When they came up for air this time, her nipples were hard and her center ached with need.

"I should go." Shawn ran her thumb over Kelly's bottom lip. "I don't know what this is between us, but I don't want to rush it. Is that okay?"

No. No, it was most definitely not okay. Kelly was going to burst into lust-fueled flames. "Of course it is. It's...sweet."

Shawn's smile held a tinge of sadness. "That's me. Sweet." She stood and pulled Kelly up with her. Once again, she gave her a lingering kiss. "Can I call you tomorrow?"

Kelly nodded and let her hand slip from Shawn's as Shawn backed toward the door. "We still have that challenge to talk over too."

"Do I get more than a cookie if I win?" Shawn asked as she opened the front door.

Kelly's knees buckled, and she sat down. Where had this version of Shawn come from? Where was the shy, awkward woman she'd been working with? "Winner's choice. You decide what you want."

Shawn grinned. "I'll think on it. Good night." She stopped as she was about to close the door behind her. "Thank you, Kelly. I had a really nice time." And then she was gone.

Kelly forced herself up and into the bedroom. She needed a very, very cold shower.

CHAPTER EIGHT

WHAT ON EARTH HAD come over her? Well, Shawn knew what had come over her, she just couldn't believe she'd acted on it. Dating a co-worker was off limits. The excuses that Kelly wasn't really a co-worker and would be moving on soon only held so much weight before she crushed them with logic. While they were working on the same project, they were co-workers. It was in the definition of the word, for fluff's sake.

She sighed and shifted in bed. Her dreams had been full of Kelly's kisses, her soft body in that white dress as it slid from her shoulders, leaving them bare as Shawn worked her way down, slowly, savoring every inch of skin, every moment. God, how she'd wanted to take Kelly up on her unsubtle offer last night. Dreams of her weren't nearly the same.

She'd let out that part of her she kept well hidden. The one confident in her sexuality, the one who managed to pick up a woman every once in a great while. She wasn't a hermit, after all. But if she went out, she went to Tulsa, where no one knew her. Or, more importantly, where none of her family would be. The last thing she needed was word to get around and cause her problems when she'd finally managed to cut ties. Otherwise she ended up in situations like the one she'd found herself in with her brother.

A situation Kelly had handled with the kind of aplomb and dexterity usually reserved for films. One minute her brother had been menacing her, the next he was on the floor with the wind knocked out of him. Aside from the family who had taken her in, no one had ever stood up for her. *Ever.* She swallowed the unfamiliar ball of emotion. But Kelly had. Both literally and figuratively, Kelly had taken charge of the situation when she'd obviously seen that Shawn had frozen in fear.

Beautiful, intelligent, kind, and brave. *What a woman.* Shawn smiled and fluffed her pillow. And damn. What a kiss. *Kisses.* There'd been more than one, and with each one, Shawn had considered asking where the bedroom was.

Shawn had the occasional fling if she came across someone who was attractive and seemed mutually interested. She enjoyed intimacy when that's what was being offered and both parties knew the parameters. When it came to anything deeper, she began to falter. And she didn't want to screw this up, even if it was bound to be short-lived. And even though she shouldn't be doing it because she shouldn't be dating a co-worker.

Groaning as she came full circle in her thought process, she got up and made a pot of coffee. She was tired, but that wasn't a surprise. Although she'd ended up enjoying herself far more than she thought she would, talking to people and being constantly aware always wore her out. Kelly's presence had made a huge difference though. What a nice surprise, that someone helped give her energy instead of sucking it away. She didn't even know that was possible.

She checked her email and social media while she waited for the coffee to brew and responded to the few things that required a response. It was Sunday, but she disliked the feeling of having something unfinished, and emails were a sore spot in that regard. She checked her box multiple times a day to make certain nothing went unread or unnoticed.

On a whim, she plugged Kelly's name into Instagram, and the profile came up right away. She clicked on it and spilled her coffee as she failed to pay attention to where the mug was in relation to the pot. Kelly in Oklahoma was beautiful. Kelly in Argentina, in Brazil, in Egypt, in India... She was clearly in her element, and she looked like a model placed on background scenes. Picture after picture showed her laughing, studying artifacts, on her knees in the dirt, standing in front of a room of people as she gave a talk... She was dynamic and stunning.

She was also rarely the one who posted the pictures. Almost all of them were posted by someone else who had tagged her in them. The few Kelly posted were usually of a pretty landscape or the cover of a book she was reading.

Her phone rang, displacing the pictures of Kelly with her name.

"I didn't know you liked poetry," Shawn said when she answered.

"I love it." The smile was obvious in Kelly's voice. "I love the way language is used to portray the complexity of life. Good morning, by the way. Always nice to know when one is the recipient of a cyber-stalking."

Shawn carried her coffee to the couch and sat down. "Good morning. I don't understand poetry, which just seems determined to cloud clear messages with indistinct wording. Like puzzles. Why create a picture only to pull it to pieces to put it together again? How tedious. Also, I dreamt of you all night. And it isn't cyber-stalking if I admit to it right away."

"Good dreams, I expect. Nothing where I'm part of a Teddy Bear's picnic that goes terribly wrong when a deranged clown with a machete shows up."

Shawn shook her head. "What a bizarre and macabre concept. It's no wonder you like poetry."

"I'm sure poets the world over would love to hear that." Kelly laughed. "Speaking of things we like, I was wondering if you'd go somewhere with me today."

"Yes."

Kelly laughed again. "You don't want to ask where we're going first? What if I drag you to a heavy metal concert?"

"It's a fundamental fact that people who like poetry don't listen to heavy metal." Shawn grinned, enjoying the chance for banter and feeling like she might be doing it right. "I don't know if that's true, actually, but it should be."

"Okay, well, then I'll surprise you. Text me your address, and I'll pick you up in an hour."

Shawn hesitated. "Kelly, last night was the most fun I've had in a while. But we're co-workers, and we really shouldn't take it beyond that. Professionally, it wouldn't look good for me to flout the rules I've put in place myself." Her stomach turned as she said it. She didn't *want* to say it. Why had it come out?

There was a moment of silence. "I won't say I'm not disappointed, but I understand and commend your work ethic. That said, I could still use a friend to spend time with. An hour?"

Shawn sighed, only mildly relieved at Kelly's capitulation. "An hour. See you then."

She set the phone down and rested her head against the cushion. Really, it was a bad idea to spend the day with Kelly. It would only make her want her more and end up frustrating them both. She should tell Kelly to pick up Bree instead.

But she didn't want to do that either. She headed to the shower, mentally sorting through her closet to figure out what to wear. The problem with not asking where they were going was that she didn't know how to dress. But she knew Oklahoma, and there weren't a lot of places to go that required the kind of clothing that couldn't get dirty.

Though she rather liked the idea of getting dirty with Kelly.

Fifty-five minutes later she was standing on her porch, watching as Kelly pulled up out front. She loped down to the truck and climbed in.

She waited, but Kelly simply looked at her. "What? Is something wrong?"

Kelly blew out a breath. "Nothing at all. You look delectable, and I was thinking of last night." She pulled the truck onto the road.

Shawn groaned. "I was trying to put it out of my mind so we could move firmly back into friendship territory."

Kelly smiled and winked. "Okay, stud. Let's change the subject then. You accepted a challenge last night. What did you see?"

Shawn closed her eyes. "Jenna is interested in Bryan, but Bryan is more interested in Gary."

"What makes you say that?" Kelly glanced at the GPS on the screen and followed the instruction to turn.

"Jenna positioned herself near Bryan whenever she could and tried to draw him into conversation. He was always polite but didn't engage much other than in brief snippets. But when Gary joined them, Bryan hardly stopped speaking and asked Gary all sorts of questions. He practically ignored Jenna, and he even turned so his back was nearly to her."

Kelly tapped the steering wheel. "Well done! You're a quick study. Anything else?"

Shawn looked over. "Pam drank water all night, and I saw her with her hand on her stomach a few times. Either she was ill or she's pregnant."

"Pregnant. Three months." Kelly turned again, frowning slightly at the GPS. "She's excited but worried about work." At a stoplight, she looked at Shawn. "Tell me what you saw in regard to Bree."

Shawn scanned her memory. "She was talking to you a lot..." She shook her head. "I don't remember seeing her much."

Kelly nodded and set off again when the light changed. "That's because she was in the kitchen talking to someone named Max. She was giggly and cute and played with her hair a lot."

Shawn considered those descriptors. "So she was flirting with him."

"Point to you."

"I noticed something else." Shawn wondered for a moment if she should say it, but they'd been honest with each other so far. "Several people were watching you. Not the way you and I were watching people. They wanted you like I wanted you." Her face went hot at the admission. "They tried to get your attention and tell you things they thought would interest you."

Kelly smiled a little. "But where was my attention?"

The realization sent a little thrill through her. "It was on me, mostly. Even when you were talking to someone else your body was turned toward me."

"We're here." They pulled up in front of a building covered in what looked like graffiti.

"I really thought you'd be against the possibility of plague. But I suppose you're used to field work in shady areas." Shawn studied the building, her skin already itching. "What is it?"

"It's a company dedicated to an immersive art experience." Kelly threw open her door and jumped out.

There was a huge metal octopus on the edge of the nearly empty parking lot. Beyond it on the ground was a painting of a giant old boombox from the eighties, complete with neon colors. A mural of a cityscape covered one wall in black and white, while another wall was covered in garish and badly done cartoon characters sitting at a table playing cards.

Reluctantly, Shawn followed Kelly to the eyesore. "Is that a vagina on the door?" Indeed, the front doors were covered in an artist's huge rendition.

Kelly tilted her head. "Well, what better way to enter a magical place than through a vagina?" She put one hand on each door and pushed.

The interior was set up much like an art gallery but one quite possibly put together by someone on an array of hallucinogens. Sculptures of a cartoonish nature were set up beside gothic type statues, and a romantic painting that could have been out of a Jane Austen novel was beside a painting with a big black splotch in the middle with the word *fuck* scrawled through it like it had been done with a finger.

"A word for the ages." Kelly grinned. "Probably one I use most often in my digs."

Shawn grimaced. "I was taught not to swear, and I admit it stuck with me. I find it crass and unimaginative."

"Yikes." Kelly shook her head, looking woeful. "You're going to find it easy to deny your attraction to me then. If I get going, I can swear like a sailor who stubs his toe while out drinking with other sailors." She nodded toward the painting. "And fuck is quite versatile, really. It can mean an actual physical act, it can mean something is great, like really fucking good. It can mean something is bad, like what the fuck do I do now. It can mean..."

"I get it." Shawn held up her hand, and Kelly started laughing. "But you can find words for all those things that aren't...that one. It's harder and more interesting."

They moved on to the other things and passed a couple discussing the merits of existential art done in acrylic paint.

Shawn rolled her eyes. "Pretentiousness irritates me."

"But is it pretentious if you believe it and find it interesting?" Kelly motioned toward a painting of a woman with more wrinkled skin than non-wrinkled skin. "You and I would discuss the archeology of her region with certainty and various hypotheses. We'd use the jargon of our field that other people wouldn't understand. We'd probably sound just as pretentious as they do to someone who didn't use our lingo or have our passion."

Shawn frowned, thinking about that. "But ours is fact-based. And useful."

"They think theirs is too." Kelly hooked her arm through Shawn's. "That's the beauty of listening to people and finding out what they think is interesting and important. We don't have to like the same things or even find them interesting. They're all stories, and we're made of them, whether we realize it or not."

Shawn pondered that as they moved from odd painting to odd sculpture. "But we have a finite amount of attention, time, and energy to give to the world. If we soak in all those stories, all the minutiae of things that don't interest us or aren't useful, then we fail to take in the things that really do matter."

Kelly headed toward a doorway at the back with a curtain hanging over it and classical music coming through. "I personally think our ability to ingest stories and experiences is infinite. We'll forget some and some will matter more than others, but there's no telling how they'll affect and change us." She pushed aside the curtain and motioned for Shawn to go in, but Shawn shook her head.

"Go ahead," she said, holding the curtain aside.

Kelly winked and went in, and Shawn followed. She stopped to stare.

Images flowed across all four walls as well as the ceiling and the floor. Bubbles looked almost like they were coming at her as they flowed over and past her. Clouds with monkeys leaping across them moved across the walls, followed by Dali type paintings that gave off an eerie feel.

She startled when Kelly took her hand.

"Come on," she said softly, leading them to a pair of bean bags against one wall.

Shawn looked around as she plopped awkwardly into the stuffed bag. Other bags and reclining beach chairs were set along the walls at large intervals so no one was too close to anyone else. All of them were taken by people who watched the strange dance of images around them.

Shawn swallowed and closed her eyes. Her pulse was racing, and her heart hammered against her chest.

"Are you okay?" Kelly whispered, her breath teasing Shawn's ear.

"I just... It's a lot." God, how she hated to admit that she could so easily be overwhelmed. "I just need a minute. I'll be okay."

Kelly held her hand gently and didn't say anything else. Slowly, Shawn opened her eyes and breathed deeply. The music had calmed in tempo and the images were more sedate. It gave her time to adjust and this time, when the music picked up pace again and the images became strange once more, she was ready for it and able to focus. She followed a parade of clowns as it moved across a wall and then behind Kelly, and her focus changed entirely. Kelly looked enthralled. Tiny lines around her eyes deepened as she smiled and followed the images across the room. She was so beautiful, it was almost painful to watch, and Shawn wanted to pull her close, drink her in, and feel whatever it was she was feeling as she watched the show.

She suddenly looked at Shawn, as though becoming aware she was being watched, and her smile softened. "You good?"

Shawn nodded.

The show's cycle started over from where they'd come in, and Shawn stood, drawing Kelly to her feet. "Where to?"

Kelly took her hand again and led them to a different doorway, all the while looking at the display. Once they were beyond the curtained doorway, she blew out a breath. "Wow. That was incredible. What an amazing way to combine the music with the images to create specific emotions."

Shawn was glad she didn't have to respond in kind when Kelly turned toward the next exhibit. It had been interesting, but she hadn't felt anything other than the initial panic.

"Here," Kelly said, handing Shawn a set of VR goggles.

Shawn held them with her fingertips. "First of all, I'm not a huge fan of virtual reality. I have enough trouble with real reality. Second, who knows how many people's sweaty faces have been against these? Can you imagine all the dead skin cells you're asking me to put against my face?"

Kelly held up a box of antibacterial wipes. "They clean them after every person, but you can wipe it down now as well. And I completely respect your decision not to do it, but I'm going in." She gave the goggles a quick wipe, slipped them on, and turned toward the next room.

Shawn continued to hold them in her fingertips as she watched Kelly moving slowly through what was a large, empty space with a lot of lights along the walls and floor. What was she seeing? Shawn warred with the desire to do it with her and the desire to remain firmly grounded in the truth of existence. With a sigh, she grabbed a few wipes and cleaned every part that might touch her face, then slid them on.

She gritted her teeth against the change in scenery. Still, she stepped forward onto the bow of a boat and fought the inclination to duck as a wave crashed over the side. Around her were floating space helmets with numbers marked on them. She focused in on number 12 and moved toward it, striding over the whirlpool moving continuously in the center of the bow. She noted the way her body reacted, jerking as though wanting to move around the danger instead of across it. While it might not be real, perception was clearly key here.

"I'm not sure you're good for my health," she said when she moved up beside number twelve's floating helmet.

"I think you have no idea how good I could be for your health, in so many ways." Kelly laughed, and a space glove appeared near Shawn's face, the colors in it sliding through the blue-purple scale. She touched Shawn's helmet and a wind chime sounded in Shawn's ears.

Intrigued, she touched Kelly's with her own space glove, which glowed through the red-pink scale, and heard the sound of a doorbell, which made Kelly laugh. They continued to move through the space together, touching a railing that set off blue sparks and stepping on enormous buttons that created the sense of the seasons as they exploded with snowflakes, flowers, autumn leaves, and sunrays.

Eventually they made their way out and took off their goggles, dropping them in a box to be cleaned for the next viewers. They headed toward the exit and out to the café in the back.

"Coffee, please." Kelly looked at Shawn. "For you?"

Shawn scanned the list of drinks. "Just water, thanks." She waved Kelly's money away and paid. "You bought the tickets for that mushroom-fueled experience in there. I can get the drinks."

Kelly sipped her coffee as she sat down at a picnic table. "Tell me what you really thought. What happened in the immersion room?"

Shawn took a sip of water and then continued to play with the lid. "I'm not sure I should tell you. There are expectations, and I don't want you to think differently of me."

Kelly frowned. "Expectations?"

Shawn motioned to herself. "Masc-presenting women are expected to act a certain way. To be strong, to be unafraid. They should be sporty and capable of fixing things in the house, they should be able to handle the spiders and laugh off fear." She shrugged, already deflating from the interesting experience. "But I'm not a lot of those things, and it tends to be a disappointment."

Kelly sipped her coffee, her eyebrows raised. "Wow. That's a lot of pressure to put on yourself. Or for other people to put on you. Do you think maybe you could just be you?"

Shawn sighed. "People don't want you to just be you. They say they do, but they don't. They want you to be the version of you they find most appealing, most acceptable." She tilted her head toward the exhibit, old wounds making her words hard. "Overwhelmed. I was overwhelmed by the combination of sounds, and images, and the new experience, as well as by being there with a woman I find intoxicating. I get that way sometimes. I just need to block out some of the stimulus until it doesn't feel like too much. Not very butch, is it? Not strong or sexy." She pressed against the plastic bottle top, trying not to let her emotions overflow.

"You've been dating the wrong women. And you've been around all the wrong kinds of people if you think that needing to take a second makes you not sexy." Kelly gave her a half grin. "I could cover you in mud and plant a flag with a picture of Trump on your head and you'd still be the sexiest thing I've ever seen."

Shawn spluttered her water. "Please don't ever do any of those things."

"Spoilsport." Kelly tilted her head again. "Okay, so initially you were overwhelmed. But your breathing slowed, and you took part. How about that?"

Shawn thought about it. "It was interesting, I suppose. As an experiment in emotions as connected to art, I imagine it holds a certain draw."

"But you didn't feel it? The way I did, I mean." Kelly simply looked curious, not in the least judgmental.

"I don't know." Shawn shrugged. "What did you feel?"

Kelly closed her eyes and her full, beautiful lips tipped in a smile. "When the clouds floated by, I felt like cool silk caressed my face, and when the clowns paraded across the walls, I remembered village fairs with Mr. Whippy and carousel music you could hear all the way down the street. When the black birds flew low against the deep thumping of the drums, I felt dread, like being at the top of a rollercoaster and waiting for the drop. And when the flowers burst out in color after color and shape after shape, I felt warm and thought of lying on a beach with nothing between me and my skin but the sun." She opened her eyes and seemed to blink away the images.

Shawn wished in that moment she could offer something similar, some experience that mirrored Kelly's. But she couldn't, and she refused to be inauthentic. "That sounds amazing. I'm glad you enjoyed it so much. Also, who is the unfortunately named Mr. Whippy?"

Kelly laughed and stretched, her top rising to show her tanned stomach. "Mr. Whippy is a kind of soft-serve ice cream. Usually served on a cone that tastes vaguely of polystyrene—"

"What's that?" Shawn asked.

"I think you call it Styrofoam?" Kelly looked thoughtful for a moment. "Anyway, your cone usually gets fed to the seagulls, if they don't rip it from your hands before you've even finished your ice cream."

Shawn shuddered. "That sounds like more of your macabre poetry."

Kelly finished her coffee and threw the cup away. "Lunch?"

Shawn followed her back to the car, thinking about how easily Kelly shared parts of herself. What must life be like, to be so open and so much a part of the world around you? Even Bree didn't have that kind of existence, try as she might to pretend she did.

The bubble Shawn had constructed around her life meant she rarely had to think about how she didn't view the world the way others did. But Kelly was drawing her out and showing Shawn's vulnerabilities to the light of day.

What if the sunlight proved to be too bright? What if Kelly decided she didn't like what she saw after all? Even more scary, what if she did?

CHAPTER NINE

THE DAY HAD BEEN surprising in multiple ways. Knowing the pressure that Shawn felt with regard to her identity was interesting but not unusual. Kelly was well aware that many masc women felt the pressure to be exactly what Shawn had described, often at the expense of being able to be vulnerable and honest about their feelings. Of course, there were plenty of butch women who were all those things that Shawn had listed too. That Shawn felt the supposed lack so deeply wasn't a surprise either. As difficult as emotions were for her, she clearly had a depth of soul that was easily stirred, try as she might to keep that from being the case.

Kelly pulled up in front of Shawn's house. Lunch had revolved around discussions of archeological significance, a topic Shawn was clearly more at ease with, and which Kelly was always happy to dive into. She had a feeling Shawn needed some time away from the more personal stuff, which was fine. There'd be months yet for them to get to know one another.

They sat in silence for a moment before Shawn finally looked at her. "I want to invite you in. I don't want the day to end. But it isn't a good idea."

"Because?" Kelly knew, but she wanted to hear it anyway.

"Because I like you too much. I want to kiss you again. And again. And then some more." Shawn rubbed her hands on her jeans. "But as I said when you invited me out earlier, that's a bad idea. It goes against policies I wrote myself. And..." She swallowed and looked away. "And you say you're attracted to me now, but eventually you'd find my quirks too difficult to deal with. I'd get attached to you, and you're going to leave for London soon. There are too many variables that involve me being emotionally invested and not knowing how to cope when it ends."

"Okay, cowboy. Slow your horse." She smiled at Shawn's frown. "First of all, yes, I think you're attractive and you're an amazing kisser. Second, I already told you that I respect your decision to keep things professional." She cupped Shawn's cheek in her palm. "And third, you deserve someone who can see how special and fabulous you are. Yes, you walk through the world differently. That simply makes you more interesting, not less. And anyone who can't see that is a fool undeserving of cold porridge, let alone someone like you." She let her hand slide away. "That said, it's true that I'll be leaving for London when our project is over, and getting emotionally attached would make things difficult. I can see that." She leaned over and kissed Shawn's cheek softly. "In the meantime, I'm incredibly glad to get to know you."

Shawn opened the door and hesitated before closing it. "Thank you for inviting me out today. I had a really good time."

She gave a sharp nod, like she'd said what she had to say, then closed the truck door and headed up the walk to her house. She gave a quick wave, then went inside.

Kelly leaned her head against the headrest for a second, then set off. She'd wanted to run her hands through Shawn's close-cropped hair and pull her close. She'd wanted to cuddle up next to her at the exhibition to let her know she wasn't alone. She'd wanted... wanted...wanted... All the innocent touches and hand holding had felt so good, and fuck it all, she wanted more. But getting involved with someone like Shawn would be hard, no question. Kelly had a temper, though she rarely let it fly, and she could be impatient as well as sharp when she was frustrated. Someone like Shawn would feel that kind of response on an almost visceral level, and that wasn't fair.

With a sigh, she headed back to her place. She'd lay in the sun and take an afternoon nap, then go find a restaurant for dinner. Alone.

Damn it. She needed to get this project done and get home.

***

Monday morning couldn't arrive soon enough. The night had been dull and long. She'd tried reading but couldn't sit still long enough to make any progress. She'd tried watching a movie, but the acting had been so atrocious she'd laughed her way through the serious parts and then given up. She'd gone out to do some shopping but found that most of the stores closed at six.

Eventually, she'd relaxed outside as dusk turned to night and the bats darted through the air like little shadows racing one another in the sky. Owls called across the light of a full moon, and the frustration and loneliness of the late afternoon had receded.

Still, as she drank coffee from yet another new coffee place, this one superior to the last but by no means perfect, she was glad to be headed into the office. She'd considered calling Shawn and asking her to hang out, but mixed messages weren't really her style, and Shawn had made her position clear. She'd thought about calling Bree, but she had a feeling Bree would probably be with Max, if the party was anything to go by. Hell, for a moment she'd even considered going over to the neighbor, Buck, and having a drink with him. But that told her just how desperate she was, so she quashed it. And so, she'd dealt with her own company and found it rather lacking in anything of interest.

She pushed open the door to the office and found Shawn already staring at the screen. Bree was beside her and gave Kelly a wide smile.

"Sounds like you guys had a great time. I'm going to have to check that exhibition out myself! I've already told Max about it, and we've decided to go next weekend." Bree's excitement shone in her eyes.

Kelly set her bag and drink down and crossed her legs, noting the way Shawn's gaze flicked to her high heels and then away again. Her jaw clenched, and she blinked hard.

Okay, so mixed messages weren't good, but it didn't hurt to know that Shawn found her attractive. She grinned inwardly and was about to turn to Bree when her phone rang. She pulled it from her bag and answered. "Jack, boss of my heart and irritation to my stomach lining. To what do I owe the pleasure of your smoker's cough?"

"Are you with Shawn?" he said, no teasing or general joviality in his tone.

"I am. As well as Bree McIntosh." She straightened. "Is something wrong?"

"Can you put me on speaker phone?" he asked, the sound of papers rustling on his end.

Kelly shrugged and did as he asked. "This is Jack, my boss in London. He's asked to speak to both of us. Go ahead, Jack."

Shawn and Bree looked at one another and then the phone, as though trying to divine the nature of the call before he spoke.

"Hi, Shawn, nice to kind of meet you. I'm familiar with your work, which is always stellar."

Shawn didn't say anything, still staring at the phone.

"Um, anyway. You're all familiar with the work going on in Denali. We've had an emergency call-out. The Broken Swan glacier–"

"That's been on the move. I read about it yesterday." Bree looked excited to be part of the conversation.

"It has. But the bigger news is that it broke last night. There's a huge crevasse, and the team out there on a different dig went to check it out." He sounded almost breathless. "There are artifacts in the break, nearly halfway down. They may be the deepest artifacts found in a glacier yet."

Shawn frowned and glanced at Kelly before looking back at the phone. "That's interesting, but how does it involve us?"

It was a good question. Oklahoma wasn't a quick pit stop from Alaska.

"Winter is coming, and there's an extremely limited window for us to get in, get what we can, catalogue it...and put it back."

Kelly closed her eyes. "I hate those digs."

"Why would you put it back?" Shawn looked from Kelly to the phone. "And that wasn't a response as to why it involves us."

"At certain dig sites that belong to tribal land, the tribes feel like removing it is disrespectful to the ancestors. They're fine with us studying it, but it can't be removed and when we're done, everything has to be put back essentially right where it was found."

"Right. And on the phone right now, I have three of the most well-known archeologists in our field."

Bree's eyes went wide. "He said three."

Kelly nodded and gave her a distracted smile. "So, you're saying you want the three of us, and presumably a larger team, to go to Alaska and dig, catalogue, and analyze as fast as we can before the storm comes in and the glacier re-ices."

Shawn sat back, her knuckles white on the arms of her chair. Bree looked like she might faint, but with excitement or fear, Kelly couldn't tell.

"This kind of break only happens once every decade, if that. For all we know, this one won't break again in our lifetimes, even with climate change acceleration. You're right, I'll have a team with you. You won't be on your own. But with Bree's photographic memory, Shawn's ability to catalogue and analyze on a dime, and Kelly, your ability to ferret out even the smallest item, along with your history of managing digs..."

Shawn blinked. "I hate when people trail off. What about those things?"

"He's saying that the three of us have the skills necessary to do what needs to be done as quickly as possible, and time isn't on our side. He wants us all on-site."

Shawn shook her head, slowly at first, and then more vehemently. "I don't do site work. You can send the images back to me here, and I'll get them done as fast as possible, although not so fast that mistakes are possible. Why the need to catalogue on site? Why can't I just use the photos of the dig the same way we're handling the Brazil dig right now?"

Beneath the stubbornness, Kelly could hear real fear. "That's a valid question, Jack. I understand how Bree's ability might come in handy for location placement, but surely the rest could be done from an office?"

"It could, in theory. But the AARG are involved, and they get what they want. And they want everything done on site, as much as possible."

Bree's eyes grew unfocused for a moment. "That's the Alaskan Archeological Recovery Group. A government system devoted to caring for the ancestry and preservation of indigenous Alaska." It sounded like she was reading from a sheet.

"That's right, Bree. And when they're involved, they want things kept close at hand. If you're analyzing data, then they want to be there to add their input and make sure you've got it right. And since we'll be on their turf, they have final say. If we want to handle the dig, then they want the experts on hand. They've agreed that anything you find can be made into a 3-D print model for museums, which is something. I know it isn't the same, but we'll still get to study the artifacts to a high degree, and they won't be forgotten down there in the ice."

He paused, and Kelly knew he was waiting for confirmation. But given Shawn's pallor and Bree nibbling on her thumb, this might be a hard sell. "Jack, you know I'm in. But I think we need to have a discussion over here." She had a final thought. "Before you go—if Shawn and Bree can't make it, do you have other people who can?"

He hesitated again. "If I say yes, then they might not come. But yes. I have a couple people who would be back-ups. But they're not at the top of their field like your current companions, Kelly. They're the best, and that's what we need right now."

"Okay. I'll call you back shortly." She hung up and stood. "We're leaving. Come on."

Shawn shook her head. "It's a work day. We have work to do. We can't just leave."

Kelly took Bree's hand and pulled her to her feet. "You should put your shoes on. City streets are notoriously filthy." She turned to Shawn. "We have a serious work-related discussion ahead of us, and that requires a change of scenery. If we were in London, we'd have our talk over a pint and a pickled egg at a pub but sadly, we're lacking in all three of those things here. So we'll settle for the next best thing." She picked up Shawn's satchel and started backing toward the door. Behind her, she heard Bree giggle slightly. "I'm holding your bag hostage."

Shawn's jaw worked, and she finally picked up the phone. "Cassandra, I'm going to a meeting. I'll be back shortly, but I'm not sure exactly when." She hung up, probably without waiting for a response. She tugged the bag from Kelly's hand. "Where are we going?"

Kelly motioned for them to follow, her thoughts twisting in a tornado. She'd done digs all over the world. She knew what they required. These two, out in the field in one of the most difficult dig sites on earth... She shook her head. It wasn't a good idea. But if this was the way it had to be, then she needed to convince them.

Twenty minutes later, Shawn and Bree sat on high barstools looking as out of place as a cat on a log floating down a river and just about as scared. The waiter placed a pitcher of beer on the table along with a bucket of chicken wings and onion rings.

Shawn looked at it all with distaste. "If you're trying to kill us before we have to go to Alaska, this should do it. And who has this kind of thing at this time of day?"

Bree almost gleefully pulled out a chicken wing and started to nibble at it daintily, her feet swinging from the barstool. "This is my kind of meeting."

Kelly grinned and chalked the pool cue. "I find that incredibly serious discussions are best had in incredibly unserious environments. It takes the pressure off and means we can speak more freely."

She bent over the table and took her time sizing up the shot for a break. From the corner of her eye, she saw Bree give Shawn an eyebrow wiggle and tilt her head toward Kelly's bent frame. For fun, she bent over a little more than necessary before she shot. When she stood, Shawn was pouring herself a beer.

"Your turn, hotshot." She handed the cue to Shawn, giving her a quick wink that made Shawn blush.

"I haven't played in a long time." She scanned the table and then walked around it. "Nine ball, corner pocket." She lined it up and shot. It went in, as did the next and the next.

Kelly would be more than happy for her to shoot all day long. Shawn's muscles bunched under her fitted button-down shirt, and she found that she very much wanted to take it off.

She finally missed and started to move around the table to hand the cue to Bree. Before she got there, Bree leaned over.

"It's a good thing this table isn't in a private place." She fanned herself with a napkin. "I hope someone looks at me that way one day." She hopped off the barstool, took a shot, missed, and handed the stick back before hopping back up and taking an onion ring.

"So," Kelly said, taking a harder shot because she knew it would put her butt directly in front of Shawn, "tell me how you're feeling about this offer. Pros and cons."

There was silence behind her, and she let them think as she took another shot.

"I've always wanted to see Alaska." Bree set the half-eaten onion ring on a napkin and then twisted a coaster in her hand.

"Okay. That's a pro. Con?"

"Bree doesn't travel." Shawn sipped her beer and winced. "This is terrible."

"Why don't you travel?" She handed the stick to Shawn.

Bree continued to fiddle with the coaster. "I can't fly. I mean, I literally have anxiety so bad I pass out. And in the lead-up to the flight, I worry myself so sick I can't function. Travel in general makes me anxious. I want to see the world, but I can't bring myself to leave the city." Tears welled in her eyes, and she looked away.

"Serious anxiety. Con. Got it." She turned to Shawn, who was standing beside the table leaning on the cue stick. "And you?"

"I like my office. I like my routine. I don't like people because they confuse and irritate me. I hate being cold."

Kelly held up her hand. "Okay, okay. You've got some cons. Any pros?"

Bree took the cue stick and Shawn picked up her beer, clearly thinking. "It might be interesting to see a dig in motion." She shook her head. "Maybe."

Bree missed her next shot and looked at Kelly. "What's it like? I mean, I guess they're all different. But what would it be like in Alaska?"

Kelly took out her phone. "Here are some photos I took on a dig there about ten years ago. It's a lot less snowy now." She handed over the phone, and Bree and Shawn looked through the photos together. She didn't miss the way Shawn seemed to take in every detail, or the way Bree looked simultaneously excited and terrified.

"He said we'd be working on a glacier." Shawn looked up from the phone. "That means we wouldn't be staying in these cabins on stilts."

Kelly tilted her head. "If I had to guess, I'd say we'll definitely be staying in something just like them. Although we use tents a lot of the time, we won't camp on the ice because of the way it's shifting. It would be too dangerous. There's a dig probably about half an hour from there, and I bet we'd stay there and commute to the glacier."

"I don't have equipment. Do we need to have our own?" Bree continued to study the photos.

The question was a good indication that Bree could be convinced to make the trip. She might have to do it highly medicated, but so be it. "A lot of archeologists have their own gear, and we can get you some things before we head out. But there's nothing to say you'd be doing the actual digging." When Bree's expression fell slightly, Kelly amended her phrasing. "Unless you particularly wanted to, of course."

"Do you think we should do it?" Shawn asked, sliding onto a bar stool. "You've gotten to know us over the last few days. Do you think we're the kind of people who belong on a glacier in Alaska?"

Kelly frowned and sat opposite them, the pool game forgotten. "There's a lot of supposition in that phrasing. What kind of people do you think go on digs?"

"The kind who like chaos." Shawn smiled a little. "The kind who enjoy adventure and who don't mind when nothing goes to plan and you have to change the way you thought you'd do things." She tapped the phone. "The kind who like to throw themselves into glacier crevasses and work all out before the glacier closes or re-ices." She raised her eyebrows. "Are we those types of people?"

Kelly took in Bree's shoulder slump and Shawn's tense jaw. She wasn't sure there was a right answer here, but she could be honest. "I think all types of people enjoy going on digs. You're right. There are going to be difficulties you'll need to overcome, and there are going to be times when it's incredibly hard. There will certainly be moments you wish you hadn't gone." She touched Bree's hand. "But I can almost guarantee it will be an experience you'll never forget, and you'll be proud of yourself for throwing routine to the wind in order to do something special."

"What about my fear of travel?" Bree asked. "It isn't just planes, Kelly. I get anxious in a car if I don't know where we're going." Her eyes filled with tears, and she brushed them away quickly.

"Well, this is a perfect moment to see how we overcome that, isn't it?" She grinned. "I say we drug you. Mildly enough so we don't have to put you in a suitcase and wheel you about, and then more so when we actually get on the plane so you sleep through the journey." She slid her phone from under Shawn's fingertips. "And we plan. I show you photos of where we're going. We have a video call with the team in Alaska and the team we'll be going with, so you get to know everyone. We look at the route we'll be taking to the campsite, and we'll see if they can video the route from there to the glacier. You'll have all the visual cues you need."

The more Kelly had talked, the brighter Bree had become. "And you'll be there the whole time?"

Kelly nodded. "Every step of the way."

Bree turned to Shawn. "I won't go without you. It's both of us or neither."

Shawn scoffed. "That's ridiculous. My work can be done elsewhere. Yours is best done on site. There's no need—"

"Both of us. Or neither of us." Bree folded her arms.

Shawn was silent for a long time, her jaw clenching and her hands busy tearing apart a coaster a layer at a time. "You know I'm going to be difficult," she finally said, glancing at Kelly and then back to the little pile of shredded carboard.

Bree's intake of breath signaled her excitement, but Kelly gave a quick shake of her head. She didn't want to jump ahead too soon. "I know you're going to have questions and plenty of things that might make you uncomfortable. That doesn't mean you'll be difficult. It means..." Kelly shrugged, unsure how to put it. "It means we better be good at communicating."

Shawn was silent once more, and the clacking of pool balls smacking against each other and quiet chatter at the bar were the only sounds. Kelly didn't need to beg. If they didn't want to do it, she'd still be working with other people probably almost as qualified. Her desire for them to go wasn't about the work. It was about them. She'd never met two people who needed to get away from the office more. She genuinely thought it would be good for them, but she wouldn't pressure them to do it. She'd said her piece.

Finally, Shawn moved the pile of destroyed coaster into her palm and left the table to throw it in the bin. Bree watched her closely, the tension clear in the lines around her eyes.

When Shawn returned, her hands shoved in her pockets, her eyes on the table, Kelly wanted to reach out and tell her it would be okay.

"We'll go." Shawn patted Bree awkwardly on the back when she jumped off the stool to pull Shawn into a hug. "But I want to be fully prepared for every eventuality."

Kelly grinned. "It's hard to be prepared that way on a dig this uncertain, but I'll do my best to help."

Shawn picked up the beer and took a deep drink, grimacing as she set it down. "Flumpit, that's bad."

"Flumpit," Kelly said, laughing. "This is your creative swearing, I take it, and not an American term I'm unfamiliar with?"

"She has a lot of them." Bree dug back into the onion rings. "I imagine you'll get to hear them when she gets cold. That's her favorite thing, isn't it?" She laughed and offered Shawn an onion ring, which was turned down with vigor.

"What about the Pedra finds? That was supposed to be the most important thing." Shawn finally made eye contact.

"We'll have to finish it when we get back." She bumped Shawn's shoulder with hers. "Guess you'll have to put up with me for longer than you'd hoped."

Shawn's cheeks went pink, and Bree giggled.

"So, what now?" Shawn asked. "Do we go back to work and finish out the day? Or do we begin getting ready today?"

"Let me see your phone." Bree passed hers over. "This video..." Kelly said, tapping away until she found it, "was done by a friend of mine. She's packing to go on a three-month dig, and she tells you what you might need, and what she would have done differently. While you're watching that, I'll call Jack and let him know the news. He'll want to begin putting our travel in place."

Bree immediately began watching the video, but Shawn held her gaze as she backed away from the table. There were so many emotions there, so many questions and worries. But when Kelly smiled, the main thing she saw was desire.

Jack answered, and she turned away to talk to him. "We're all in."

His sigh of relief was audible. "When can you go?"

"I'd be ready tomorrow, obviously. But we've got two dig virgins, so we'll need to get them kitted out. And they're going to need some hand holding too. That means I have some homework to do to make them comfortable." She wondered for a second how difficult this was really going to be. Was she leading them into a situation they'd regret? She turned and looked at them watching the video. Bree's hands were going as she talked, and Shawn clearly kept trying to shush her to hear what the woman on the video was saying. Rather than looking upset, she looked intrigued. "I can't get home for tea. You understand what that means?"

"I'll get some shipped to the team going with you. I'll ship twenty tons of tea to you in Alaska for making this happen. Anything else?"

She could think of ten things offhand, but this wasn't the time. "I'll send you a list tonight. Best guess, I need three days to get things under control here."

"Perfect. That gives me time to assemble the team going with you."

She rolled her eyes. "You haven't already contacted people?"

"I wanted to wait until I knew you were going. If it wasn't going to be you, I had to change the team." Papers rattled noisily. "The University of Aberdeen has a crew headed to their satellite campus there. I'll have them assigned to you."

"Good. They can bring some proper biscuits as well. And a few tins of mushy peas, please."

"Revolting. Send me anything else you think of."

She continued to watch Shawn and Bree talk. "I assume you'll be taking care of their costs with regard to kit."

He hesitated. "That's not really protocol–"

"You're asking two office-based researchers to head into one of the harshest environments we work in. Protocol can fuck itself with a gravy boat." Kelly grinned at her wording. Shawn would've flinched for sure.

"Yeah. Okay. I hear you." He sighed dramatically. "Send me the bill, and I'll get it taken care of."

"Good man." She waved when Shawn looked around for her. "I'll email you tonight and call you tomorrow with an update."

"You're a good woman, Kelly, no matter what people say about you." He laughed and she joined in.

"And you're not nearly the wanker people think you are. Speak to you tomorrow." She hung up and headed back to the table.

"This one or this one?" Bree said, showing Kelly a couple trowels.

"You okay?" she asked Shawn, while pointing at the correct tool.

Shawn nodded slowly. "I think so. I'll probably change my mind a million times before we leave though."

"Understandable." She tilted her head toward the door. "How about we go back to the office and work on the Brazil finds for the rest of the day? Then tonight, we'll have dinner and make lists of what you need."

Bree looked briefly disappointed as she put away her phone. "I don't know how I'll be able to concentrate on anything other than this."

"Shawn? Is that plan okay with you? Or would you rather skive off work—"

"No!" Shawn swallowed. "Sorry. No, I think it's a good idea to go back and get things in order. I'll need to talk to everyone and reallocate responsibilities." She seemed to bite the inside of her cheek. "Do you know how long we'll be gone?"

Kelly shook her head. "I don't, but I don't think it will be too long. Glaciers are temperamental things, and with it being so late in the year, we'll lose daylight as well as be watching for storms. As soon as the glacier becomes too unstable or the storms come in without a break, we'll be done."

Shawn sighed. "This is exactly what I was afraid of. That wasn't an answer with any kind of meaning. You may as well have answered with something about astrology."

"I'm an Aquarius." She winked when Shawn groaned.

"I'm a Pisces." Bree laughed and slapped Shawn on the back. "Shawn is a Leo." She waved her hand to indicate Shawn's body. "As you can see. Concerned with appearance, always right—"

"And great hair." Kelly lightly touched Shawn's hair, only for her to pull away with a frown. "Lions don't like their manes being touched."

"Nonsense. It's all ludicrous, non-factual nonsense. The stars have as much to do with our personalities as...as...carrots have to do with paint." Shawn stood and started heading for the door.

"There's a tribe in South America that uses mashed carrots to dye clothing. So maybe that's not as good an analogy as you think it is." Kelly laughed at Shawn's eye roll. "Do you believe in anything you can't explain?"

Something flickered in Shawn's expression, but it was gone too quickly for Kelly to parse it.

"No. Everything can be explained somehow. Even emotions are often down to fight or flight."

Bree walked ahead of them toward Kelly's truck, and Kelly tugged on Shawn's hand to get her to stop for a second. Gently, she cupped Shawn's face in her hand and leaned close to her ear. "And what about what you feel when I do this?" she asked, lightly nipping Shawn's earlobe.

Shawn hissed slightly. "Biological response. Lust," she murmured.

Kelly chuckled and let go. "Okay then. If anything occurs that you can't explain, you're required by law to share it with me."

Shawn looked puzzled. "There are no laws requiring the sharing of that kind of information."

"There are when you travel with me," Kelly said, backing toward the truck.

Shawn sighed, shaking her head. "How am I supposed to understand laws you make up yourself on a whim that have no real relevance?"

As Shawn opened Kelly's truck door for her, she leaned closer.

"You'll just have to pay attention, handsome." She got in and grinned at Shawn's grumbling as she shut the door. This was going to be hard, but it was also going to be a hell of a lot of fun.

CHAPTER TEN

A MOUNTAIN OF CARDBOARD boxes sat in Shawn's living room, waiting for attention. She stared at them from where she sat at the dining room table. The night before, she and Bree had gone to Kelly's place and done all their shopping online with next day delivery after they'd made clear, functional lists. That had been enjoyable, for the most part, and she'd even managed to shut off the bit of her brain sounding a claxon alarm that this was not just a bad idea, but one right up there with glass hammers and prune milkshakes. This was going to turn her ordered, stable life upside down. And for what?

Kelly. Shawn groaned and rested her head in her hands. She was pretty sure no one else on the planet could have convinced her to do this. But it hadn't been anyone else on the planet. It had been Kelly, who'd breezed into their lives almost like she belonged there, made them laugh, set Shawn's body on fire, and was now leading them to a chasm in Alaska.

Last night every one of Shawn's senses had been on overload. Kelly had sat shoulder to shoulder with her on the couch, and Bree was on the other side. Heck, Shawn wasn't even sure what she'd ended up buying, thanks to the scent of Kelly's subtle perfume and the way her leg kept pressing against Shawn's every time she leaned over to look at Bree's computer.

The phone rang, jerking her from the memory of how badly she'd wanted to kiss Kelly deeply. Her cat, Marvel, jumped from her lap and headed toward the phone as though he was going to answer it. That was illogical, of course, and fantasy movies were just movies, but she'd admit privately that it would be very cool if the cat did, in fact, answer the phone. She'd read a book once where the cat wore glasses and read a newspaper. She had a feeling she'd enjoy a conversation with that type of cat.

"What kind of people are you hanging around with now? What have you gotten yourself into?"

All warm feelings fled at the crisp, iceberg tone of her mother's voice. "What are you talking about?"

"How could you let some woman beat up your brother? He's your family. Not these terrible people you spend time with."

Surprised, Shawn couldn't help but grin a little. "He grabbed the woman in question, and she defended herself. She had every right to do so." The momentary pause on the line meant Shawn's brother had blamed the big bad lesbians and hadn't mentioned the fact that he'd deserved what had happened. *And a lot more, really.*

"Well, you should have called off your dog. You know full well he didn't mean nothing by it, and besides, you should have stood up for him."

"He was being nasty to me as well, so I felt no need to say anything to him at all. She defended me the way you never did." Shawn bit her lip, shocked at the words that seemed to have come out all on their own. Maybe Kelly was a good influence after all.

"Here we go again with the pity party. Poor Shawn was misunderstood." She coughed, a harsh, wracking sound. "That's life, and you know full well how we feel about your lifestyle."

"I do. Which is why we don't talk anymore. Did you really call just to tell me my brother's ego is hurt because he got his butt whooped by a woman?"

Again, there was a moment's hesitation. "I'm sick. Might need a kidney. The whole family is being tested for a match. I need you to get down to the hospital too."

Shawn felt the tremble that always began deep in her chest, a vibration that spread like ripples until it flooded her whole body. Within seconds, her hands were shaking. "So, I'm not good enough to be part of your life—I'm not good enough for anything, according to you—but my kidney might be good enough?"

"As a child, it's your duty to obey and respect your parents, Shawn. You'll do no less than your siblings, just as God wills." There was iron in her voice now, a tone Shawn knew all too well.

Shawn saw Kelly's car pull up outside. "I'll see if I have time." She hung up and set the phone on the charging cradle after glancing at the notifications to make sure there wasn't anything she was missing or needed to pay attention to. Her mother certainly wasn't one of those things.

When Kelly knocked, Shawn had to take a deep breath to try and stem the shaking in her hands. She didn't want Kelly to think she'd fall apart at the smallest thing. It was hard enough silencing her inner critic that said someone like Kelly wouldn't have any real interest in Shawn without appearing weak too. How the hell was she going to survive this?

"Hey there, travel buddy. You ready to take on the world?" Kelly gave her a quick kiss on the cheek.

Shawn grimaced. "That doesn't sound like fun in the least. And I'm seriously doubting why I've said yes to this. Tell me again."

Kelly laughed, and Shawn frowned at her. "Ah, you're serious." Kelly sat on the arm of the armchair but shifted quickly when Shawn moved toward her, intent on moving her into the right position in the chair. "You're doing this because it will be good for our science overall. Because you're going to be there helping me as we make some truly remarkable discoveries—"

"You can't know they'll be remarkable. There may be nothing but fragments." Shawn was never sure how people came up with the assertions they made about the future.

"If they were barely fragments, then we wouldn't have been called. And enough fragments put together make up a whole, and that's part of the fun. But the team there think whatever has been exposed is worth digging up, even with the expense and danger involved." She winced. "We'll be well geared up though, so no worries about the danger."

"There's danger on any dig site, right?" Shawn sat on the couch across from her. "I spent a lot of time listening to an archeologist's podcast while I was working out this morning. He said you just have to be prepared."

"He's right. You can't be prepared for every single eventuality... I mean, I didn't know that we'd set up camp near a ground-dwelling hornet's nest until someone tried to dig a hole for a loo stop." Kelly laughed and shook her head. "You don't want angry hornets down there, let me tell you."

Shawn flinched and felt her legs tighten in sympathy. "Was the person okay?"

"She had to go to the hospital and stayed for a few days. The guy laughing at her and kicking dirt at the hornets got stung even worse, and I admit to thinking karma played a part in that."

"Karma is something made up so people feel better about the things that happen to other people. They rarely think what happens to them is their own karma, unless it's something good." Shawn wanted to pull Kelly across the small distance between them and ignore the mountain of boxes and the impending trip. But now, they were not only going to be co-workers on a more literal level, they'd also be sleeping near one another.

Before she could broach the issue of sleeping arrangements, the door was flung open.

"Bears. Are there bears? No matter how big I try to be, I'm not ever going to look big enough to scare away a bear." Bree threw her bag on the couch and headed to the kitchen, quickly coming back with a mug and a muffin in hand.

"You shouldn't get within three-hundred yards of a bear and if you do, that's why we bought bear spray." Kelly winked at Shawn and then turned her attention to Bree.

What did the wink mean? Was she sharing some information that Shawn didn't understand? Was there an inside joke? Or was she being sexy? Because she was sexy, for sure. But the wink didn't seem like a "let's go to bed" wink. Shawn ground her teeth and focused on the packages. This was a bad idea.

"And we'll be in groups big enough that the bears will stay away unless they smell food. Honestly, this time of year they're heading into hibernation, so we're unlikely to see any at all." She turned to Shawn. "Are you okay?"

"You winked." Shawn shrank a little inside when Kelly looked confused. "I don't know what it means."

Kelly seemed to think for a moment. "It meant it was okay that our conversation was interrupted when Bree came in, and that we'd continue it later."

Shawn blew out a breath, relieved. "Thank you. But we don't need to. Spiritual stuff like that doesn't really interest me."

"Shawn!" Bree smacked Shawn's leg. "Just because it doesn't interest you doesn't mean it doesn't interest other people. And sometimes you just have to put up with other people talking about things that they like."

Shawn groaned, tired of the conversation. "You always say that."

"And it's always true." Bree stuck her tongue out, making Kelly laugh.

"This is going to be a great trip." Kelly looked around. "Where should we start?"

Bree started to stand, but Shawn pulled her back onto the couch. "Not you." She stood, ignoring Bree's pout. "We do this methodically, laying things in piles so we know what belongs to who so we can account for everything."

"Not one to just rip into birthday gifts then, eh?" Kelly grinned, but it faltered when Shawn grimaced.

"We didn't celebrate birthdays. Mine, anyway. Birthdays were for kids who were normal and had friends to invite over." Shawn picked up a large package, one of two that size, and guessed it was their sleeping bags. When she noticed the silence behind her, she looked over her shoulder. Their expressions were...well, something. "What?"

"I severely dislike your familial relations more with every bit of information you share about them. Vile creatures." Kelly's cheeks were flushed, and she flicked at the edge of a cardboard box. "We'll find a way to make up for that if I have to fly here every year just to celebrate it with you."

The warm, happy feeling that flooded her chest was new, and Shawn wasn't sure what to do with it. She took the box to Bree and put it on her lap. "Start here." She got the matching box, and they opened them to reveal a pink sleeping bag for Bree and a navy blue one for Shawn. Both were designated useful for extreme temperatures.

Shawn took the bags and set them beside one another against the far wall, then handed Bree another package. Item after item was added to each pile, and Shawn couldn't fathom how they'd need it all while working on a glacier. Neither she nor Bree needed a pick-axe. After all, Bree was just observing, and Shawn would be entering data. But Kelly had insisted.

"Before you use those, make sure we show you how. You wouldn't believe how many people don't use them right and believe me when I say you don't want to be close to someone who swings one without warning." Kelly stood and lifted the side of her T-shirt to reveal an inch-long pink scar.

Shawn wanted to touch it. Really, really wanted to touch it.

"Okay. Everything we ordered is here, and now we can get it packed and ready to go." Kelly handed Shawn her phone. "Those are our travel details."

"Already?" Shawn asked, reading every line and committing it to memory. She handed it to Bree and knew she'd do the same.

"When I called and said you'd agreed, things got underway pretty quick. The team have been notified and are ready to go, and the team already in Alaska will meet us at the airport."

Shawn looked over when she heard a strange sound and realized it was Bree, breathing too rapidly. She took her hand. "Hey now. We're in my house. Nowhere near a plane yet. Feel the carpet under your feet. Think about the color of the desk at work.

Smell that cinnamon bread thing you like so much." She worked through the sensory steps she knew would work, and soon Bree's breathing was back to normal.

Kelly waited until Bree had wiped away her tears and then knelt in front of her. She held out a small vial. "I promised we'd help with the anxiety. I had these overnighted from a physician in London. It's strong, and it'll relax you to the point you feel like you're made up of nothing but clouds and starlight, which means you *have* to be aware of the dosage. You can start taking it tonight. Two drops in a glass of water before bed, then the same tomorrow morning and night, right through until we get to Alaska."

Bree held it to her chest. "What if it doesn't work?" she whispered.

Kelly sat back on her heels. "Then I'll hit you over the head with something and knock you out that way. You'll be unconscious and when you wake, your head will hurt so much you won't be able to think about anything else."

Shawn looked from Bree to Kelly quickly, and her anxiety lessened when Bree laughed. "That doesn't sound like a good idea."

Kelly tilted her head. "No, probably not."

Shawn took in the pile of stuff they needed to pack. "We'd better get this done."

"We aren't leaving for two days. You've got time." Kelly resumed her position on the couch, this time tucking her feet under her.

Shawn blinked. "That amount of time is two days. What if we need bigger suitcases? What if something is missing? If we don't do it now, then we run the risk of not being prepared." And they'd already discussed the need for that. Had Kelly already forgotten?

Kelly held up her hands. "You're right. I should get out of your way and let you two get ready. I have some things I need to prep anyway myself."

Shawn didn't want her to go. But there was no reason for her to stay. She and Bree were certainly capable of packing on their own.

Asking her to stay would be nonsensical, even if her emotions said otherwise, so she didn't say anything at all.

"Do you have to go?" Bree looked up from a pack of carabiners in her hand. "We could use the company, I think." She looked at Shawn, who nodded.

Kelly wiggled her butt so she sank deeper into the couch. "In that case, I'm all yours."

Again, that warm feeling filled Shawn, but this time, she recognized the feeling of desire that spread through her. She squashed it under the analysis of her new thick, fleece-lined pants.

She folded everything carefully, putting things in individual packing cubes and zipping them shut so she knew where things were. She had labels too, and she wrote in neat, clear writing what was in each bag. Contentedly, she listened to Bree and Kelly talk about some of the digs Kelly had been on and things she'd found. The excitement and passion in her voice were almost enough to make Shawn think she'd made the right decision about coming along on this trip.

Almost.

Shawn nodded, looking over her neatly packed case and deciding it was what it should be. Then she looked at Bree's.

"Aren't you going to fold anything?"

Bree's forehead creased. "What do you mean? Everything *is* folded."

"I can't... No. That's just... No. Move over." Shawn ignored Bree's protestation and continued to scoot her out of place until Shawn was in front of the case. She tipped it over and emptied everything out.

"Hey!" Bree pushed her feet against Shawn's legs. "I was almost done!"

"If you were five years old and in charge of packing, then I'd agree. But you're not, and you're not." Shawn began methodically repacking the case.

Bree huffed and stood. "Fine. I'm ordering Mexican for lunch."

When Shawn went to protest, Bree cut her off. "Two against one."

Kelly shrugged. "I like Mexican."

Shawn grunted and went back to her organizing. It was only when Kelly's perfume floated to her that she realized she had moved to her side on the floor.

"I like the way you take control in order to make things right for someone else," she murmured, drawing her finger along Shawn's forearm.

Shawn shivered and watched the finger's progression up her arm and over her bicep before it began its way back down. "I can't help myself," she finally said.

"Nor should you." Kelly's lips were soft against Shawn's cheek.

All she had to do was turn. Just a little, and she could taste Kelly's lips again. She could feel Kelly pressed against her and hear that cute little moan Kelly made when she was turned on.

"Oh my god. It's like leaving two horny teenagers together." Bree came back into the room holding a pitcher of iced tea and three glasses.

Kelly laughed and eased away. "I've been accused of worse."

Simultaneously irritated and grateful for the interruption, Shawn focused on the task at hand.

"Have you had any whirlwind romances, Kelly? I imagine you have women following you around all the time." Bree poured the iced tea.

Why did she have to ask that? Shawn would be quite happy never, ever knowing that Kelly enjoyed women of the world when it was Shawn who would quite happily press Kelly into a bed and enjoy her for hours at a time.

"No big romances, no. I enjoy company on a dig if it's on offer, but it's always temporary. I never fall for anyone. I don't have the kind of life that allows for something deep and meaningful." Kelly sipped her drink. "It isn't something I've been interested in really. My parents have what I consider the perfect marriage, and until I can find something, or someone, who fits me as perfectly as they fit each other, I won't be settling down."

Shawn frowned, thinking of her own family. She wouldn't have to wait long at all for something better than what they had. Heck, the one night stands she enjoyed had more going for them than what her parents endured. "Your parents like each other?"

"A lot of people's parents like each other, Shawn." Bree made a face as she sucked the lemon in her tea. "Your family isn't a beacon of relational harmony."

Kelly huffed. "If your brother was anything to go by, I'm afraid I'll have to agree. I'd not be interested in meeting them, I don't think."

Old shame flooded areas long strewn with emotional wreckage, and Shawn felt her face flush. But there was nothing she could say to refute it either. So she said what came to mind. "My mom called right before you got here. She needs a kidney. I'm supposed to get checked to see if I'm a match." Why had she shared that? She'd dealt with her oversharing quirk a long time ago and now kept most everything to herself. But then, Bree understood her, and she was going to be spending a lot of time with Kelly, so maybe she could let the mask slip, just a little.

"I hope you told her to get her kidney from a cow ill with the kind of virus that causes severe diarrhea and vomiting. And possibly a form of vertigo." Kelly crossed her arms, her eyes narrowed.

"I'm not sure why I'd tell her to do something so irrational. But I did tell her I'd see if I had time." Shawn finished folding and packing the last shirt on the pile. "I don't think I will though."

"Did you tell her we're going to Alaska?" Bree asked.

Shawn heard the telltale tone of Bree's voice that meant she was asking something but not outright asking it. "No. Why would I?"

"Just wondering." Bree glanced at Kelly, who shrugged a little.

Shawn waited but no more information seemed to be forthcoming. "You're doing that thing that means you're saying more than I'm understanding. Explain, please." When neither of them seemed inclined to do so, Shawn sighed with frustration.

The doorbell rang, keeping her from saying anything more. She went and got the Mexican food, which she had to admit smelled enticing, and took it into the kitchen.

"A lot of people would tell their family members if they were going somewhere that had the potential to be dangerous, or even just to let them know they were going to be away. But you don't have that kind of relationship with your family, and we respect that." Kelly bumped Shawn lightly with her shoulder. "Sometimes it takes other people a while to figure out that their way isn't the only way. That's all."

Shawn let her shoulders drop. "I can understand that. And I don't need to tell them anything." She began opening the containers. "What's next?"

They took their food into the dining room, and Shawn sat at the table. When Kelly and Bree moved like they were going to sit on the couch, she cleared her throat. "Meals are eaten at the table."

Kelly's eyebrows quirked slightly, but she turned and joined Shawn. Bree sat on the other side.

"Next, you put in place things to keep your life in order while you're gone. Get someone in to water your plants, to take care of your cat, to check your post. Things like that."

"I'm putting Marvel into a cattery with excellent reviews. I'm taking her there tonight." Shawn shook her head as she ate. "I don't like doing it though, and it's another reason this is a crazy idea."

"She'll get to make new friends." Bree moaned as she took a bite of enchilada. "I've got my mom coming to check my mail. She tried to convince me to change my mind for over an hour last night. She kept telling me about all the things that could go wrong and asked me about my vaccines. I explained we were going to Alaska, not a foreign country." She looked at Kelly over her fork full of dripping food. "That's right, right? I mean, I know the states can be really different from each other."

"There's a certain irony to an American asking a Brit just how different their states are from one another." Kelly's smile was gentle, and she was clearly teasing. "Honestly, Alaska is pretty different in some ways. They're closer to Russia than they are the States, and there are still quite a few native tribes there. The conditions mean they're tough and quite self-sufficient, if I had to generalize." She laughed. "But there's a Starbucks and they have Tinder, so it isn't like we're headed straight to the wilderness."

Shawn blew out a breath and let her shoulders drop an inch or two. "I was thinking we'd be without cell service."

"Oh, we will be. All we'll have is a satellite phone." Kelly pulled Shawn's open laptop over and started typing. "Look. This is Denali Base Camp. We'll fly into Anchorage and then take a small plane to the base camp. We could drive, but it would take about five hours, maybe more if there's a storm, and with time being of the essence, we want to get there as quickly as we can. That's where the archeo team already in place will meet us—"

"Wait." Bree's hand trembled as she pointed to a spot on the screen. "You're telling me we're taking a toy plane over a mountain range covered in snow, where we're going to land...on snow." She turned a shade slightly paler than Shawn's walls.

"I promise it'll be okay. I've landed on a river barely big enough for the plane, which was also infested with crocs. And these pilots do this all the time. They probably won't even be drunk."

Shawn and Bree stared at Kelly, who began to laugh.

"You guys are too easy. I promise it will be fine. Honestly, the pilots do this all the time. Climbers at Denali are one of their biggest tourist attractions. Over a thousand each year, I believe." She took Shawn's hand. "I promise to watch out for both of you. If I think there's real danger, I'll pull us out."

They ate in silence, and Shawn was glad for the time to pay attention to the thoughts on a spin cycle in her head. She was also glad that Kelly continued to eat but didn't let go of Shawn's other hand.

Shawn's phone rang and she glanced at it, but when she saw her mother's name, she ignored it. Bree looked at the phone too and grimaced.

"You know you don't owe them anything." Bree scooped a tortilla chip through some guacamole. "Especially a body part."

Shawn knew that but not how to respond. She shrugged.

"How did you two meet?" Kelly asked, pushing her plate away.

Bree grinned. "Shawn wanted to take me home and do the nasty."

Shawn choked on her mouthful of rice and shook her head vehemently.

"I knew she was a tiger." Kelly laughed and rubbed circles on Shawn's back until she stopped coughing.

"That's not true." Shawn took a deep breath and sipped her water. "We were at a college function–"

"An LGBTQ function," Bree said, waving a chip.

"You're gay too?" Kelly looked surprised.

"Bi. I'm mostly about the person, not the wrapping." Bree looked at Shawn. "You were saying?"

"Before you interrupted me." Shawn narrowed her eyes slightly. "We were at a function, and it was one of those networking things. I'm awkward now but back then, I could barely speak to anyone I didn't know. But staying in my room alone night after night was getting me down, and I was still coming to terms with my sexuality in relation to my religious upbringing. Once I was there though, I was frozen. I watched everyone laughing and talking and I wanted to say something, but I couldn't."

"And I saw this gorgeous little butch thing standing in the corner looking like a seal surrounded by orcas, so I went and said hi." Bree made a face at Shawn when she rolled her eyes at being interrupted again. "She didn't say much, but I could tell she was going to be my lifelong friend."

"And that's been the case," Kelly said, squeezing Shawn's hand and then letting it go.

"It turned out we were in a lot of the same courses, and as people with similar IQs, we understood one another well." Shawn tilted her head and looked at Bree as she remembered. "No one had ever made the attempt to get to know me like Bree did. I think she may have saved my life actually. I was in a dark place, and the isolation was getting worse."

Bree wiped the tears from her eyes. "You do say the sweetest things sometimes."

"But you didn't want to date her after all?"

Shawn tucked her hands between her knees. This was far more personal than she'd planned on being. "I did ask her out. That much is true. Not to take her home, not like that. I mean, she was the only other gay person I knew."

"And isn't that what every girl wants to hear?" Bree put her hand over her heart. "It wasn't that I wanted you, I just didn't have anyone else."

Kelly laughed. "Not really the prequel to putting a ring on it, eh?"

"Anyway," Shawn said, stacking their empty plates. "She turned me down. She'd met someone else from the group and was already exclusive."

Bree picked up some dishes too. "Ah, the best and most dramatic three months of my life. I was desperately in love and saw forever in her eyes. Until she saw forever in someone else's."

"The romances of a twenty-year-old." Kelly laughed, placing dishes beside the sink. "I had a few of those myself."

Shawn was content to listen as Bree and Kelly shared snippets of their young dating lives. Her thoughts drifted to her time in college and how alone she'd felt until she'd met Bree. She finished what she was doing and tuned back into the conversation.

"I did my undergrad at Oxford, my postgrad at York, and my doctorate at Cambridge. I was out in the field more than I was in the classroom." Kelly snapped the towel at Shawn's butt, making her jump. "All of which means I love getting dirty."

Shawn felt the heat rise in her cheeks at the thought, and she quickly doused it with thoughts of sleeping in the cold. She had a feeling she'd be doing a lot of that in the near future. Maybe she should bring ice packs for her sleeping bag.

CHAPTER ELEVEN

THE EARLY MORNING SKY was slowly becoming a child's fingerpainting of pinks and blues as Kelly watched from the airport window. Yesterday, she'd made a last-minute change to the flight after seeing Bree's panic attack in action. This trip was going to be hard enough. No need to add a crush of bodies to it. And a bit of luxury before heading into the frozen north would be nice.

Shawn and Bree came walking along the empty corridor. Shawn looked puzzled, but Bree looked like she might be off in wonderland already.

"Good morning," Kelly said, wishing she could lean forward and give Shawn a morning kiss. But the day after they'd spent the day packing, Shawn had sent a text saying she was sorry, but there really couldn't be anything between them, and she'd appreciate if Kelly stopped flirting with her, as it made things more difficult. Kelly had known that was Shawn's position but figured light flirting wasn't a problem. Apparently, that wasn't the case.

"Why are we in the wrong section of the airport?" Shawn asked, holding up her phone. "You changed the meeting place."

"I did." She looked at Bree, who looked back with a dazed glow. "I chartered a private jet. I know how hard this is for you, and you shouldn't be squished in with a ton of other people for your first flight."

Bree swayed. "That's nice. Isn't she nice, Shawn? I like nice. It rhymes with ice. I like ice too. Which is good, since I'll be walking on it soon."

Kelly reached out and took Bree's elbow. "Good to know the meds from the UK are working. Let's board, shall we?"

Shawn hesitated, her hand white-knuckling her bag. "I was ready for the regular flight. I hate changes I'm not prepared for."

Kelly sighed a little internally but reminded herself to be patient. "I'm sorry. It was a last-minute decision on my part for the sake of comfort." She motioned to the jet sitting outside. "I thought you'd like it too. No people breathing down your neck, our own bathroom, nice and quiet. There are five other people already aboard, the team joining us on the dig."

She waited, somewhat impatiently, as Shawn processed that. Finally, she nodded and moved like she was ready. Relieved, Kelly led Bree down the gangway to the plane. Even drugged though, Bree had started to shake a little and her eyes widened.

"I can't fly. I mean, if the plane falls from the sky, I don't have wings," she whispered loudly to Kelly.

"None of us do, lovely. And the plane isn't going to fall out of the sky. It's going all the way to Alaska."

Bree balked slightly as she stepped through the doorway, but then she brightened as she slowly took in the interior. "Hello, other people! I'm Bree, and I can't fly."

There was a titter of laughter, and Kelly nodded appreciatively when one of the team came forward, took Bree's bag, and then led her to a large, plush seat. Kelly turned to Shawn, who looked stunned.

"I was expecting something very different," she murmured.

"Surprise!" Kelly gently pulled Shawn forward. "I'm sitting there. I thought maybe you'd want the seat across from me?" She pointed toward the two deep seats with a table between them.

Shawn glanced from them to the other empty seats. "I don't think I want to fly backward. Sitting backward, I mean."

Of course. Kelly should have thought of that. "Fair enough. I'll sit backward and you can take that one."

Shawn gave a sharp nod after a second and put her bag in the overhead bin. Kelly turned and ducked her head into the cockpit. "All ready to go on our end."

The pilot, an older woman with short hair, dark skin, and a dazzling smile looked her over. "You're the boss." She winked, and Kelly smiled back.

It wouldn't do to get used to that kind of service, since she wouldn't splurge on a private jet again, but the thoughts of how a pilot could entertain her during a long flight would be a nice way to pass the time should Shawn decide she didn't feel like chatting. Not that Kelly couldn't talk to the rest of the team too. Before she took her seat she looked down the aisle. Bree was fast asleep, even with members of the team talking around her. Perfect.

Shawn was scrolling through her phone and didn't look up when Kelly sat down.

"Can I ask you something?" Kelly said after a few minutes.

Shawn finally looked up. "Yes."

"You seem really attached to your phone. I rarely see you go for very long without looking at it. What is it that you find so fascinating?"

"You don't?" Shawn asked, her eyes darting to the phone on Kelly's side of the table.

Kelly held it up, showing the beastly old thing with the cracked face. "I use it for an occasional photo or to take a phone call. I might check email if I'm expecting something. But other than that..." She shrugged. "It's just a tool like any other."

Shawn gingerly set hers down, almost like she was afraid it would disappear. "This is my tie to the world. I get knowledge, articles, news. I hate being out of the loop, so I check my email all the time to make sure I'm not missing anything. And I hate making people wait for a response if they've sent me something that requires one. I always respond as fast as I can."

As though it knew it was being talked about, it pinged with a notification. Kelly shook her head. "It's so Pavlovian. It dings and you look. It dings and you check it. It dings and you look at a photo or some such thing. Like you're being trained to take an electronic leash."

Shawn's frown deepened. "But I like being connected to the world this way. I like talking to people all over the globe about things like deep space or new discoveries in Egypt."

Kelly shrugged, wondering if she was pushing too hard. But healthy disagreement wasn't a bad thing. "Okay, but what about the constant pings for attention? Couldn't you decide when to look instead of being told to?"

Shawn's fingertips rested lightly on the edges of her pristine phone as she contemplated. "I like knowing when new information is available. Like I said, I don't want to miss anything."

"Doesn't it mean you never get any peace? I bet you even have it with you when you work out."

Shawn flushed. "A lot of people do. It's not like I'm the only one."

The engine rumbled, and the flight steward went past to check their seatbelts. "No, that's true. It seems like most people should have their screens permanently implanted in front of their eyes. Like Cyborg."

Shawn looked up, a small smile on her lips. "*Justice League*." She looked out the window at the swiftly retreating ground. "I think that would be amazing actually."

Kelly groaned. "And then you'd be half in this world and half in that one."

Shawn glanced at her and then back out the window. "Nothing new."

Once again, Kelly was struck by the shadow of loneliness that clung to Shawn like a second skin. Although she'd clearly been able to mingle with co-workers at Kelly's party, it was obvious the only person in the world she was close to was Bree. Kelly could think of any number of people she could call on a moment's notice if she needed someone to talk to. Not that she was particularly close to any one person, maybe, but there were people out there if she needed them. Including, of course, her parents. She hadn't thought to call them while she was in Oklahoma, and now she'd be in Alaska for who knew how long. She'd have to rectify that situation as soon as she got back.

Chay Clipwell moved from the back of the plane to the seat opposite them the moment the seatbelt sign turned off.

"Shawn, this is Chay. She's our site manager for the dig, and she's been working almost non-stop since we got the call to head out. She and the others back there are part of the University of Aberdeen archeology team." Kelly gave Chay a smile that acknowledged their history. They hadn't seen one another in several years, and their enjoyment of each other had been brief but satisfying. Like most of her relationships, it had ended the moment she'd left the dig site for the last time.

"Good to see you, Kel. Shawn, nice to meet you. I read your paper on the variabilities of human existence in the Fjords in the Archaeological Papers a few months ago. Fascinating take."

Shawn looked genuinely surprised. "I don't think anyone has ever told me they've read my articles. I just write them to pass the time."

Chay's eyebrows rose, and she glanced at Kelly. "You write professional articles just for something to do?"

"Why wouldn't I?" Shawn tapped on the sides of her phone as though using it to ground herself.

"Um...anyway. I thought we'd discuss some site stuff before we get there." Chay held up a thick folder. "It's a doozy."

Shawn pushed away from the table. "I'll sit in the back with Bree."

Before Kelly could protest, Shawn had moved to sit on the couch at Bree's feet and was already focused on her phone before she'd even sat down. Kelly sighed and motioned to the recently vacated seat. "Let's talk."

Chay shifted into the seat but left the file closed. "You brought math people to a glacier fight."

"Weird sentence, but yeah. Jack wanted them to come because of the AARG demand." She looked over Chay's shoulder at Shawn's strong, handsome profile. Brow furrowed, shoulders tight, she looked far too stressed for a luxury plane.

"Already on the prowl?" Chay grinned wryly when Kelly looked at her. "I know that look, Kel. I got to see it aimed at me once or twice a million years ago." She turned to look over her shoulder, then refocused on Kelly. "I get it, in a way. For you, I mean. Not my type, obviously. But she doesn't seem like the kind to go skydiving or hiking across tree limb bridges with you."

That was true, so why did Kelly find it irksome that Chay would say so? "I think you wanted to talk about the dig?"

Chay held up her hands in defeat. "Touchy about the truth when it comes to emotion. Same old Kel." She opened the file and pulled out a map. "Here's the dig site."

Kelly focused and they discussed the various parameters of the dig. She kept going back to the idea that Shawn and Bree would both be so insanely out of their elements. It wasn't just going to be cold. The glacier was shifting and cracking almost constantly, and the ice work was going to be dangerous. Shawn could maybe stay behind and do the statistics analysis when the team got back to camp, but that would slow things down. And she needed Bree's perfect memory in order to get the items out, cataloged, analyzed, and put back as fast as possible. That meant they both needed to be on the ice with her.

"Did the team who found the dig site send any photos?" Kelly asked as she continued to scan the paperwork.

"They weren't equipped. They're working near the Kahlitnu dig and heard the split from where they were after an intense ice quake, so they went to check it out. Sunlight caught on an artifact sticking out of the ice, which is the only reason they saw it and went out to investigate. But they're not glacier-ready."

Kelly nodded. That made sense. Glacier excavations were a specific area of archeology that weren't for the faint of heart. Even really adventurous archeologists usually kept to land. Once again, she looked over Chay's shoulder at Shawn, who was sitting with her head back and her eyes closed. With her frown gone and her face relaxed, she was even more good-looking, if that was possible.

Chay closed the file after reorganizing it. "Kel, we've known each other for a long time, and I think I have some latitude to speak freely?" She waited for Kelly's nod. "Your focus has to be spot-on, babe. Distractions are a bad idea out there on the ice, especially when you've got novices with you. Hell, not even novices. Have they had any field training at all?" At Kelly's shrug, she shook her head. "It's one thing to have a good fling on a normal dig. But this isn't normal. The glacier is in motion, there are storms moving in, and the whole damn thing could become unstable at any second. You lose focus," she thumbed over her shoulder, "and it could be disastrous."

Kelly sat back and raised her arms to rest her hands behind her neck in an attempt to ease the tension. "I hear you. I want to throw something at you for being right, but so be it."

Chay gave her a wicked grin. "Hey, if you're still hard up after the dig, I'll be available to scratch whatever itch might be left over. You're just as gorgeous as you were all those years ago." She stood and twisted, doing her own stretching. "We should probably have a team meeting if you're up for it."

"Let me get a drink. I'll be right there." She watched as Chay went to the back of the plane where the others had congregated. Only then did she notice that Shawn was watching her. What was going on behind those guarded eyes? She smiled and went to the front of the plane to get a few drinks. Then she headed back and took the seat near Shawn. Handing over the bottle of water, she said, "You okay?"

Shawn swallowed a long drink of water. "Thank you. I'm okay. Flying doesn't bother me as much as the thought of the work that isn't getting done while I'm gone." She tilted her head toward Bree. "I think she's waking up. Should we let her?"

Kelly nodded and waved for another bottle of water. "I think so. If she freaks out, we can give her more of the meds, but I'd like to see how much of her anxiety is present once she's already in a situation."

Shawn looked down as Bree's feet twitched at her side. "You think she's faking it?"

"God, no. Of course not. It's something she said the other day that got me thinking. She said her mum was trying to talk her out of it, saying things about crashing and illnesses. I just wonder how much of Bree's fear is due to her mum harping on about tragedy."

Shawn shifted when Bree began to stir. "I've never thought of that. Her mom is... You know how some really small dogs shake and snap all the time, even if there's nothing going on around them? That's Bree's mom. She's nice, don't get me wrong, but you've never seen someone so nervous about just...being."

Kelly couldn't help but wonder if Shawn saw any correlation with herself but chose not to say anything. It wasn't really her place, after all. She wasn't a therapist. She wasn't even a fuck buddy. Now she was just a colleague and acquaintance. What a depressing thought.

Bree mumbled something and wiped at her face. Her eyes fluttered open, and everyone chatting stopped to watch, like looking at a bear in the zoo about to come out of hibernation. She'd make a very cute little bear, Kelly thought absently.

She looked around, her gaze bleary, until it landed on Shawn and Kelly. "Are we in a living room? Are we already in Alaska?"

"No, lovely. We're on a special plane. This is the team we'll be working with." Kelly motioned to the others, who gave faint hellos.

Bree's head snapped around, and she looked out the window. She instantly went pale and began to sway. "Oh my god..."

"Hey." Chay moved in front of her and took her hand. "Hi. How are you? I'm Chay."

Bree looked slowly away from the window and at Chay instead. Her hand went to her hair, and she attempted to smooth it down. "Hi," she said softly.

"Hi. Do you know how a car works?" Chay asked, softly stroking Bree's hand.

"I... No. Do you?" Bree asked, blinking like she was still trying to wake up.

"Nope. Not a clue. I use the pedals and the steering wheel and off it goes. I use one every day, and I never worry about how it works. It gets me where I'm going." She tilted her head toward the window. "I don't know how planes work either. But they get me where I'm going, just the same way a car does. And the view is way better."

Tentatively, Bree looked away from Chay and out the window. In a moment, she was nearly sitting there with her nose pressed to it. "Look how small everything is! That river must be enormous if it looks big from up here." She continued to ramble on, her excitement growing.

Shawn looked at Kelly. "You were right."

Kelly smiled at Chay and mouthed, "Thank you."

Chay nodded and let go of Bree's hand so she could move back to her seat. Kelly turned to the rest of the team, who'd also watched the exchange respectfully. She knew all of them, to varying degrees. They were experts in their fields, just as she was, and there was no question they all knew what they were doing.

"I don't think any Marvel superheroes ever looked as good as this team does." She grinned at the groans and laughs sent her way. "I've had a really good meeting with Chay, our site manager, about what we're going up against." She motioned. "Shawn and Bree are joining us as stats folk. They're going to be site crew, there to analyze and produce the data because this is a retrieve and replace dig." She nodded at the groans. "I know. As our Finds Manager, you're going to have your hands full, Gianna. I expect you and Shawn to be working together as quickly and efficiently as possible. Once the artifacts are out of the ice, we'll tray them and bring them to you for cataloging and photographing, with the long-term goal of 3-D printing the artifacts for further research. I'm not sure how we're going to go about putting the artifacts back where we found them. Pam? As our glaciologist, do you have any ideas on that?"

Pam turned her open laptop toward them. "I wish I had better news, but the temps have dropped rapidly. They're rising in the daytime which will make retrieval easier, but if you want to place the artifacts back where you found them, you'll have to do it before the area you pulled them from refreezes."

Kelly sighed and pinched the bridge of her nose. "So at the end of every day, before the temps drop again, we need to get the pieces back in place. Bree, that means you'll be on stage as we pull things out and as we replace them." She looked at the team. "Bree has a photographic memory that's truly phenomenal. I've had the chance to see it in action over the last week, and you won't believe how much easier this is going to be because of it."

Bree finally looked away from the window. "Thanks, Kelly." When she saw the rest of the team gathered for the meeting, she slipped away from the window and sat facing them, her cheeks pink. "Sorry."

"No need to apologize for being anxious, or excited, or any other number of things," Chay said. "That means you care, and caring in our line of work matters an awful lot."

Kelly tried to hide the smile that rose when she saw the way Chay and Bree looked at one another. Chay might have warned Kelly about staying focused, but it looked like she was going to have to fight for that herself.

"That leaves Dave and Rena, our enviro and geo archs. Anything to add on this front, guys?"

Dave and Rena always came as a package deal. They'd been a couple for twenty-five years and never married because "it was an outdated institution meant to force people to stay together." They stayed together because they wanted to not because of some tradition that said they needed to. Kelly had heard their declaration multiple times over the years. She wasn't sure she agreed, but since marriage had never figured into her life plan, she didn't need to know.

They looked at each other. "Nothing from us until we're on site, Kel. Every glacier has its own personality and issues, so we'll do an onsite analysis the moment we get there." Dave waved toward Pam's laptop. "Pam says the glacier is unstable, and if that's the case, we'll need to do some drone scans before we step foot on the ice to check for other fissures."

"Are there tribes in the area?" Pam asked. "Anyone else we need to be concerned about out there on the ice?"

Bree raised her hand a little. "Um, can I say something?"

Kelly threw a peanut at her. "You're part of the team, Bree. You say whatever you want to, whenever you want to."

Shawn rolled her eyes. "Probably not a good idea."

Bree ignored her. "I did some research while we were preparing to come along. There's the Koyukon tribe, who are in the Athabascan region and most likely to be in the area we'll be in. The Tanaina may be nearby as well. There are actually a lot of different tribes in that region, but at least four of them are going to be far north of us."

The team looked impressed, and Kelly was glad they already saw Bree's value to the expedition. "So, we'll be on the lookout for any tribes hunting or fishing in the area, although I'm sure they're far more aware than we are about the need to be careful when a glacier is on the move."

"Strange saying." Shawn was rubbing her thumb and forefinger together, her gaze unfocused. "It doesn't really move all that much, and yet people say it's moving. Or calving, like a cow. But it isn't giving birth. It's dropping a piece of ice into the water. Or in this case, just splitting itself into sections temporarily."

And now the team looked confused. Chay's eyebrows rose as she looked at Kelly.

"As you may know, Shawn is the director at the Oklahoma Archeological Center. She created the program they've currently got in place, which is foremost in the field of statistical and descriptive statistics for archeological finds. It's an exceptional system they've got set up."

Shawn nodded but didn't add anything further. There was an awkward silence, and Kelly went on. "Rigging is going to be imperative. We'll set up the finds and meal tent well away from the crevasse, and we'll need to dogsled back to camp each night."

Shawn looked up. "What? Why not truck or snowmobile?"

"Nothing with an engine is allowed in Denali. The planes are allowed to land at base camp, but no motorized vehicles are allowed anywhere else in the park. They passed a law against it some years ago in order to keep the place pristine."

Shawn stared at her for a long moment and then refocused on her shoes.

"The team at the K dig have already arranged for our cabins to be ready so we'll be up and running as fast as possible, and the dog sled teams will be available the whole time." Kelly put her hand over her mouth as she yawned. "We should get some sleep. Once we arrive, it'll be all hands on deck."

"Idioms," Shawn said softly, shaking her head.

Kelly stood. "We could find some amazing things on this dig." She held up her hand when Shawn went to protest. "Or we could find fragments. Regardless, we'll be looking at items that haven't been seen for a very, very long time. This is going to be fucking awesome."

There was a general cheer of agreement, and Bree went back to looking out the window. Shawn stood.

"Can I come back and sit with you again?" She looked toward Chay, who'd moved to sit beside Bree. "Unless you'd like her company instead?"

Kelly tilted her head toward their seats. "Watching body language and interpreting, are we?"

"Maybe?" Shawn shrugged and slid into her seat. "I could be wrong. I doubt I'm very good at it yet."

"What do you think it is between us?" Kelly asked more out of curiosity than anything else.

"I think...I think you like each other. Your bodies were turned fully toward one another, and you gave her that smile you give someone when you're attracted to them." Shawn frowned and turned her phone over and over in her hand. "I think you're comfortable with her because you laugh and smile easily, and you leaned toward her while you talked."

Kelly reached across the table and gently pulled the phone from Shawn's hands and set it aside so she could take Shawn's hand in her own. "You're right. I do like her, and at one time, I was attracted to her. We enjoyed each other's company quite often on a dig that lasted nearly six months. And then we went our own ways, as we so often do in this profession. I still think she's a lovely person, and I'd go so far as to call her a friend." She squeezed Shawn's hand when she didn't respond. "But I'm not currently interested in fun frolic in the frozen wastes, if that was of any concern."

Shawn looked up quickly. "I can't be concerned about it because there's nothing between us. I mean, there's attraction, obviously, but nothing else, so I have no right or reason to be jealous, or any other emotion, about you and someone else." She swallowed and ran her hand over her hair.

It sounded like maybe she'd rehearsed that reasoning multiple times, given the way it came out. "True. But sometimes right and reason have little to do with emotion." She let go of Shawn's hand, wishing she could instead reassure her that there was more to what might be between them. But she couldn't because Shawn was right. There wasn't anything, and as Chay had said, focus was paramount right now. And, like her relationship with Chay, anything with Shawn would come to the same end. It would float into the past as surely as the items they'd find and replace, lost forever.

CHAPTER TWELVE

A BAD, BAD, SO very bad idea. Shawn couldn't let go of the sentence that repeated itself like a chorus in her mind. The plane had been amazing, and Kelly was right. It was so much better than flying on a regular plane crowded with people. She'd been able to sleep, stretch, eat...all without worrying about banging into someone. What it also meant, however, was that she could watch Kelly and her old friend laughing, working, and eating together.

And it made her stomach turn.

The landing had been grim though, and Bree's momentary relaxation when it came to traveling came to an abrupt end when turbulence shook the plane, and it dropped through the air before climbing again. She'd turned deathly pale and started to silently cry. Shawn had been about to unbuckle her seatbelt and go to her, even though it was against the rules, but Chay had beaten her to it. She'd spoken in soft, low tones that made it impossible to work out what she was saying, but Bree had seemed to relax and had wiped away her tears. Shawn had done her best to breathe through it and found that concentrating on the deep V-neck of Kelly's sweater had helped distract her from the certainty of imminent death.

There was no question everyone was relieved to get off the plane. Light, nervous laughter and more than a few deep exhalations accompanied the sound of the door opening. Shawn was glad she wasn't the only one somewhat undone by the experience.

But when she stepped out of the plane, she immediately wanted to get back on it, no matter how turbulent the flight.

It was freezing.

Quite literally, freezing. There were long, thin icicles hanging from the rooftops, and a thick mist swirled in the wind, blowing ice crystals into her cheeks. She pulled her hood up and tucked her hands inside the slightly too long jacket sleeves. *Such a bad idea.* She followed the group quickly to a waiting van and breathed easier when she was hit by a blast of hot air.

"Welcome to your tropical holiday. I'll be your cruise director and if you need anything, I'll be sure you can't find me." The driver looked in the rear-view mirror and laughed.

Shawn frowned and looked out the window. Why was she doing this? She could be drinking coffee at her desk right now, everything aligned and where it should be, including her.

Kelly's voice drew her attention, and she listened as Kelly asked questions about their destination and timing. *Kelly.* That's why she was here, and that was the most ludicrous thing in the world. They weren't a couple. They weren't anything. Sure, it was logical that she attend this expedition because she had the ability that no one else did. But that wasn't really why she was here. It was because of the woman with long, silky hair, and eyes that made her think of magic. Not to mention the body that moved in sensual, erotic ways in her dreams.

And because of that silly infatuation, she was going to freeze to death in Alaska.

They pulled up at a miniscule airfield with several banners that advertised companies making the flight to Denali Base Camp. Small planes were arrayed nearby, somewhat obscured by the mist. They made their way inside the hangar that doubled as an office, and Shawn shivered so hard it hurt.

"You okay?" Kelly asked, pulling her coat tighter around her.

"It's so cold. I'm cold." Shawn clenched her jaw, hating to sound so weak.

"It's actually only in the low forties but with the windchill, it feels like the low thirties. I'd forgotten what it's like to work somewhere this extreme. Brazil was hot and humid, but that was easier to deal with." Kelly reached out and wiped a bit of moisture from Shawn's cheek, leaving it tingling.

"I can't!"

The sound of Bree's high-pitched exclamation drew their attention, and Shawn quickly moved to her side. Chay was standing there with her hands in her pockets, clearly at a loss, and Shawn couldn't deny the feeling of satisfaction that someone else couldn't just barge in and make everything okay again.

"Hey." Shawn took Bree's hand. "Talk to me."

Bree took a shaky breath. "That landing was awful. I hate the way it made me feel. I don't want to fall out of the sky. I don't want to die." She choked out a small sob. "I'm sorry. I can't get on that tiny plane. It will be like holding onto a kite in a tornado."

Shawn looked beyond her at the plane, which did, in fact, look rather like a toy that wouldn't be up to the wind and freezing rain that had assaulted them on the way in. She swallowed. "I don't like it either. I hate it, in fact. But everyone else is going to get on that plane and get to the dig site. We've got to do the same, or we'll get left behind. And what was the point of coming all the way here if we were going to chicken out anyway?" She dipped her head so the others wouldn't hear her. "I don't know about you, but I don't want these people thinking I was a waste of their time."

Bree studied her, her watery eyes clear. "You're right. But I'm going to need some of Kelly's medicine to get through it." She bent and dug in her case for the little vial and then dripped some on her tongue. "Together?" she asked, holding out her hand.

"Together." Shawn took it and squeezed and then turned toward Kelly. "We're okay."

Kelly nodded, her expression unreadable, and then turned to the pilot. "Let's do it."

As a group, they filled out the necessary forms, including weight so that they could be seated in the most optimal position for a plane so small, and that didn't make Bree any happier, but the effects of the medicine were hitting, and she let Shawn do the writing when hers became scribble.

Once the forms were in and the pilot had done his calculations, they headed out to the plane. Their bags were stowed, and they climbed the stairs into the small, spartan interior that was nothing like the beautiful jet they'd just flown in on.

Bree and Shawn sat beside one another, and although Shawn was fine to hold her hand and try to distract her, she wished she was sitting beside Kelly, who was next to Chay. Both of them seemed utterly at ease. Once again, Shawn was reminded just how far out of her league Kelly was. Women comfortable with flying into a storm and rappelling down ice didn't fall for women who liked cozy desk jobs.

The plane taxied down the runway, bumping and bobbing, and Bree made little noises of distress, but her eyes were glazed over. The plane shot into the air, rattling like it might just fall to pieces, and there was nothing to see outside the windows but clouds and shards of ice hitting the glass. Her stomach lurched as the plane dropped and rose, dropped and rose, and she gritted her teeth to keep her eyes from watering. No way in hell would they see her cry or panic, even if she wanted to do both.

She looked at Chay, with her short hair shaved on the sides, her lazy grin, her relaxed posture with her long legs out in front of her, crossed at the ankles. Envy, green and bitter, swished through her. What she wouldn't have given to be that kind of butch. One tall and confident and oozing sex appeal. She was the kind who did social media videos and got thousands of likes, just for looking at the camera and smiling, for flump's sake. What would that be like?

At five foot nothing and stocky, not to mention awkward, Shawn would never know. *That* was really the kind of woman Kelly went for. Shawn was a novelty, a local yokel to spend time with while she was in a place she couldn't think of as anything other than a backwater.

A cloud came over her. *Such a bad idea.* At least back home she could have gone on pretending that maybe Kelly really did find her attractive for some reason. Now, that possibility had been deftly smothered.

The flight went fairly quickly, and it wasn't long before they were landing. Shawn looked out the window and her pulse raced. There wasn't a runway. None. Just a long, flat patch of snow between two mountains. She gripped the armrests hard and noticed that Chay looked a little stiffer too. At least there was that.

The plane hit the ground, jumped, hit the ground again, and then rolled to a stop. No one spoke for a moment, and then the cockpit door opened, and it seemed to release the collective breath they'd been holding.

"Another landing without a heart attack!" The pilot grinned as she looked around. "Off you go! I need to get back to base before the storm hits."

Everyone went into motion, and Shawn drew Bree up to her feet. She stood and looked around, still dazed. "I guess that wasn't so bad," she said, looking at Shawn.

"Nope. Not bad at all. Come on. Time for the next journey." What she wouldn't give for that to be a hotel with a soft, warm bed, a restaurant with healthy food, and a hot shower. Instead, they headed down the stairs and across the snow to another building, and the sound of the dogs was clear even from a hundred feet away. As was the smell.

The group went in and were greeted by two women behind a plain wooden counter. The women, who said they were "mushers," explained how the sleds worked and what to expect. One of them looked at Bree and frowned.

"Is she okay?"

"Medication for the plane. She'll be fine, but she's a little unsteady on her feet." Kelly gave Shawn a quick smile. "We'll hold on to her, won't we?"

Before Shawn could respond, the musher was making notes on a clipboard. "We'll add a sidecar to the sled and strap her in. Everyone needs to be aware of their own center of balance, and we can't take the risk that she'll fall off. It might slow us down a little, but we'll manage."

Shawn kept her expression neutral, but she was glad a sidecar was an option. She didn't like the idea of having to ride a dogsled for the first time while also worrying about Bree falling over or out.

"We've got three sleds for people, and two sleds for all your gear. Your stuff has been taken from the plane and is loaded up, so you just have to decide who is going on which sled. Make sure your hood is pulled up, your gators are fully zipped, and your snood is pulled up over your nose. Cover as much as you can, as it's going to take about forty-five minutes to get you to your new home away from home." The musher turned away, leading the group outside.

"Want to ride with me?" Kelly asked as she moved to walk beside Shawn.

"Yes." Shawn wished she was the kind to play it cool, but she couldn't help being direct.

"Excellent." Kelly turned to the others. "Each sled takes three, so Shawn and I will take one, and you guys can split up on the other two, one of which will have Bree in the sidecar."

Was it her imagination, or did Chay look...something? Irritated? Jealous? Some expression had flashed across her face, but Shawn wasn't good enough at reading emotions to know what it was. Someone like that wouldn't be jealous of her, surely. But maybe irritated that she wasn't the one riding with Kelly. That would make sense.

With a sense of pride that she shouldn't have, she sat in the rear seat of the three-seat sled, and Kelly sat in the seat in front of her. Ahead of them, the team of dogs barked and shifted, looking restless. Once the other mushers on the sleds gave a hand signal, the sleds set off one at a time, and Shawn acknowledged the exhilaration that came over her as the wind whipped past them and the dogs barked and ran. Kelly looked over her shoulder, and her eyes crinkled in a smile.

"Isn't this amazing?" she called out, her hair whipping out from the sides of her hood.

Shawn was disappointed when she turned back around. She liked being the focus of Kelly's beautiful gaze. Instead of thinking about that, she looked around her. Enormous mountains climbed up to the sky on either side of them, jagged, ragged peaks covered in white and streaked with gray rock. There was no other color. No green trees, no bushes, no weeds or flowers. White snow, gray rock, gray sky. The only color was that of the sleds and their passengers.

It was magnificent.

Shawn had never felt the need to use that word, not even in relation to the archeological finds she recorded. Words mattered, and she didn't like the way people used them willy-nilly, as though they meant something they didn't. Magnificent was one of those words, and she'd never come across something that seemed to warrant that description.

This did.

She felt so small, so insignificant, but in the best way. She'd never dreamed of being able to see something this extraordinary. She reached out and put her hand on Kelly's shoulder, wishing she had the words to express how grateful she was that Kelly had convinced her to do this. She might feel otherwise after the cold and barrenness became overwhelming, but in this moment of awe, she wished she could crush Kelly to her and say thank you in a more intimate way.

Kelly reached up and held Shawn's hand to her shoulder. It was a simple gesture, but it made Shawn's stomach flip anyway.

The ride was over too soon, and Shawn was pleasantly surprised when she saw where they'd be staying. She'd assumed it would be the thick canvas tents she'd seen on so many websites, but these were actual cabins built on high stilts.

While their gear was being unloaded, they huddled together as a group.

"Cabin three, at the end there, sleeps four. Cabins' one and two sleep two, and they're all twin beds."

"As the site manager and dig director, I think you and I should share a space so we can stay on top of things." Chay's arms were crossed, and Shawn didn't miss the quick glance thrown her way.

Kelly hesitated. "Makes sense. Shawn, why don't you and Bree take cabin two, and the rest of you can take cabin three? We'll meet up for dinner in cabin one in an hour."

Without any further discussion, the group headed toward their separate quarters. It made sense, of course. She and Bree worked together. They were friends and were both out of their element. But the fact that she wouldn't be bunking with Kelly left her feeling almost as hollow as knowing that Kelly would be sleeping near Chay instead. Would their old romance flare up again? And why shouldn't it?

Because I want it to be me.

"Wow." Bree looked around as she flopped into a chair, the medicine clearly starting to wear off. "I thought this would be way worse. Look, there's a real fireplace."

Shawn put her suitcase on the bed. Good to know Kelly and Chay would be warm. She looked over her shoulder at the noise of metal and a *thunk*. Bree dropped a large piece of wood into the fireplace and lit a match. She held it to the end of the trunk, but it went out without doing anything. She tried again, and again, but no luck. She sat back on her heels, brow furrowed.

"I don't think it should be this hard."

Shawn peered into the metal container beside the fireplace. "You're supposed to put the kindling under it, and light that. Then the piece will catch." She dug some out and placed it carefully beneath the log, then lit it and turned away.

"You couldn't tell me that while I was wasting matches?" Bree pushed herself to her feet and dragged her suitcase noisily across the floor to her bed.

"You didn't ask." Shawn left her clothes in the packing cubes but set them in the drawers beside her small bed.

"Right." She flung open her case. "Are you going to tell me

what's wrong now, or do I need to wait for the cover of darkness so you don't feel exposed?"

Shawn sighed and crumpled more paper to throw into the fireplace. "I wanted to sleep with Kelly. I mean, share a cabin with her. To get to know her better." She ran her hand over her hair.

"I won't take that personally, because I wouldn't have minded a little snuggle time with that Chay woman. Wow. What a body. And those eyes? Luscious. She looks like the kind of woman who would have sex while in the middle of rock climbing."

"Great." Shawn roughly shoved her case under the bed. "Flipping fantastic."

Bree ducked around Shawn and sat on her bed. "Are you jealous?"

"What's to be jealous of? Their previous relationship? The fact that she's everything I've always wanted to be but never will be? Or that they're sleeping in a cabin together, and there's nothing between Kelly and me, so there's no reason for her not to sleep with that Adonis of a woman because she has no interest in a muscular hobbit with anxiety and a touch of OCD?" Shawn ran out of breath, her face hot and her hands clammy.

Bree blinked. "Whoa. Okay. So there are some things I clearly missed while I was knocked out. Give me details so I can make a reasonable analysis, please."

With that kind of direction, it was easier to talk, so Shawn recounted the conversation with Kelly on the plane, as well as what she'd observed of their body language throughout the trip.

Bree got up and started unpacking. "Well, I'm not feeling great about my attraction to Chay now either. But it wasn't like I've already made out with her, so at least there's that." She shook out a thermal blanket and laid it across the bed. "First of all, I think you're way more into Kelly than I realized, and I'm sorry because I know how it feels to be into someone you can't have. Second, you made it clear to her that you don't want a relationship with her. It's unfair of you to want her not to be with someone else when you've said, plainly, that you won't even kick the tires."

"So juvenile." Shawn grimaced and laid back on the bed with her arm over her eyes. "That's what I keep telling myself. I have no right to feel this way. But I do, because she's different than any woman I've ever known and she makes me feel *more*, and I don't know what to do with it."

"You treat it rationally, like everything you do. You have to believe in the truth of it, and the truth is, you put the line in the sand, and she agreed not to cross it. Now we're here, at the end of the world, and instead of thinking about the work, you're obsessing about a woman you're sending mixed signals to. Probably during the most dangerous moment we'll ever experience." Bree stood with her hands on her hips, staring down at her. "If we were still in Oklahoma, I'd tell you to talk it out, to tell her you're confused and uncertain. But we're here, and she's going to have her hands full of work. Something you understand very well. So set the personal aside, just like I will, and focus."

Impulsively, Shawn stood up and pulled Bree into a hug. "I'm so glad you're my friend."

Bree hugged her back tightly. "And I always will be. You good now?"

Shawn nodded and let go, embarrassed by the flash show of emotion. But having someone to talk these things out with meant the world to her, and now she could do as Bree said. She'd get focused on what mattered. Her dating life hadn't been an issue before, and it definitely didn't need to be one now.

They finished unpacking, and Shawn repacked the bags they'd take with them to the dig site and set them by the door for the morning. Sunrise was at 8:11 a.m., and it didn't set until 7:24 at night, even this late in the year, and they'd likely be out the entire time.

"Time to go to Kelly's for dinner." Bree stood and pulled on another three layers of clothing.

Shawn did the same. The temperature was forty-six degrees, and it often got colder than that in Oklahoma in the winter. But the wind and ice were bitter, making it feel far worse. The thought of going out in it, even just to the cabin next door, made her bones ache. It had, after all, been in the low eighties when they'd left Oklahoma. The change felt extreme.

Together they dashed over and up the many stairs, and Shawn held the door open for Bree when they heard a cacophony of voices coming from inside. She had to yank it closed against the wind. When she turned, she was surprised to see more than just their own crew looking back at her. She stayed still, wondering if she'd made some kind of faux pas already.

Bree smiled and waved, obviously feeling no such compunction. "Hi, everyone! I'm no longer drugged."

There were general cheers and laughter, and Chay came forward and took her coat. Before Shawn could offer hers too, Chay had turned away to hang it up. She shrugged and placed her coat beside Bree's on the rack as she and Chay headed into the group chatter.

Kelly's hand on her back made her stumble slightly.

"Glad you came over. I wasn't sure you'd be up to more people time." Her tone was low, and she stood close.

Shawn took a half step back, much as she wanted to take one closer. "I'm hungry, and I know we need to get along with everyone." She couldn't help the quick glance at Chay, whose shoulder was pressed to Bree's.

"Getting along on a dig like this one is imperative, that's for sure." Kelly led the way to the small kitchen area. "I grabbed you a bottle of water."

Shawn took it, grateful for the kind gesture. "It smells good in here."

"The other team got here first and put on a pot of chili. On digs like this, you do what you can to help the next team along. It's a courtesy thing." Kelly sat on a high stool. "The other people here are with the K team who found the crevasse. They'll head back as soon as we've eaten, since they have to be back at their dig in the morning, and they know how tired we'll all be after our travel day."

Shawn nodded to show she was listening, but Kelly hadn't said anything that needed her input, so she stayed quiet.

"Are you okay? You seem a little distant." Kelly turned toward her and lightly touched her hand.

Shawn eased away a little, trying to put a bit of distance between them. "I'm fine. I talked to Bree, and now I understand how to handle things."

"What—"

Before Kelly could ask her question, someone Shawn didn't know tapped on a glass with a fork. "We just wanted to welcome team Broken Swan to our pretty little piece of Alaska. If you need anything, don't call. We won't answer." There was general laughter, and Shawn smiled a little. "Seriously though, we're fifteen miles west of you, but if you need us, we're on the red line."

Shawn looked at Kelly for clarification.

"The red line is an emergency phone powered by a generator and a satellite, so we can always call for help." Kelly's smile looked a little tighter than usual.

"And we always pray we never have to use it," the person speaking said. "Your food delivery will be here tomorrow while you're out, but we made enough chili for you to have leftovers until the day you leave. Whenever that may be."

Shawn could only hope it wouldn't be long. All these emotions and new ideas were draining. She wanted her old life back. She'd seen something beautiful, and that was great. Now she could go back to her desk and routine. But as she looked at Kelly, she wondered how that routine would ever manage to feel satisfying again.

CHAPTER THIRTEEN

KELLY SAT ON THE top stair leading to her cabin and watched her breath fluff into the air, backlit by the orange sunrise breaking over the snowy peaks. The tea in her flask warmed her inside and she was grateful for it. Jack had been true to his word and sent along a big box of Yorkshire Tea, along with some digestive biscuits and three tins of mushy peas, which she'd save for the moment she could savor them. At some point today, it would get into the forties but right now, it was below freezing, and she was about to spend the day working on the ice. The hot drink helped settle her nerves a little.

None of that, however, was on her mind. After the gathering last night, where Bree and Shawn had received plenty of tips and stories about field work, everyone had left. Chay and Kelly had unpacked and gone over the plans for today one more time. She hadn't missed the welcoming look in Chay's eyes, nor the way her touch had lingered a moment longer than necessary. She'd thought that Chay might be interested in Bree but apparently, she hadn't set aside the heat they'd created a few years ago.

And at any other time, Kelly would have welcomed having a bunkmate, especially when they had a private cabin. Chay was still sexy as hell, and they worked well together outside the bed too, which meant focus wouldn't be an issue when they were out on the ice.

But that wasn't what she wanted, and when she'd been lying in bed, unable to sleep, it had been a surprising thought. Shawn looked so sweet, so vulnerable, and her expression was far too easy to read. Her jealousy of Chay was as obvious as a chalk line on a black board, and her acknowledgement that she'd discussed her feelings with Bree meant she was having a hard time. What was Kelly supposed to do about it though? Because Chay was right. Kelly couldn't be worried about Shawn's comfort or emotions when they were on a project with so many unknowns.

The cabin door opening pulled her from her thoughts.

"Porridge?" Chay asked.

Kelly nodded and the door closed again. On the other hand, maybe enjoying what Chay had to offer would get her mind off Shawn and the awkward impossibilities between them. But wouldn't that be using Chay? Shaking her head at the thoughts which didn't deserve space in her mind right now, she stood and brushed the light dusting of dry snow from her pants before going inside. Chay had stoked the fire, and it was almost too warm inside. But that heat would linger for a while and make it easier to warm the cabin up again when they got back tonight.

She pulled the porridge to her and nodded thanks as she began to eat. Neither she nor Chay were morning people, which again made it easier for them to bunk together. Eventually, she got up and cleared the dishes, and then poured coffee into both their flasks for the day. She added digestives too, willing to share only because Chay had become a fan of the dry, crumbly biscuit on their last dig.

"You ready?" Chay asked as she pulled her thick wool sweater over a thermal shirt.

"Ready as I can be, I think." Kelly zipped the gators. "You?"

"Excited actually." Chay hefted her rucksack over her shoulder. "I can't wait to see what's out there."

It was the enthusiasm Kelly needed to hear, and she grabbed her own pack. "Me too." She grinned and waved Chay out ahead of her.

Shawn and Bree were already standing beside a dogsled, talking to the musher and giving the dogs cuddles. Shawn pressed her face to a dog's muzzle and was rewarded with licks and a roll for a belly rub. She glanced up at Kelly and gave an open, happy smile, which was then quickly shuttered as she looked away and back to the dog.

It's for the best, Kelly reminded herself, and said good morning to Bree.

The gear for the expedition was extensive, and she and Chay went over it, checking off items on lists as it was piled on two different sleds. Every item mattered. The rest of the team came down from their cabin and before long, they were on their way. This time, Kelly and Chay rode in a sled, leaving the others to sort out the seats among them. She forced herself to pay attention to the terrain. Not that there was a lot to take notice of in particular. That outcropping over there looked like a bird's head, complete with long beak. The one over there looked like half a spaceship. Markings like this could be imperative if they got caught in a blizzard or something and needed to find their way.

Within about half an hour, the sled slowed to a stop.

"Here you go," the musher said, jumping from her perch. "The crevasse is about a hundred yards that way."

The team gathered at the subtle edge where the packed snow met the glacier ice. Only the dogs made any noise as the group took in their surroundings. Almost as one, they jumped when a loud popping, hissing sound shattered the air.

Bree squatted as though her legs had given out. "Can someone explain?"

"Like we said on the plane, the glacier is moving, and that movement is creating splits in the glacier itself. Picture an ice cube with a large crack in it, from the top down. It's wider at the top, and as it breaks away lower down, you hear it. Similar situation here." Pam scanned the ice ahead of them. "We'll probably be hearing it a lot until it snows enough to fill the initial crack and freeze up again."

"Okay, folks. First things first." Kelly turned to address the team, old training coming back to the fore. "Pam, Dave, and Rena, I'd like to get a full lay of the land. Send up the drone and get some readings so we know how often the ice quakes are occurring. We need to know if there are other crevasses or ice pits in the vicinity before we set up the tents."

They set off to do as they were told, Pam with her insulated laptop already open and Dave holding the drone and control.

She turned to Bree and Shawn. "In an active area like this, you have to be aware of where you're putting your feet at all times. Fresh snowfall can hide an ice pit, where a new crevasse may be developing, or where the original crevasse has begun to send off shoots of new ones, like tree branches. When we're out on the ice, we'll be roped together so that if someone should slide into a trench, the others will be there to stop it from becoming a disaster." She pulled some tools from her bag. "If someone shouts and starts to fall into a crevasse, the other people rigged to them will fall to their stomachs in the snow. You'll dig these," she held up two snow axes, "into the snow and hold tight. When all motion has stopped, we'll figure out the next step depending on how far down the crevasse the person has gone."

She couldn't make out anyone's expression given that she could only see their eyes, but they were enough for her to see the stress. "I won't say it's unlikely or that it won't happen. We have to be prepared for anything." She held up some climbing gear from the bag. "For the dig itself, we'll be rappelling into the crevasse. We'll be held by an anchor like this, which we'll put in with a mallet. Rope ladders will also be in place, but they'll be secondary, as we don't want to place too much stress on the wall of the crevasse and risk it splitting. Along the lip of the crevasse, we'll have these pipes, which our ropes will run over so we don't dig into the ice with the ropes and create friction as we come in and out. The trays will also be attached by ropes that someone at the top will bring up and out when we shout for them to do so." She paused, wondering how they were taking in the load of information. Really, it was probably too much to give people without years of training. So be it.

Bree raised her hand tentatively. "Where am I going to be?"

Kelly wound the rope and began repacking the bags. "I'm not sure, to be honest. It depends on how deep the artifacts are, how well you can see them from the lip, and whether or not you can make note of the areas from up high. If you can't, then you'll have to come down with us." She smiled, hoping Bree could see it in her eyes. "Essentially, you'll just be sitting on a swing while the rest of us work."

Bree didn't look convinced.

"Shawn, you'll be at the finds tent waiting for things as we bring them out. Gianna is our finds person, but she's going to be in the crevasse as well and will only come out when there are enough trays for her to begin logging everything. In the meantime, you can be doing what you do." She waited for Shawn to respond but nothing was forthcoming. "Shawn?"

"Yes?"

"Does that make sense?" Kelly didn't have time for extra explanations or hand-holding.

"Of course." Shawn's tone sounded a little offended. "You didn't say anything that required a response."

Kelly shrugged. "Okay." She turned to look at Dave, Rena, and Pam, who were still focused on what they were doing. She was eager to get out on the ice, but they couldn't risk moving so fast that they ignored danger. Close by, she heard Chay mumble, "Math nerds to a glacier fight."

Shawn left the group and went over to the others. As far as Kelly could tell, she simply stood and listened and watched, and they didn't seem to mind at all. Soon, it was clear they were sharing with her, including her in the discussion and answering her questions. Kelly sighed softly. She had to cut Shawn some slack, and she couldn't let her impatience and temper loose. It wasn't fair.

Soon, they all walked back. The drone footage came up on Pam's screen.

"We're in a good location. There are a couple suspicious dips on the other side of the split but on our side, we don't see anything of note. The crevasse itself seems to be about thirty feet wide and approximately ninety feet deep. That's lots of good room to work and not too deep if we need to do a rescue." She pointed to one section. "I don't like the look of this part here, where it looks like we might have an offshoot but as long as we stay well away from it, I think we'll be fine." She looked up. "All in all, I think we're in for a smooth ride."

Kelly breathed a sigh of relief. "Okay. We all have to carry as much as possible on a dig like this, so take the one marked with your initials and strap it on to your back, and then take a smaller pack and carry it on your chest. Pam, have you identified a place for the tents?"

Pam nodded and shrugged on her pack. "I'll lead the way."

Chay and Kelly went into action, using the system of ropes and carabiners to connect everyone. She thought Chay might have pulled a little harder than necessary on Shawn's rig, but she couldn't be sure, and she needed to focus on the people she was hooking up. Soon, everyone was attached so that there'd be about six feet between them. Bree looked a little hunched under her heavy pack, but Shawn looked at ease with the fifty-pound pack she wore. There was no question her gym workouts were going to come in handy.

"Let's go."

Pam set off and the group fell into line behind her. Awkwardly at first, as people tripped and slipped in the snow and then the ice, but soon they all came to terms with the spiked grips attached to their boots, and the lines stayed taut as they moved carefully in a line. Pam stayed at the front, followed by Chay, and Kelly brought up the rear. That way, the most experienced people were watching the group and checking for pitfalls. It was only when Pam held up her hand for them to stop that Kelly took a deep breath and released her shoulders.

"The tents can go here." Pam unhooked her pack, and the others did the same, releasing their ropes as well. "I was scanning throughout the walk, and the ice is solid all the way here. When we head to the crevasse, I'll do the same."

"Tents first." Kelly moved to one bag and Chay went to the other.

"Can I help?" Shawn asked as she moved to Kelly's side. "I've had some experience with tents."

"Fantastic. The poles consistently piss me off." Kelly yanked the offending metal out of the bags and handed them over.

She and Shawn worked silently, and it was clear that Shawn knew what she was doing, which made it far easier. She watched as Kelly drilled the anchor holes for the first two corners, then took over for the other two. When it came time to pop it up, Dave came over to help hold it in place while Shawn pegged it into the ice like she'd done it a hundred times before.

"Nice. It looks like half of a giant orange soccer ball, doesn't it? Who knew you were so handy?" Kelly said, her breath puffing into the air even through the snood.

"I knew." Shawn turned away and went to help with the other tent, which was flapping haphazardly in the wind, with Bree trying to catch it to no avail. Chay looked on, clearly bemused as she unloaded gear from the other bags.

Why did Shawn's words feel like a rebuke of some sort? Kelly shook it off and started unloading the gear for tent one, which wasn't a whole lot more than portable bench seats to sit on and a couple of camp stoves, along with cups and bowls. There were also a few thermal blankets for people to wrap up in during breaks, as well as first aid kits. In a corner, she rolled the various rigging apparatus into coils, making sure they were all unknotted and ready to go.

Once the second tent was up, the whole group lugged bags into it. Tables were set up to handle the finds, trays were piled high ready for the artifacts, and the computers were set up right in the middle, away from the tent walls so they'd have the best chance of staying warm. Space heaters on ice wasn't a good idea unless they wanted to melt the ground beneath them and go for a very cold swim, so special thermal covers were tucked around the machinery to keep it from freezing.

It was past midday and finally warm enough to feel like she could lower her snood. She noticed the others had already done so.

"Okay, folks. Ass in hands time." Chay waved them toward her.

Bree laughed. "I have no idea what that means. Whose ass should I be grabbing?"

"It's a rough way of saying you can kiss your ass goodbye if you don't pay attention." Chay grinned and leaned on a climbing pole.

Shawn frowned, her arms crossed so her hands were under her armpits. "That makes no sense."

"It does when you've done it as long as I have." Chay motioned behind her. "We're heading out there now. We follow Pam's lead. If she says stop, we stop. If Dave says he sees something weird with the drone, we stop. If Rena notices some anomaly in the ice, we stop. Once we're in the crevasse, you listen to me or Kelly. One of us will be in the gap with you, and one of us will be at the top, watching. We'll take turns with the rigging in order to pull people out. Going down is far easier than coming out. Climbing out, you have to come all the way up, and then lever yourself over the lip as well. That's when a lot of falls happen, so take your time. Never rush, and if you're worried, you have to speak up. There's no room for error or ego."

Kelly could have sworn she heard Shawn make a noise, but when she looked over, Shawn's expression was blank as she listened to Chay.

"We rope up again as we walk out, and once we're there, we'll decide how to rig as we go down." Chay looked at Kelly. "Anything else?"

"This is a small group, and we all need to pitch in however we can. Roles out here are more fluid, and you may need to do things that you wouldn't normally do." She turned to Shawn. "You're strong, and that will be useful in helping people out. Plus, it would be helpful if you could assist in putting in the peg lines along the crevasse. I'll explain what they are and where to put them."

Shawn nodded, her expression thoughtful. "I'm happy to help."

"What about me?" Bree looked tiny and uncertain. "How else can I help?"

"You've got an amazing attention to detail. Take note of how we're setting things out, who is where, and how long they've been working. Although we need to work fast and hard, it isn't worth dehydration or hypothermia. If you could help Chay with looking out for everyone, that would be immensely helpful."

Bree nodded, looking a little relieved. "Will do."

Kelly grinned at Chay. "Let's go find the treasure."

They were soon rigged up again, packs in place, and the group made their way carefully toward the crevasse. When they reached it, there was a long period of stunned silence.

"Wow," Bree finally said softly. "I had no idea it would be so beautiful."

Kelly wasn't sure "beautiful" was the word for it. It seemed far more than that. Below the layer of dirt-flecked white snow, it became a glorious turquoise blue, marbled through with swirling layers of yet more white. Rather than being purely vertical, it almost looked like an ocean wave, frozen in time, bending and sweeping outwards and down.

"Magic." Shawn peered down, her voice carrying softly on the still, frozen air.

Kelly had to agree. But when the light shifted and caught something that looked metallic, she pulled out of the moment. "Right. Let's get to work."

Kelly and Chay gave the orders, along with clear explanations of what gear should go where. It wasn't a discussion, and it wasn't gentle. They moved around each other easily, and it was good to see Shawn and Bree being careful. The others worked with the economy she expected, and it wasn't long before the lines had been laid and the rope ladders put in place at intervals into the crevasse.

Kelly fixed her rappelling gear into place, checking and double-checking every carabiner and line, and then Chay checked them as well. She stepped over the poles placed along the lip and tentatively tested the edge. It held firm, and she gave a thumbs-up before she stepped off the edge and began to lower herself down, with Chay slowly feeding the line, ready to grab it if the lip gave way.

She was only two feet down when she saw what had caught the other team's eye. "We've got a spear!" she shouted up and smiled at the resulting cheers. Slowly, she made her way further down and spotted far more items, some sticking out, some barely shadows deeper in the ice. When there didn't appear to be more, she started tracking sideways after shouting up that she was moving that direction. Her line moved smoothly overhead, and she continued to see items all along a similar vertical plane, not more than two feet higher or lower than the main layer. She marked everything sticking out with a red flag that slid into the ice almost too easily, and it was only then she noticed the dripping water sliding down the walls to the bottom.

"Coming up!" she yelled and began to raise herself hand over hand using her winch system until she reached the lip. She took the hand outstretched and hauled herself out.

Breathless, she looked into Shawn's eyes and forgot to breathe at all for a second.

"So? What's down there?" Chay and the others gathered around her, breaking the spell.

"It's incredible. The first thing I saw was a full spear—not just the head, but the whole thing. It looks like the shaft might be bone." She shook her head and then shook out her arms, which were tingling. She hadn't had to do a climb like that in a while. "I planted about twenty flags, and that's just the stuff sticking out, waiting for us to pull it. There's more around every piece."

The excitement was palpable and set-up resumed at a faster

pace. Kelly took the time to explain the different types of knots and ropes to Bree and Shawn, who listened without comment and then repeated the knotwork until they had it down. Gianna and Chay were roped up and waiting at the lip.

"Kelly, I need to show you—" Pam gasped and looked at the mountain beyond them.

A rumble, like a two-ton lorry heading their direction, started low and began to echo, building in intensity. Kelly's stomach dropped.

"Ice quake! Away from the lip! Everyone down!" She dropped, yanking her ice claw from her belt and slamming it into the snow. Beside her, Shawn and Bree did the same.

"Shit!"

Kelly looked over her shoulder just as Gianna slipped over the lip. Chay's body jerked as she took the weight of Gianna's body, and Kelly felt the ropes tighten around her.

The ice shook, and showers of snow fell from the mountain sides around them, sending plumes into the air like small snow bombs going off, beauty belying danger.

Soon the rumbling stopped, and everything grew quiet again. Kelly looked over her shoulder. "Gianna! You okay?"

"I'm okay!" came her reply, echoing off the crevasse into which she'd fallen. "I'm good to come up when you're ready."

"Right." Kelly kept her axe in place and used it as a handhold to get to her feet. "You two next, then Pam, Dave, and Rena. Chay will go last once we're all ready to support her, so she doesn't go over with Gianna. Be ready to take her weight."

Braced, they all did as they were told. Chay moved gingerly, clawing her way away from the lip on her hands and knees, until she finally stood and braced herself. The others held the ropes as Gianna brought herself up to the lip, and then Chay grabbed her and helped her out.

Kelly knelt in the snow. "Well, that was an exciting first foray."

Nervous laughter met her statement. Bree flopped backward

into the snow. Shawn stood looking at the crevasse, her expression impassive.

"Let's try this again. Pam, can you and Dave get some readings, please? Rena, you too. Let's make sure nothing has opened up beneath us, okay?" They nodded, and she turned to the others. "Shawn, I'd like you and me to go down first. Let's get the horizontal lines in and everything pegged. We'll start digging tomorrow. For now, I want to let the ground settle before the rest of the team go in there."

Chay waved. "Um, hello? I'd think you'd take in the person who knows how to do this instead of a person more used to a keyboard than a mallet."

Shawn crossed her arms. "You don't know me. You have no idea what I'm used to."

Chay rolled her eyes, and Kelly held up her hand before the pissing match began. "Chay, I'm taking Shawn down because I need you up here in case there's another quake. One of us needs to be topside at all times with the ice being this unstable. Shawn is strong and capable, or she wouldn't be here." She made sure there was no room for argument in her tone and was glad when Chay just nodded.

Kelly led the way and Shawn followed. At the lip, Kelly showed Shawn how she was going to drop in and where to place her feet.

"Ready?" Kelly asked, and Shawn simply nodded, mirroring Kelly's movements.

They stepped off, with Gianna and Chay feeding their lines as they moved slowly down the vertical blue ice wall.

"Stop there!" Kelly shouted and felt her line go taut. "So, we're going to put in some horizontal lines. We won't use them unless absolutely necessary, but they're a good safety measure if our own rigs give out and we need to grab hold of something on the wall. They're also good for marking where we've been so we know where to pick up again next time. We'll mark the beginning and ending areas where we see artifacts with black-tipped sticks and then during the dig, we'll mark the finds with blue-tipped sticks."

Shawn nodded and held out her hand. "You place the pegs, and I'll mallet them in."

The plan went smoothly, and Kelly found that working beside Shawn was easy. She didn't act like she knew any better than anyone else. She listened carefully and did exactly as she was asked. They worked in silence, the voices of the crew above occasionally filtering down.

"Are you glad you came?" Kelly asked as they came to what appeared to be the end of the artifact section.

Shawn frowned, carefully tapping in the peg. "It's only the second day. I'm not sure yet."

She'd been hoping for something a little more...exuberant maybe. But she should have known better. Shawn wasn't an exuberant kind of person.

"Does that disappoint you?" Shawn asked as Kelly knotted the line around the peg.

"No." Kelly tilted her head. "Maybe. I was hoping after seeing this," she motioned to the artifacts sticking out of the ice, "you'd be more excited. But that's my issue, not yours."

Shawn sighed softly, her breath puffing out in front of her. "I'm sorry. I'll be excited once I've had time to process. I kind of, I guess, take everything in first, and then I think about it later. Emotion is secondary to understanding." She gave Kelly a small smile. "I'm glad that my workout routine means I'm not feeling the strain the way Bree is."

Kelly laughed. "To be completely honest, I knew this was going to be way out of your comfort zones, but I hadn't considered how physically demanding it was going to be. Poor Bree."

Shawn grinned. "She'll be fine. It will be good for her. She'll appreciate our office even more after this."

"And what about you? Think you'll get bitten by the field bug?" Kelly placed the final peg and wished they weren't wearing gloves when their hands touched.

"It's hard to say. This is indescribably beautiful." She glanced at Kelly and then back at the ice. "On many levels."

Kelly warmed but before she could reply and get herself in trouble, a shout came from above.

"Hey, Kel, can you guys come up? We've got visitors."

Kelly and Shawn exchanged a glance and then began the slow climb up, with Kelly giving Shawn tips that she didn't really seem to need. In fact, she seemed pretty comfortable with the whole setup. A thought occurred to her.

"Shawn, have you done other climbing before?"

She nodded as she moved the winch system. "There's a rock wall at the gym I like to use sometimes."

Kelly sighed internally. Of course. "But I didn't ask you the question, so you didn't think to offer up that information. Doesn't having things explained to you that you already know irritate you?"

Shawn paused in her upward movement, looking confused. "Why would listening to someone else's knowledge irritate me? There's nothing to say they don't have information I don't. Even if it's minimal, in a situation like this it could be important."

Kelly quite desperately wanted to lean over and kiss her, hard. How rare it was to come across someone so intelligent with so little ego. Instead, she ducked her head. "Even when it's Chay giving you the information?" she whispered.

Shawn grunted and started moving again. "You might find I have my limits."

Kelly laughed, and they continued their climb to the top, where people were waiting to help pull them up and out. She shook out her arms and winced at the tingling in her hands and feet. She hadn't realized she was getting that cold. She'd been so relaxed working next to Shawn that she'd failed to pay attention to safety.

"Looks like you might need to get warm." A woman waited for Kelly and Shawn to move away from the opening. "Let's talk in your tent."

Kelly nodded and led the way. She hadn't given much

consideration to the issue of having someone from the tribal nations join them, and she hadn't considered waiting for them back at the campsite. It was a foolish oversight that hopefully wouldn't cause any trouble.

Once inside the tent, Shawn immediately turned on the propane heaters for the pot of hot water, and Kelly changed into another jacket, looking up in surprise when Shawn wrapped a blanket around her before taking one herself. Finally, she looked at the couple who'd come to talk.

The woman had smooth, light brown skin and thick, dark hair pulled into a tight ponytail. She wore a thick puffer jacket, leather pants that looked soft and were probably made from caribou, if Kelly had to guess, and solid hiking boots. The man with her was similarly dressed, but the deep lines in his face and his shock of white hair made it obvious he was far older.

"I'm sorry for our lack of hospitality," Kelly said, gratefully sipping the coffee Shawn handed her. "We were so excited to get out here—"

"No apology necessary." The man gingerly lowered himself into the chair opposite Kelly. "It's an exciting time. We knew we'd find you when we needed to."

Shawn leaned forward. "You're with the council who want to put the items back in the ice instead of into a museum."

He nodded. "I'm Morris Jette. The Koyukon have lived in this area for many generations. The land is part of who we are, and when we leave parts of ourselves behind, we become part of the land that sustains us."

"But aren't we closer to the Dena'ina tribal lands than yours?" Shawn frowned at Kelly when she nudged her with her foot. "Shouldn't the Dena'ina be the ones deciding?"

"The AARG is made up of members of all the Athabascan tribes." The woman's expression didn't give anything away, and her tone was neutral. "I'm Grace Jette. Grandpa Morris is a tribal elder."

Shawn looked at Kelly. "That didn't answer my question."

"If I'm understanding correctly, the Jettes are here on behalf of the council as a whole, meaning they've been given the go-ahead to speak for all the tribes, including the Dena'ina." Kelly could only hope that Shawn's directness didn't make the council want to pull the permission for the dig.

"That's right." He studied Shawn. "You're not happy with that decision."

Shawn simply looked at him.

"Like many archeologists, Shawn is saddened that the beautiful items will be returned to the ice instead of made available for people to see and learn from in the years to come." Kelly had grown somewhat accustomed to Shawn's inability to respond to things that weren't direct questions but to strangers, it must seem rude.

"Nokinbaa," he murmured, still looking at Shawn.

Grace looked surprised but didn't say anything. She turned to Kelly. "We understand. But this isn't your land, and we honor those who came before us by keeping what they left behind as part of the land. We were told you'd respect that, and the 3-D printing would suffice as a compromise for you to come out and do the research."

Kelly finished her coffee, wishing there was more. Or something stronger. "And we will. We've brought an expert with us who will be able to make sure the items go back to where they were pulled, assuming of course that the ice is still capable of that."

Grandpa Morris finally looked away from Shawn, who looked bemused. "We understand that exact placement may be virtually impossible once the pieces have been moved. As long as they're in a reasonably similar position, we'll be happy."

"Will you be joining us at the site?" Kelly asked, wincing at the sharp tingling of feeling returning to her fingers and toes.

"Some days, yes. We're interested in seeing what you've found." Grace's smile lit up her eyes. "I read up on you. Some of your finds have been truly magnificent."

"I'm not an owl." Shawn's abrupt insertion brought the conversation to a standstill.

"What?" Kelly asked.

"You understood?" Grandpa Morris nodded and pushed himself to his feet. "Then you are exactly what I saw you to be." He patted Grace's shoulder. "Let them get back to work. We'll come back in two days to see how things are going."

Grace gave Kelly a genuine, if somewhat puzzled, smile, and they left the tent.

"What was that about?" Kelly turned to Shawn, trying not to be irritated by the way she was with people. It wasn't her fault. But still...she would have liked to talk to them further.

"That word he used. Nokinbaa." She pronounced it slowly, uncertainly. "It means snowy owl. I thought that's what it was when he said it, but it didn't make any sense, so I was thinking about it. But that's what it means. Why did he call me an owl?"

Kelly stretched. "I don't know. Owls have spiritual significance in a lot of cultures. I'm not even going to ask how you know a tribal dialect spoken by only about a hundred people on earth."

"A hundred and fifty, approximately. But what does an owl have to do with me?"

"I don't know. Let's get back and see what the others are doing." In another time and place, Kelly would have been happy to sit and chat about what Grandpa Morris might have meant by it. But right now, she didn't have any answers, and they were burning daylight. If Shawn wanted to talk about things like that, they'd have to do it in the cabins after dark.

It was impossible to ignore the hurt look in Shawn's eyes, which she quickly shuttered as she turned away.

CHAPTER FOURTEEN

THERE WAS A FEELING that Shawn hated more than any other feeling in the world. It twisted and turned inside her, making her wish she could pull it out, drop it at her feet, and stomp on it.

That feeling hit harder than usual when she saw the flicker of irritation and heard that same dismissive tone in Kelly's voice that she'd experienced for so much of her life. To this point, Kelly had seemed to get it. From the start, she'd been kind and gentle, and Shawn had felt seen in a way that rarely happened. But since they'd been in Alaska, that patience had already worn thin, and if anything, the brief meeting with the tribal people seemed to have made it worse.

The feeling writhed, tormenting her stomach and heart, tightening and making it hard to breathe, just as it had all last night and into the morning while she was getting ready for today's work.

She gritted her teeth as Chay, Dave, and Bree descended into the crevasse, and she concentrated on the rope sliding through her hands, on the weight of the bodies being lowered, on the crunch of the snow under boots as the others moved around. Anything to ignore the feeling of being not enough, yet again.

Kelly, holding Chay's line, looked relaxed now. If she was still irritated, it didn't show. But then, she was...ephemeral. That was the right word, Shawn thought. Not moody, necessarily, just changeable. She didn't seem to hold onto things the way Shawn did. Not that she knew her all that well really. This might be her more real personality, and the one she'd been showing them in Oklahoma had been transitory, a kind of mask. Shawn knew all about masking. She'd been doing it all her life in an attempt to fit in.

It never seemed to work for very long.

"Tray ready!" Dave shouted from below the ice ledge.

Pam moved to the line dedicated to the trays, a thick orange piece that was flat instead of round. She brought it up slowly, and when it got to the edge, she loop-locked the line and went to the edge to pull it the rest of the way out. She took it to a sled, wrapped it in a soft blanket, and then went to Shawn.

"You're up! I'll take the line, and you can take the tray back to the tent and start doing your thing."

More relieved than she wanted to be, Shawn nodded and headed to the sled. She was about to kick off, glad to be putting all these people behind her for a while, when Kelly's voice stopped her.

"Shawn, be careful, please. You're on your own from here to the tent. Be extra alert for any shifts in the ice. Any kind of soft spots or lines need to be checked out before you go over them." Kelly's smile was small, her eyes serious. "I know it isn't all that far, but still."

Shawn studied her for a second. The bright sky behind her highlighted the lighter strands in her hair. It would feel so good to run her hands through them. But no. That was nonsense, and she needed to get a grip. She turned away and set off, pushing the small sled along almost like a skateboard. Once she got to the tent, she carefully unloaded the tray.

Out of habit, she pulled her phone from the zip pocket of her jacket. There was nothing to be checked though. No signal at all meant no email, no social media, no...anything. She ran her fingers over the screen, feeling the loss of connection to the world where she felt most comfortable. It was a strange, bereft feeling, added to by the vast white space she was occupying with people who would only find her irksome at best and useless at worst.

Well, there was a simple way to combat the worst. She'd prove her usefulness. She lifted the tray to the table and uncovered it. The contents were fascinating, and a thrill began to slip through the anxiety.

A nine-inch knife made of metal and bone sat to the left of what might have been an ancient piece of sled. Next to that was a piece of leather that looked like it might have been part of a shoe. She opened the computer, sat down, and took photos of the items from every angle with the professional camera already hooked up to the laptop. Then she placed it on the stand that allowed a camera to scan every inch of it for the 3-D printing later. Every item was tagged with a piece of tape with the location, item number, and time found. Shawn entered the data quickly, along with keywords to search for similar items once they were connected to reality again. Gently, she picked up the knife and turned it over, studying it intently. The grooves and markings along the bone handle weren't just from the ice or wear. She tilted it, then used a light to look closer. The markings were pictures, not dissimilar to the ancient cave art found in other parts of Alaska.

What did it mean? Shawn sat down, the implications overwhelming. Could it be that something so ancient had risen so high in the ice? She shook her head. That was the wrong path of inquiry. Just because she was traveling with people who were happy to jump to conclusions without scientific proof developed after rigorous testing didn't mean she needed to be that loosey-goosey with her ways. No, she'd continue to enter the data sets and include keywords that might tie the pieces to others. That was the way she'd always done things, and it was the way things worked best. Gianna, as the Finds Manager, would authenticate Shawn's input later. Possible exhilaration tamped down, she finished the entries for the pieces, carefully placed them in a longer, covered tray in the back, and then headed back to the site with the empty tray.

When she arrived, the team had switched again, and this time Kelly, Pam, and Rena were in the chasm, with Chay, Dave, and Gianna holding the ropes. Shawn placed the empty tray in a line, ready to be lowered once the other had been pulled up.

"You didn't bring the items back?" Chay asked, glancing at the tray. "We need to put them back in the ice."

Shawn bristled at the tone, one she knew well. "I'm not stupid. The pieces are extraordinary, and the tribal people today said that as long as the pieces were in the general area, they would be happy. I thought the rest of the group might want to actually look at the pieces before we put them back. Bree is exceptional at what she does and won't have a problem making sure things are where they need to be." She crossed her arms. Chay might be a lot of things that Shawn wasn't, but when it came to work, Shawn knew what the hell she was doing. And thinking of what other people might want rather than what protocol required was already unusual enough to make her feel itchy inside. She didn't need Chay second-guessing her abilities or making Bree feel less-than.

Chay's eyebrows rose a little. "That's great. Thanks. What did you see when you looked at them?"

For reasons she couldn't explain to herself, Shawn didn't want to share what she'd seen with Chay. She wanted to share it with Kelly. Okay, so maybe she didn't need to explain it explicitly to herself. She wanted to see that light in Kelly's eyes when she got excited, and she wanted to be the one to put it there. Tangentially, at least, since it would be the artifact she'd be excited about, not Shawn. It still counted.

"You'll have to check it out for yourself. I wouldn't want to spoil the surprise." Shawn gave a quick smile and turned away when the shout came that they were sending up more pieces. This time, a spear came up and over the edge, followed by Gianna. Shawn gave her a hand out and then carefully picked up the spear.

"There's a tray ready to come up too," Gianna said, her hands on her knees as she caught her breath after the climb.

Shawn set the spear on the sled, then raised the next tray. After tucking it in place, she held the sled steady as Gianna stepped onto it. "I'll take the snowshoes and meet you there."

Gianna nodded and set off. Shawn watched as she seemed to sway just a little before righting herself.

"What is it?" Chay asked. "You look worried."

"Do I?" Shawn frowned, wondering what her own expression looked like. "Gianna just looked a little wobbly, that's all."

Chay glanced over her shoulder at the retreating sled. "We'll keep an eye out. Any time you see something like that, say something. It could be nothing, but making sure everyone is okay is important."

"Yeah." Shawn strapped on the snowshoes. Kelly's question earlier, about becoming irritated when Shawn was told things she already knew, came back to her. As she'd said, when it came to Chay doing it, there was no question it rankled. She didn't say anything else as she started tromping toward the tent. Walking in the giant snowshoes was awkward and made her thighs ache, but she liked the challenge and had already worked it out pretty well by the time she reached the tent. When she got in, she instantly noted Gianna's pale face and bluish lips. Her hands were shaking as she went to pick up an artifact.

"Hold up there." Shawn quickly unlaced the snowshoes and moved to Gianna's side. "Sit down for a second."

"We have...have...to..." Gianna's stutter got worse as her teeth chattered.

Shawn ran to the tent next door and grabbed a propane heater and pot for water, as well as a big mug. She returned to find Gianna curled in on herself in a chair. First, she wrapped Gianna in both of the available blankets, tucking them tightly around her. Then she got the water boiling and soon put a hot cup into her hands.

"Thanks," Gianna whispered, barely visible through the blankets around her. "I don't know why I'm so cold."

"Because it's below freezing, and you've been hanging by ropes between walls of ice." Shawn shrugged. "Seems pretty straightforward."

Gianna's laugh was hoarse. "Well, when you put it that way."

They looked up when the sound of the others coming their way floated into the tent. Shawn moved to the artifacts and started setting up, uninterested in watching Kelly and Chay come in together. But it was Bree and Chay who came in first, laughing, both dusted in snow.

"I'll be the one to throw the first snowball next time," Bree said, shaking the snow from her hair.

"I'll be watching," Chay said, giving her a lopsided grin before looking at Shawn. Her expression darkened when she looked at Gianna. "What's wrong?"

"She got cold." Shawn didn't look up from the artifacts.

Chay moved to kneel in front of Gianna. "Fingers."

Shawn watched from the corner of her eye as Chay took off Gianna's gloves and checked her hands. She held them for a while between her own, then she did the same with her feet after she'd taken off Gianna's boots and socks. Her fingers and toes were all a brilliant red. Interestingly, she didn't rub them the way Shawn would have thought to, if she'd thought to do it at all.

Chay turned on Shawn. "What the hell were you thinking?"

The others, who'd been busy looking at the artifacts, stopped what they were doing.

"What do you mean?" Automatically, Shawn took a step back and immediately hated herself for showing weakness.

"I told you to say something. The moment you saw that Gianna was in distress, you should have come and gotten me. It's *my* job to make sure everything and everyone here is safe. Not yours. You don't make a decision that everything is okay because you've wrapped her in a couple blankets."

"Chay, hold on—"

"No, Kelly. I know you've got a soft spot for her, but I'm not going to let her put others in jeopardy because she doesn't know enough to ask for fucking help." Chay's eyes were narrowed, and she shrugged off Kelly's hand.

Unable to figure out what to say in the face of Chay's onslaught, Shawn balled her hands into fists in frustration.

"Hey now." Bree stepped in front of Shawn, her hands up.

"Shawn did exactly what I would have done. This is our first time in the field—"

"And that's the problem, isn't it?" Chay sighed and rubbed at her temples, her shoulders dropping. "You guys really have no idea how to work outside an office. You shouldn't be here."

The moment Shawn saw Bree's shoulders hunch forward, anger replaced her inability to deal with conflict. Gently, she pulled Bree back and put her arm around Bree's shoulders. "We said as much, Chay. You think we don't know that we're out of our element? You think this was easy for us?" She motioned to Kelly, who was watching the argument but not saying anything. "You're right. We don't know what we're doing, and we were assured that we'd be okay, that we could learn what we needed to once we were here. I'm sorry I didn't come running back to our big bad savior in the snow when Gianna got cold. I know now that you need to be told, and it won't happen again." She removed her arm from Bree's shoulders and stepped in front of her. "But I'll be darned if you're going to make us feel like poop because we're not Lara Croft wannabes."

There was a snort of laughter from someone, but Shawn didn't see who because she wouldn't break eye contact with Chay. The moment was tense, and Shawn hoped with all her being that Chay didn't throw a swing, because if she did, they were well-matched, and it would be messy. Not to mention extremely unprofessional.

Suddenly, Chay laughed. The tension in the tent popped like a balloon, and it seemed like everyone started to breathe again.

"Okay, Shawn. I hear you. Gianna's going to be fine. When we're back at the cabins, we'll have a talk about hypothermia and safety protocols so we're all up to speed." She leaned forward, close enough to whisper, "Just don't forget who's in charge, eh?" Moving away, she looked around. "Who do I need to fuck to get a hot drink around here?"

Behind her, Shawn heard Bree sigh, and she turned around. "You okay?"

"I don't know if I want to have sex with her or run from her." Bree's smile was a little tremulous. "I don't think I've ever seen you step up to someone like that."

"I don't think I ever have." Shawn was glad she still had gloves on so she didn't have to wipe her sweaty palms on her pants. "But I wasn't about to let her make you feel bad." She smiled a little. "I'm not sure I understand the desire to bed her though. She's intense."

Bree rolled her shoulders, and her usual smile returned. "That kind of intensity has its uses, believe me." She looped her arm through Shawn's. "Let's see what we've got, shall we?"

Together, they moved to the tables with the artifacts laid out. There was a lot of conjecture and unsubstantiated claims about the pieces, but Shawn decided silence was the better part of knowledge for the moment. None of the claims were going in the computer, so they could say whatever they wanted. She caught Kelly's eye. "Do you see the handle on the first knife you pulled out?"

Kelly frowned and peered more closely. "There are a lot of ridges in it."

Shawn shook her head and motioned. "Look." She held the piece carefully, tilting it under the lamp.

Kelly looked more closely and gasped. The smile that lit up her whole face was exactly what Shawn had hoped to see. It was worth any peeing contest with Chay, just for this moment.

"Shawn! That's amazing!" Kelly took it and shifted so she could see it better. "We might have missed it altogether."

The others crowded around, and Shawn backed off, glad to let them analyze and debate the origins of the piece.

Kelly looked over her shoulder. "We might have put this back without having really looked at it. Thank you."

Shawn ducked her head. "Sure." *Take that and stick it in your craw.* She didn't look at Chay just in case her expression gave her away.

"It's such a shame that it has to go back into the ice." Rena looked genuinely sad. "Do you think they'd change their minds?"

Kelly took a seat next to Shawn. "I don't think so. Do you?"

Shawn glanced at her, incredulous. "You think I'd know better than you?"

"Well, he did call you an owl. Wise and—"

"Intense." Chay finished the sentence and knelt to check on Gianna again.

Shawn inwardly flinched but kept it hidden. She couldn't let Chay get to her again. And how weird that she used the same word to describe Chay. "No, I don't think so. Spirituality is deeply engrained in isolated cultures, often more so than in cultures which are more centralized and well-populated. They made it clear how they feel about it and although the finds are exceptional, I don't see how that will make it less important to them that they remain with their ancestral lands. 3-D printing and photographs will have to do."

"Damn." Dave had continued to look over the finds with a magnifying glass. "If I had to guess, I'd say we're looking at something from one or two hundred AD." He looked up. "How would they know? I mean, if we didn't replace it. They aren't here. They don't know what we've found and what we haven't. If a couple pieces didn't make it back into the ice..." He shrugged.

Before Shawn could object, Kelly shook her head. "We're not tomb raiders, Dave. As much as I get where you're coming from, we don't do our work through deception. It would taint anything we found."

He didn't look convinced when he turned away to continue his examinations.

Shawn breathed a little easier. No matter how conflicted she felt about Kelly, at least she could sleep easier knowing she wasn't a deceiver. Bree caught her gaze and gave a little nod, as though she understood what Shawn was thinking. She probably did.

"In the meantime," Rena said, "let's get the absolute best images we possibly can. Gianna and Shawn, since you two are the computer people, do you think you could rig something to do that?"

It wasn't easy, and it wasn't pretty. But together, Gianna and Shawn moved computers, cables, and the available lighting into a position where the pieces could be slowly and closely photographed and videoed in order to get the level of detail they needed. It was painstaking work, and Shawn barely registered when the rest of the team headed back to the crevasse, leaving them to do what they needed to. It seemed like no time at all when they came to take the trays back so Bree could give directions as to where to replace the items they'd found so far.

Soon after, Bree came in shivering and tried to stretch, but that was made more difficult by the layers of clothing. "I'll be glad to lay in front of the fire like a cat tonight."

Gianna nodded, her color better. "I hear that."

The rest of the team returned too. "Time to head back to camp," Kelly said. "We don't want to be out here after dark."

The computers were packed up, and the trays with the remaining artifacts were bundled carefully onto a sled so they could be photographed and analyzed in the cabin before they were put back the following day. Most everything else was left behind for tomorrow. The tents were zipped closed, and the group trudged, slower this time, back to where the sleds and dogs were waiting.

"Cutting it close," the musher said, watching as everyone settled. "We could do with about an extra thirty minutes tomorrow, okay? Dark settles in fast here."

Kelly apologized, and the group set off. Shawn and Bree rode together, neither saying anything, and Shawn soon realized the others were quiet too, and only the sounds of the dogs and sleds echoed over the snow around them.

Once they were back at the cabins, Kelly thanked the dog team and then turned to the others. "Come on over to our place for chili if you want to. Gianna, I'd like you to come over so we can check you out, okay? If you're not joining us for dinner, we'll see you at the same time in the morning."

Chay held up her hand. "I'd like Shawn and Bree to come over for some first aid training."

Shawn didn't want anything to do with anyone tonight. She wanted the peace and quiet of their cabin so she could process the day and everything that had happened. But one of those things had been, apparently, her lack of knowledge about how to treat someone who was too cold. "I'll need half an hour."

"Perfect." Kelly lightly touched her arm. "See you soon."

Shawn took a step back, then another, until she turned and headed to their cabin. She heard Bree's footsteps crunching on the icy snow behind her. Once they were inside, silence continued, and she was thankful Bree didn't feel the need to chat. She got the fire going, and it wasn't long before the cabin started to feel a little warmer. She and Bree pulled chairs up in front of it, and Shawn closed her eyes.

"I've never felt so inept." Bree's voice was soft.

Shawn rolled her head to the side, too tired to lift it. "What do you mean? You did everything right."

"That's not what I mean." Bree toed the wood in front of the fireplace, steam rising from it as it warmed. "Yeah, I did what they expected me to do, and that's great. But the ropes, and the way they work together as a team... It's a lot. I mean, it's impressive, for sure. It's just... I don't know."

Shawn rolled her head back and stared into the fire. "We're not one of them."

Bree sighed. "Yeah. It's like hanging out with the cool kids at school but knowing you're not actually part of the group. You're an outsider, and that's exactly how they see you."

Shawn nodded but didn't say anything. It hurt in a way she was familiar with. An old, dull ache in her chest that reminded her, yet again, that she wasn't part of Kelly's world and didn't belong in it. By the time this expedition was over, it would be easier to deal with the fact that Kelly was out of her league in a million ways that made it so they wouldn't work.

The ache intensified.

"The Alaskan elder. He called me an owl. It's bothering me." Shawn changed the subject to hide the other emotions she wasn't ready for.

Bree raised her eyebrows and looked at the ceiling for a long moment. "I can see that."

"Why?"

She motioned vaguely toward the sky. "They're loners. Most owls don't have flocks, and they're protective of their territory. They're sharp, intelligent, and metaphorically, they're wise. You're all those things."

"But why call me one? What's the point?"

Again, Bree considered before answering. "Sometimes comparing yourself to something else can help you see parts of your personality you might not see otherwise. You're an owl—do you want to be a loner? You can't help being wise and intelligent. But maybe understanding that's your nature can help you accept it." She finally turned to look at Shawn. "See?"

Shawn nodded, taking Bree's words onboard. The assessment was a logical one, and the extended explanation made sense. In fact, she found she rather liked being compared to an owl when it came down to it. Better than something like an anteater or a puffer fish.

"Thirty minutes is up." Bree pushed herself from the chair with obvious effort. "Come on."

Shawn followed and they made their way into the wind, which had picked up and was blowing snow in pretty, stinging waves through the frigid air. Kelly's cabin was warm though, and all the others had gathered. The smell of chili made Shawn salivate, and her stomach rumbled in response.

Kelly held up two bowls. "Come on, champions. Feed the soul."

She and Bree took the bowls with thanks and found empty seats. "I'm pretty sure things like church are meant to feed the soul.

FRAGMENTS OF THE HEART 165

Food is meant for the body."

Kelly took a seat on the floor next to Shawn, stretching her legs out in front of her. "Food is good for the body, but haven't you seen the way cultures come together over meals? They share stories, they talk about life, they take on one another's distresses. Food is used as medicine as well as a way to communicate your love for someone." She looked up at Shawn and gave her a sweet, soft smile.

Shawn choked on her chili.

"Agreed." Chay scraped her spoon around her bowl. "My family gets together at least once a month for dinner. My mom's enchiladas are the best you've ever had, and she takes hours to make them. It's a sign of love and affection, and I'll always associate that dish with her."

Shawn thought about it. "But that's familial affection. The soul is nebulous at best. Affection and the sharing of food is an animal's way of developing a pack. It's evolution. It has nothing to do with whatever a soul is."

There was quiet for a moment. "So you don't believe in the soul?" Kelly asked, looking up at Shawn.

"I don't get what it's supposed to be, or how it's different from things that we can categorize." Although Shawn was always happy to avoid small talk, this felt like dangerous territory. But they were all scientists here, right? "We have personalities. We have likes and dislikes, we have behaviors borne of childhood experiences and the elements we're brought up with. Those things create who we are. They're easily categorized and explained. The idea of a soul seems redundant and used mostly for religious purposes."

"I disagree." Chay grinned when Shawn rolled her eyes. "I think it's the combination of all those things you mentioned plus the way our emotions run us that create a soul. It's the way your energy touches the energy of others and the world around you that defines a soul. It doesn't have to do with religion."

"I like the idea of soulmates." Bree set her bowl aside and drew her knees up to her chest. "The idea of someone meant to be with me, someone who's destined to come across my path and sweep me off my feet appeals to me." She smiled at Chay, who smiled back with a softness in her gaze that Shawn hadn't seen before.

Shawn shook her head. "You've always been a romantic. I don't know how you allow the idealistic part of you to marry up with the scientist in you."

Rena, holding Dave's hand as they sat next to each other on the couch, held up their hands. "People don't have to be one thing or another. They can be a crazy mix of ideas that don't seem to mesh. Dave is an atheist through and through and probably agrees with Shawn. I'm a romantic, like Bree, and I think we were meant to be."

"We're stardust." Kelly said, rolling up from her place on the floor. "Our compositions are made up of the same stuff that makes up galaxies. Who's to say that your stardust isn't a soul looking for stardust to match it and create something even more beautiful, like the aurora borealis that dances through the sky?"

Shawn didn't agree, but the way Kelly said it and the way her eyes sparkled as she did meant Shawn wasn't about to argue the point. She was simply too beautiful, and it made all the words disappear.

"Now." Kelly planted her hands on her hips. "I believe Shawn and Bree have some training to do."

And just like that, the bubble popped. The very last thing in the world Shawn wanted to do was listen to Chay instruct them on anything at all. Bree stood quickly though, and Shawn groaned silently as she followed. She walked past Kelly, who gently stopped her progress.

"Before you go tonight, can we talk?" she asked.

"Sure." Shawn's skin tingled under Kelly's touch, even through layers of fabric.

Kelly's hand slid off, slowly, and she smiled before turning to the group, who moved off the subject of the soul and onto the finds of the day. Gianna booted up the computer, and they gathered around it. Shawn wanted to head that direction, but a throat clearing made her look over.

"Come on, scout." Chay's crossed arms and the way her eyes flicked from Shawn to Kelly made it clear she knew what Shawn was thinking.

"I'm not a scout. I never have been." Shawn sat at the small dining table with them.

"That doesn't surprise me." Chay tapped the PDF on the iPad in front of her. "Let's start."

Shawn managed to pay attention to the lesson on working in extreme temperatures, and it was actually interesting and useful, and she understood why Chay had gotten so irritated with her earlier. Gianna could have lost fingers or toes if she'd been allowed to get any colder, and if she'd chafed them, there was a minimal possibility of a heart attack, which would have been on Shawn's shoulders. Now that she knew, there'd be no question of how to react in the future. Throughout it all, she'd been aware of Kelly's voice and position in the room. If only there wasn't an unbridgeable gap between them. Firelight flickered over Kelly's face, highlighting her beauty and reflecting her passion. Memories like this were what Shawn would hold on to in the lonely nights when Kelly was long gone.

CHAPTER FIFTEEN

THE RADIO CRACKLED TO life, making everyone look up. "Sled shed to Broken Swan expedition."

Kelly headed for it, her heart sinking. A call this late at night couldn't be good.

"This is Kelly with the Swan expedition. Go ahead." She looked at the worried expressions around her. All except Shawn, who simply looked curious.

"Sudden storm has blown in and looks like it's here for a while. We won't be going out tomorrow. Sorry."

There was a collective groan from the group. If this was the start of storm season, today may very well have been it. Not to mention the finds they marked yesterday could be completely covered over by morning, let alone by the time they went back out.

"Thanks for letting us know. Keep us updated tomorrow?" Kelly said.

"Will do. Also, be aware there's been a wolf pack sighting in the area. They probably won't come anywhere near you but watch for them anyway."

Kelly signed off and set down the radio. "Well, we have a day off now. We can get together tomorrow and go over the finds, but it looks like we're cabin-bound until we get the go ahead. At least we can sleep in."

She was glad to see some smiles and nods of assent. The group began to disband back to their cabins.

Chay stood. "I'll walk Bree back, since you wanted a word with Shawn."

Kelly gave her a warning look. She'd clearly been

eavesdropping, not that there was a ton of space in the cabin. But there was a devilish glint in her eyes that she recognized all too well. "Remember that conversation we had on the plane."

Chay shrugged. "Do as I say, not as I do?" She laughed and slung her arm around Bree's shoulders. "Let's leave the serious people to do their serious talking."

Bree giggled, her cheeks turning a cute shade of pink. "I'm all for leaving serious behind."

They left, and Kelly stood looking at the closed door for a moment. She and Chay had decided that focus was paramount. But if the expedition had already been shut down, then maybe they could afford to relax a little.

"Should I go?" Shawn asked.

Kelly turned. "I'm sorry. I was just lost in thought." She sat on the couch and waved Shawn over. "Come sit with me."

For a second, it looked like she might say no, but then she rose and came over. "You wanted to talk to me?" She motioned toward the door. "About something serious?"

She draped her feet over Shawn's lap and was glad when Shawn automatically started to rub them. "No. Not really. That was Chay being Chay."

"Not *really* implies *something*. Not nothing."

"I wanted to check in. It was quite an intense day. Are you okay?"

Shawn frowned, her hands seemingly on autopilot as she rubbed Kelly's feet. "I'm fine. Thank you."

Kelly wiggled her toes. "Hey. How are you *really*? I'm asking because I want to know."

Shawn flinched a little. "Do you, though? Because I'm pretty sure you got frustrated with me earlier. And that's okay. I know I can be hard to take. But you don't have to pretend."

Kelly pulled her feet away, as much as she wanted to leave them in Shawn's capable hands. "What are you talking about?"

Shawn was silent for a while, her gaze focused on the fire. "When the tribal people left, you had that tone. The one that says,

'Shut up and just be normal, Shawn.' I've heard it all my life, and I know what it sounds like. And I know that when people use it, it's because they're tired of me being me." She shrugged. "I'm not complaining or having a pity party, as my mom used to say. It's a statement of fact, that's all."

It wasn't just a statement of fact though. Kelly could hear the tangled thread of old pain in her voice and see it in the way Shawn held herself so still, as though prepared for a blow of some kind. And having met her brother, it was probably just as literal as it was figurative. She moved closer and cupped Shawn's cheek.

"I'm sorry if I got impatient today. You're right. Working with you in Oklahoma has been relaxed and easy, but to be honest, I'm not known for being relaxed."

"But you are known for being easy?" Shawn grinned a little, her glance flicking to Kelly's face.

"Sometimes." Kelly laughed and pinched her cheek. "I have a temper, Shawn. I've been told I'm rather exasperating to work with in the field. It's all guns firing, and I demand a lot from the crews I work with. I don't have a lot of time for discussions of a nature that don't have to do with digging things up unless I'm spending time with the natives of the area. Then I have all the time in the world." She drew her fingertips down Shawn's cheek to her lips. "Fire and water. Both powerful, both capable of destruction."

"I take it you're fire," Shawn said, holding Kelly's hand and biting the tip of her finger.

"Let's find out." She stood, pulling Shawn up with her.

"Kelly." Shawn stopped their forward movement. "You have to know I want you. I've wanted you since you walked into my office. But we said we couldn't do this because we're co-workers. And now, with all this going on," she motioned toward the cabin next door, clearly meaning Chay, "it isn't a *better* idea than it was when things were simpler."

Kelly tugged Shawn toward her and pulled her in for a long, deep kiss full of promise. Shawn's hands settled on her hips, then moved up her back.

"It isn't a good idea, Shawn. But the storm may have just sunk our expedition, which was why we had a ticking clock on it. And here and now, we're alone. I want you. When we get back to Oklahoma, we can revisit our office rules. For now, let's enjoy Alaska rules." She kissed her again, harder this time, and moaned when Shawn's hand rested on the back of her neck.

Shawn reached down, grabbed her ass, and lifted her. Kelly wrapped her legs around Shawn's waist and continued the kiss as Shawn walked them to the bed. She lay Kelly down and then quickly started taking off layers. Kelly did the same and swallowed hard when Shawn stood there in nothing but her tight boxers and sports bra. Firelight flickered over her defined abs and the long length of muscle in her legs. Her biceps flexed as Kelly looked her over.

"I don't think I've ever been looked at like I'm about to be devoured." Shawn crawled up the length of Kelly's body, nipping, licking, and sucking as she went. "You're so flipping beautiful."

"I think it's a crying shame you have to cover that body of yours with clothing. You should walk around naked for the rest of time." Kelly turned her head to give Shawn better access to her neck.

"I'd get cold." Shawn's hand moved under Kelly's hair and gently pulled, exposing the front of her neck and making her moan. She bit and sucked, her thigh pressed between Kelly's legs.

"Speaking of," Kelly said, already breathless and loath to move. "Let's get under the blankets."

Shawn shifted, pressing her leg a little harder into Kelly before getting off the bed. Kelly yanked the blankets aside, slid under them, and held them up for Shawn.

Shawn looked over her shoulder. "What if Chay comes back?"

"Then she'll get a hell of a show. Or she can join us." Kelly burst out laughing at the look of horror on Shawn's face. "I'm kidding. If I know Chay, she and Bree are already further along than we are."

Shawn frowned and looked toward the door again.

"Hey." Kelly waited until she had Shawn's attention, and then she moved so Shawn could see her fully. "Show me what you've got."

With what sounded almost like a growl, Shawn slid into bed and pulled the covers over them. Her hands were everywhere in just the right way, and Kelly wondered if they'd burn a hole right through the bed, she was so hot. The way Shawn pinched and twisted her nipples made her want to cry out, but she pressed the pillow to her mouth and pushed her breasts harder into Shawn's almost possessive touch.

"Please," she whispered. "Jesus, Shawn, please fuck me."

Shawn captured one of Kelly's nipples in her mouth and sucked hard as she entered her with two fingers, pushing deep and slow. Kelly wrapped her hand in Shawn's short hair, biting her lip to keep from screaming as Shawn pushed in deeper and harder, fucking her so...so...right. Her fingers twisted inside her, pressing, and Kelly yanked the pillow over her face as she cried out, her orgasm crashing through her like a tidal wave. She grasped Shawn's wrist and held her still as she rode out the crest and came down the other side.

Slowly, she let go of Shawn's wrist and let her hands flop to the bed. "Oh my god," she muttered, the pillow still over her face.

Shawn raised the edge of the pillow and peeked under it. "Sorry, I didn't catch that. Can I come in?" Lifting the pillow, she moved to lay beside Kelly, and set the pillow back down on the sides of their heads. "Did you call me God? It's happened before." Shawn grinned, and there was an easy light in her eyes that was almost never there.

"I think you broke me. I've not had an orgasm that good in a long time." Kelly threaded her thigh through Shawn's so they were pretzled together.

"You're so stunning, Kelly. Your curves, your skin, the way you smile, the way you laugh... The best artist couldn't come up with anything as beautiful as you." Shawn's fingers trailed lines of tingling desire along Kelly's stomach and thigh. "I don't think I could get enough of you." Her hand became firmer. "In fact..." She flipped Kelly onto her stomach, laid on top of her, and pushed inside, again deep and firm.

Kelly wasn't sure what words came out of her mouth. Most were probably nonsense. But she didn't care as long as Shawn didn't stop. When Shawn wrapped her arm around Kelly's waist and pulled her up so she was on all fours and then drove into her, rocking her body in time with her thrusts, Kelly gave in and cried out as she pushed onto Shawn's fingers, letting Shawn take her weight as she held her in place. Shawn's thumb hit her clit.

"Come for me," she murmured.

Kelly's body responded, jerking as she came hard, her head thrown back as she saw stars behind her eyelids, and there was only Shawn, inside her, around her, murmuring words Kelly couldn't make out.

Slowly, Shawn lowered her back to the bed, onto her side, and pulled the covers over them. She wrapped herself big spoon-style around Kelly, her arm holding her close. Kelly drifted off into a post-orgasm haze, comfortable, warm, and feeling strangely cared for. There was no reason for that. She had sex all the time. Why did this feel different?

Sleep had just begun to draw her under when Shawn said, "Tell me about your tattoo?"

Kelly involuntarily flexed her lower back, covered in ink. "Why don't you tell me what you think it means?"

Shawn shifted, probably to look at it more closely. "The broken hourglass is spilling sand. So that's clearly something to do with time escaping? The saying along the lines of the cracks reads, *tempus fugit, amor manet,* which means time flies, love endures. But there's nothing here that would indicate love, I don't think. No hearts, or cupids, or anything."

"For me, that's where the birds circling the hourglass come in. My parents told me that no matter where I flew to in the world, their love would always be right there with me." She shivered as Shawn traced the delicate black lines, drawing it so Kelly could picture the whole thing.

"It's beautiful."

Kelly turned over to face her. "No ink on you that I can see." She grinned and snapped at Shawn's sports bra. "Unless you're covering it."

Shawn gave her a wry smile. "No ink here. Can you imagine what I'd be like with someone trying to stick a needle in me? I barely tolerate it at the doctor. And I'd be so stressed out about them possibly making a mistake, or it not being absolutely perfect, that I'd end up in an anxiety attack and they'd have to stop anyway." She brushed some stray hair from Kelly's cheek. "But I can appreciate the talent of good art on someone's skin, even if I don't always understand the meaning." She tilted her head, looking thoughtful. "But there's often meaning. So what worries you about time escaping? I understand the parental love bit, even if I haven't experienced it."

Kelly pillowed her head on her arm. Shawn's eyes were so expressive, and she had no idea that was the case. Right now, she looked like any genuinely interested lover. Hair mussed, a light flush to her skin, expression kind and caring. Kelly's heart ached at how lovely it was to be looked at and really seen.

"Time is slippery, isn't it? We live our lives by it. Wake with the alarm, go to work for a specific time, eat lunch at noon, go home at five, go to the gym at six, eat dinner at seven, go to bed at ten. And then wake up and do it all over again. Suddenly, time is gone. You spend your whole life working just to spend the last decade or so of retirement trying to fit in everything you've wanted to do all your life. It's quite depressing really. I became aware of how desperately sad it is when I was doing my degree at uni. The professor was about to retire. He was old, and cranky, and jaded. He was also seventy, and he'd always wanted to see the Seven Wonders of the World. But by then he had heart problems that meant he could no longer fly. He'd waited all his life to see the world, and when he finally stopped living by the clock, it was too late. Time had run out." She shook her head, thinking of his sad smile when she'd met him in the coffee shop and he'd urged her not to teach but rather to go out into the world. "It's because of him I became a field archeologist instead of going into teaching. I can't imagine how different my life would have been."

Shawn did that thing she did, where she looked from eye to eye. "You'd have been in an office and completely out of your element when a beautiful woman walked in and dragged you out to freeze your rear end off in Alaska."

"And I wouldn't have met one of the most unusual, interesting women I've come across in a long time." Kelly kissed her softly, eliciting a quiet sigh.

"Unusual isn't always a good thing," Shawn whispered against her lips as she shifted so she was partly lying on top of Kelly. Her hand moved to cup her breast, and she squeezed.

Kelly pushed into her touch and let her eyes flit closed. "I think it's one of the best things."

***

The wind crashed against the cabin and the blowing snow obscured any view from the window. Kelly lay contentedly in Shawn's embrace, enjoying the warm comfort under the thick blankets. It hadn't been all that long since she'd woken in a woman's arms, but somehow this felt different. Marta had been damn good in bed, full of Latin fire and passion. And the women before had all offered their own unique takes on the sensual dance done body to body.

But this was different. Shawn had been, as she always seemed to be, *more*. She'd stroked every inch of Kelly's body, studying it like it was a piece of art. Or, even better, like it was an artifact, something to be cherished and understood. Nothing she'd said had been cliché but rather, it all seemed to come from a place of absolute honesty. When she said she thought Kelly was beautiful, it wasn't a line. It wasn't something she said to just anyone. And Kelly felt that compliment in a place inside she rarely let anyone touch.

"What time is it?" Shawn asked, her voice thick with sleep.

"I have no idea, and it doesn't look like we'll need to worry about it today." Kelly rolled over to face Shawn. "Good morning."

Shawn's arm tightened around her. "Good morning."

"I want coffee, but it's too cold out there. I guess we'll just have to stay in bed all day." Her hand slid up Shawn's thigh to the edge of the boxers she'd slept in.

Shawn darted from beneath the covers. "Cripes, it's cold." She ran over to the fireplace and quickly got a fire going, then draped a throw around her shoulders and got water boiling for coffee. The whole time she bounced from foot to foot on the cold wood floor.

"As adorable as that is, you could come lay back down while it brews." Kelly held up the covers, waiting.

"It's almost ready, and I don't think I've got enough courage to get out of bed again once I'm warm." Shawn tugged the blanket tighter. She turned and had just pulled a mug down when there was a rumble.

The ground shook and from a distance came a cracking sound, like a giant dropping a glass from a great height. Shawn held onto the counter until the shaking stopped and the noise faded away.

"Another ice quake." Kelly got out of bed and dragged the comforter along with her. Grabbing the radio, she called the dogsled base. "You guys feel that?"

"We did. Dogs are going nuts. Sounds like we've got a new break somewhere too."

Kelly watched as Shawn tiptoed back to the bed to keep from putting her feet all the way down on the floor. Carefully, she climbed in holding both cups of coffee. "We'll send out the drone as soon as the storm passes to see what's going on. Any reports on how long it will last?"

"Should pass by around midnight." Dogs yelped and barked in the background. "Give a shout if you need anything. Stay inside."

Kelly shuffled back to bed in the comforter and climbed in. "I should have gotten radios for the different cabins. I didn't think we'd need them. Rookie error."

"I'm sure everyone is fine." Shawn held the propped pillows in place for Kelly. The single bed was too small for them to fit in comfortably, but since comfortable wasn't really the main idea, that didn't matter. "Hopefully the tents are far away from whatever break in the ice has occurred."

"Thank you for this." Kelly sighed happily as she took a sip. She didn't want to think about the possible destruction of the site. "And I don't think I've ever seen you drink coffee."

"I don't, usually. But this trip is all about new things I won't do back home." Shawn smiled over the rim of her cup, but there was no denying the hint of sadness in her eyes.

"Are you feeling estranged from the world without your phone?" It had only been two days but for someone like Shawn, that probably felt like a lifetime.

"Honestly? Yeah. I keep reaching for it only to find that there's no signal. I've looked through my photos about fifty times over the last two days. Not knowing what's going on out there makes me feel...out of control, I guess."

"But are you in control of any of it anyway?" Kelly asked. At Shawn's look of confusion, she continued. "I mean, you can check your emails and read the news and scroll through all the social media platforms, but that isn't you being in control, is it? You're taking it in, but it will happen with or without your ingestion."

Shawn appeared to consider that. "Maybe that's true of the news and social media. But my email is something that needs my attention. My work is part of who I am. If I'm not there, how do I know things will get done? Isn't that why you oversee a dig?"

The cabin creaked as a gust of wind slammed into it. Kelly waited, pondering her answer as she waited for the noise to abate a little. "I oversee a dig because I love watching it happen and yeah, there are often questions I need to answer. But when I leave the site to go into town or do whatever I need to do, then I trust the people I have in place to do their jobs. I never assume anyone isn't up to the task until they prove otherwise."

The quiet stretched out, but it wasn't uncomfortable. She knew full well that Shawn liked to process her answers, and since they weren't out in the field where time was a luxury they didn't have, she could relax and let her do her thing.

"I never thought of it as not trusting them to be good at what they do." Shawn shivered and pushed deeper under the blankets. "I always thought of it as being a good boss."

"Well, there's no question you're that as well. It was clear at the party that people respect you. If you were a prat, no one would have come, and they certainly wouldn't have hung around talking to you." She laughed when Shawn winced at her language. "Don't you ever find it exhausting, always needing to know what's going on in the world, with people you don't know?"

"Politics are important. Not knowing what's going on is choosing ignorance." Shawn took Kelly's empty cup and dashed out of bed, to the pot, and back again with more coffee and a bottle of water in the blink of an eye.

Kelly hadn't even needed to ask. Shawn did small things like that all the time, almost as though they weren't even conscious decisions. She had a caretaker's soul. "Now, that's true. But I can choose when to find out what's going on in the world, when it suits me and doesn't take me out of the moment. But you seem to be rarely away from your phone."

Shawn rolled the icy bottle of water between her hands, seemingly unaware of, or at least unbothered by, the cold against her palms. "It's an escape," she said softly, her brows furrowed and a faraway look in her eyes. "If I'm focused on the cyber world, the world around me isn't so flipping big." She shook her head, her short hair falling over her forehead. "Using my phone allows me to control the flow of information. I decide what to look at, what I want to read, who I want to interact with. But out here, people come to me. They talk to me when I don't want to talk. They get the social cues and the niceties that mostly escape me. All my life I've done all I can to fit in. I temper my tics and try to hide my OCD, I mimic other people's ways of being as much as I can, like an actor on a stage. That makes people less uncomfortable around me." She closed her eyes and let her head drop back against the pillows. "But it's exhausting. When I'm alone with Bree, or on my phone, I can just be me."

Kelly ached inside at the loneliness and depth of sadness threading through Shawn's words like streaks of marble lacing her emotions together. "I hope you know you can be yourself with me too."

Shawn rolled her head to the side to look at her. The smile she gave her was a sad one. "It's nice you think that, and you probably want it to be true. But we saw yesterday how you react when you see just a particle of me that doesn't fit with how you operate." When Kelly started to protest, Shawn took her hand. "It's not a judgement. It's just how things are. I'm used to it. And to be fair to you, you've been way better than most."

It was a backhanded compliment, and Kelly wasn't sure how to respond. So she changed the subject. That was always the easiest thing to do. After setting her coffee cup aside, she turned over and once again slid her hand up Shawn's thigh. "Let's focus on something else."

Shawn's hand covered hers, stopping its upward trajectory. "Kelly, I—"

"Are you stone?" Kelly moved her hand away. "I'm sorry, I didn't think to ask."

"No, no. It's not that I'm stone." Shawn ran her other hand through her hair as she sat up. "It's that thing about being butch. I know a lot of people think butches shouldn't want to be touched, and it makes them less-than somehow." She looked over her shoulder. "I don't generally receive. It makes me feel too...soft."

Kelly blew out a breath. "You really do worry too much about what other people think and what gender expectations there are. I've been with *a lot* of butch women who loved being touched." She grinned at Shawn's eye roll. "Shawn, you don't have to conform to anything in a labelled box. You decide who you are, how you present, and what you like. And fuck anyone who wants to put you in a cage. Unless, of course, that's your kink."

Shawn studied her for a long moment, her breathing a little faster than usual. Then she slowly lay back and, trembling, placed Kelly's hand on her thigh once again.

Honored at the trust being placed in her, Kelly decided it was best to move slowly. She slid her hand over Shawn's crotch, on the outside of her boxers, and was rewarded with a soft groan. "Will you tell me how you like to be touched?" Kelly asked, pressing a little harder.

"Soft." Shawn swallowed, her eyes tightly shut. "Soft, slow circles."

Kelly could handle that. She slipped her hand inside the boxers and found Shawn's clit already rock hard. She jerked at Kelly's touch and pulled her close.

It had been a long time since Kelly had truly watched a lover's face. She enjoyed their bodies, the noises they made, the way they reacted. But watching the vulnerability in Shawn's expression as she relaxed and let Kelly make her feel good tugged on heartstrings she didn't even know were there. "How could you ever think you're anything less than fucking gorgeous?" Kelly whispered.

Shawn jerked into her touch, one fist gripping the blanket, the other hand firmly gripping Kelly's waist. "Please don't stop."

Kelly continued, matching the speed of her strokes to Shawn's hip movements, and then pressing when Shawn moaned and thrust hard against Kelly's hand before sinking back into the bed.

Gently, she removed her hand and curled up against Shawn's side, resting her head on Shawn's chest. Shawn pulled the blankets over them and then pulled Kelly tight against her.

"Thank you," Shawn whispered. "It's been a while. Sorry it was so fast."

Kelly grinned, tracing patterns on Shawn's stomach. "Are you a one-and-done?"

Shawn laughed. "I am, I'm afraid. Not like you who can get there over and over again. Which I'm a fan of, incidentally. In case that wasn't clear."

"Oh, you made it very clear." Kelly snuggled in and let her eyes drift closed.

When she woke again, she could see her breath. "Damn." She started to get out of bed, but Shawn tugged her back.

"I'll do it." This time she wrapped a blanket around herself right away. The fire was lit in record time, and then she turned to Kelly. "Food?"

"God, yes. I'm starving." She fumbled on the bedside table for her watch. "No wonder. It's already mid-afternoon."

Shawn held up two tins of soup. "Not exactly gourmet, but will it do?"

Kelly yawned and nodded, then reached for her sweats and sweatshirt. "I'm going to use the loo." The cabin was already warming, but when she looked outside, she could still see nothing but white. "It's like being stuck in static."

"It's like being stuck in a snow storm in Alaska. Much the same thing, I imagine." Shawn smiled a little as she poured the soup into a plastic bowl.

Kelly couldn't argue with that. She stepped into the small shower, wishing it was big enough for two, and got clean while hoping she'd still have plenty of time to get dirty again later in the evening. When she came out, toweling her hair, the smell of hot soup made her stomach growl. Shawn was already sitting at the table, her phone beside her, open to the photos.

Kelly sat down and started eating. "Thank you for getting this ready."

Shawn nodded. "I don't eat a lot of canned food at home. Too many preservatives. But this tastes perfect right now."

"So you do a lot of cooking?" Kelly could easily picture Shawn moving methodically around the kitchen, with no wasted effort.

"Some. Easy stuff mostly since it's just me."

"Have you ever had a long-term relationship? Someone who lived with you?" Kelly knew she was prying, but if you couldn't ask these kinds of questions when snowed in and after fantastic sex, then when could you?

"Two." Shawn's shoulders rose a little. "Both women were good people. Amber was ambitious and got a job in New York, and obviously I wasn't going to go with her, and Kim was...well, Kim wanted a lot. Material things, emotional things. She liked drama and when things were stable she'd find a way to create chaos. She hated that I'd duck conflict instead of fighting with her. Needless to say, she moved on."

"Nothing unusual then." Kelly finished the soup and wished there'd been some bread to go with it. "And do you miss having that kind of stable partner in your life?"

"No." Shawn grimaced. "Sometimes. Like this." She motioned with her spoon. "Sitting and talking to someone after great sex when the intimacy feels good. That's nice." She picked up Kelly's bowl and rinsed both out. "You already said you don't do long-term relationships, so I won't ask."

Kelly remembered that conversation and had a strange sense of embarrassment that she couldn't quite understand. She'd never been shy about the fact that she only enjoyed brief encounters. But there was something about Shawn that made her want to appear deeper and more stable than she really was.

"So, I guess this thing between us is temporary then." Shawn kept her back to Kelly as she looked out the window at the snow.

"Is that okay?" Kelly left the table and wrapped her arms around Shawn from behind. "Last night and today have been amazing, and I hope we can continue to enjoy each other. But I'll leave and go back to London, and as you said about your ex, you're not about to uproot yourself and move to another city." Shawn stiffened in

Kelly's embrace. "God, not that I'm asking you to up and move away with me after we've known each other for a week. I'm not that much of a lesbian cliché. I just mean, with regard to your question about long-term—"

"I get it, Kelly." Shawn turned in her arms, her hands still on the countertop. "You never made any claims otherwise, and you're not responsible for my feelings. I suppose part of me was wondering if you might be interested in trying something long-distance."

Kelly slowly pulled away and shoved her hands in her pockets. "Honestly? Long-distance relationships are a recipe for disaster. Eventually, one or the other person gets tired of being alone. They either step out on the other person, or they grow more and more resentful until it erupts in flames and the relationship burns down spectacularly. It's easier to walk away and stay friendly before that kind of nightmare even begins."

Shawn picked up a spoon and began to fiddle with it, as though uncertain what else to do with her hands. "Wow. And I thought *I* didn't like conflict. You cut off connection just in case conflict even thinks about developing. Not that conflict itself thinks. You know what I mean." She shrugged. "I'll be another one of the many butches you've slept with and enjoyed. And that's okay. I shouldn't have mentioned it at all. It isn't like I've been under the impression that I could be what you want or deserve."

Kelly gritted her teeth, trying to hold back her temper. Shawn's tone was matter of fact and non-judgmental, but her words hit their target anyway. "And what is it you presume to know I want or deserve?"

Shawn looked surprised at Kelly's sharpness. "Someone like you. Someone adventurous, capable, athletic, and intelligent. Someone willing to jump off the edges of waterfalls and dig trenches in ancient rainforests." She motioned around them. "Someone willing to fly to Alaska and rappel into an icy crevasse at a moment's notice."

As quickly as her temper had flared, it was smothered under

the gentle honesty of Shawn's response. "You were right there beside me on that flight to Alaska."

"Yeah, but that's a one-time thing, isn't it? It wouldn't be a way of life for me the way it would for you. And why would you want to hang around for some desk jockey who likes her routine, and doesn't like her food mixed up, and who feels like the color yellow sticks in her teeth?" Shawn stopped, her hand pressed to her stomach. "I think I'll head back to my cabin."

"A one-time thing doesn't have to be an emotional black hole, Shawn. Surely you have flings too?" Why had this romantic interlude turned into something so fraught?

"Sure I do. I go out, enjoy someone, and go home. But this is different. You're different. I don't take the time to get to know the people I have encounters with. We both know what's going to happen. It does, it's usually good enough, and then we part ways."

"But you've gotten to know me, so it can't still be good?" Kelly was having some trouble working out just why Shawn was holding on so tight. "Can't it be better because we know each other?"

Shawn sighed and pinched the bridge of her nose. "Not for me. I mean, getting to touch your body that way was extraordinary. And I'll never, ever, forget the way you look when you orgasm or the feel of your skin under my fingertips. But because I know you and I like you, I want more. But I can't have more, and that hurts. In here." She tapped her chest. "Maybe that's a lesbian cliché. Maybe it's just a human wanting to explore a connection with another human who seems really special, and so it's disappointing that it won't happen." She shrugged, looking wrung out. "I'm sorry this turned so heavy. Like I said, I'll head back to my cabin."

"It's snowing so hard we're going to have to shovel our way out." Kelly stood slowly and held out her hand. "Come lay down with me and we'll keep talking."

Shawn stared at her hand for a long moment before taking it. "This feels like a mixed message."

"It might be." Kelly led her to the bed, and they crawled in, still fully dressed. They lay facing one another, and Kelly felt better when Shawn rested her hand on Kelly's hip. "First of all, I'm sorry you're disappointed or hurting in any way. I'd never want that."

Shawn didn't say anything.

"Okay, so we're approaching this thing between us from very different angles. If I lived closer, if I wasn't used to being a nomad, then I might stick around and see what this is between us. You're so special, and you really have no idea." Kelly cupped Shawn's cheek. "Tomorrow, we'll go back into the world and go back to being colleagues. And, I hope, friends. Today...let's just be together like the outside doesn't exist."

Shawn's eyes were glassy as she turned onto her back and pulled Kelly against her. "If that's what you want."

They lay in silence for a long time, no sound but the wind to interrupt their thoughts. In truth, it would have been easier if Shawn had gone back to her cabin, if only so Kelly could break something and get out her frustration, a reaction she didn't want Shawn to see. Was she making excuses? Long-distance relationships really were too fucking hard, and she really was going back to London. Those were facts. But people made long-distance relationships work all the time, and that was a fact too. Eventually someone moved though. Someone gave up their home, their job, their freedom, and settled down with the other person. And as far as she could see, neither she nor Shawn would be doing that. And why should they when they barely knew one another?

So that put an end to their fledgling romance. Didn't it?

CHAPTER SIXTEEN

SHAWN WOKE TO A scratching, scraping noise. She blinked against the light streaming in and nudged Kelly. "I think someone is shoveling their way to the door."

Kelly pulled her pillow over her head. "Tell them I've become a bear and won't be coming out till spring."

Shawn smiled, then her heart dropped as she remembered the conversation from yesterday. They'd talked a little more in the night about their families, about their likes and dislikes. It had been shallow talk though, and for some reason, that made the ache a little worse. She swung her legs out of bed, glad she'd put socks on to sleep, and went to the front window. Three people were shoveling a path to their door, and she could see others doing the same at the cabin next door.

"It's the dogsled team, I think." Shawn stretched and headed to the bathroom. Once she was done, she studied herself in the mirror. There were bags under her eyes and her hair stuck up in every direction. She took the time to try and tame it, not that anyone would see it under her beanie and helmet. Would they be going home today? The thought of spending another day in the cabin with Kelly created conflicting feelings. She wanted what little time they might have together, if only to look at her and be in her presence. But on the other hand, it was like handing a child an ice cream cone and then telling them they weren't allowed to eat it. She shook her head at the weird analogy. What she wouldn't give to have internet access right now, so she could dive into her emails, into her various social networks, even into work articles, and lose herself in a world that wasn't the complicated one around her.

There was a pounding on the door, and she heard Kelly open it. Voices were loud and there was laughter, and Shawn wondered if anyone would notice if she simply hid in the bathroom all day.

"Hey, can I get in there?" Kelly asked from outside, with a quick tap on the door.

Shawn sighed. So much for hiding. "Yeah, sorry." She avoided eye contact and slipped past to finish getting ready.

Before long, the rest of the group had assembled, along with the sledding group who had come to dig them out. Chay and Bree came in, with Chay's arm around Bree's shoulders. The cabin was crowded and noisy, and Shawn considered slipping out and heading back to her own cabin.

"No, you can't leave." Bree sat down beside her. With her flushed skin and bright eyes, it was clear she'd had a good night. "And you don't look nearly as happy as I thought you would."

It wasn't a question, so Shawn didn't respond. She shrugged and watched everyone interact.

"So, what's wrong? What happened?" Bree asked, tapping her leg.

"I don't want to talk about it. Not here, anyway." Shawn watched as Kelly and Chay laughed together, and her stomach clenched. Were they laughing about Shawn's illogical desire to develop a real connection? Probably not. They weren't the kind of women who did that sort of thing, were they? "Did you have a good time with Chay?"

Bree blew out a big breath. "Did I ever. That storm has my eternal gratitude, and it was good that it was so loud." She giggled behind her hand. "I don't think I've ever made that much noise."

"Will you see her again? After this trip, I mean."

Bree shrugged. "I don't imagine so. She said she's going to spend the winter in Madagascar. I'm pretty sure Oklahoma isn't on the route."

"And that doesn't bother you?" Shawn frowned and glanced at Bree.

Bree tilted her head, looking thoughtful. "I never thought it would be something serious. I like her a lot, and it would be fun to date her. But that isn't in the cards, and that's fine." She turned more fully to face Shawn. "What's going on, babe?"

Before Shawn could answer, Kelly's voice rang out over the din.

"Okay, everyone. Listen up." The group grew quiet and turned their attention to her. "That storm dropped a hell of a lot of snow, and I'm sure several of you felt the ice quakes."

"Were they quakes? I thought it was just my cabin." Chay grinned and winked at Bree, who blushed furiously.

Kelly rolled her eyes. "That said, we're going to head out to the base area and see how the tents and such fared, and we'll send out the drones to see what the dig site looks like. If there's any chance of going in for a final look, I'd like to try. But anyone uncomfortable with that is more than welcome to stay here."

Shawn took a breath to say she'd stay behind, but Bree pinched her leg.

"You're going," she murmured. "We both are."

Shawn grimaced and looked at her boots. She wasn't going to argue in front of all these people.

"All right. Gear up, and we'll meet outside in fifteen minutes."

Shawn stood up and headed toward the door behind Bree.

"Shawn?" Kelly put her hand on Shawn's arm before she could leave.

She stopped and waited, trying to ignore how beautiful Kelly looked in the morning light. Chay leaned against the kitchen countertop, clearly watching them.

"Are we okay?" Kelly didn't let go of her arm. "Waking up with you was nice."

Shawn swallowed against the ball of emotion in her throat. "We're okay. We have to be, don't we? Colleagues and friends." She gently pulled away. "See you shortly."

The cold, crisp air helped clear her head as she went to their cabin. She winced when she stepped iinside. "It smells like sex."

"As it should." Bree laughed as she pulled on extra layers and got ready for the chill outside.

Shawn did the same, wishing that it was Kelly getting ready with her instead. She liked watching the way she moved.

"So, in a nutshell, what happened? Why aren't you glowing with post-coital endorphins?" Bree asked as she pulled on her pink beanie.

"We had sex, and it was good. Great, even. The best sex I've ever had, several times over."

Bree waited, eyebrows raised. "And that's why you look like you just watched a sad movie?"

"I...I think I'm in over my head. I'm already attached. I want more. A lot more. More time, more sex, more of her attention. I want to be with her and see if we could maybe have something real. But she's not interested in that. For her, it was just sex. Like you and Chay. I seem to be the only one with an issue." Shawn let it out, knowing Bree would understand her frustration. "You know I have no issue with no strings sex. But this felt special and different, and I hate how it's making me feel now." She sat and rested her head in her hands. "I'm ridiculous. I knew full well that this would be a mistake, and now that it's been proven, I'm angry with myself."

Bree sat down beside her and rested her head on Shawn's shoulder. "I'm sorry that you're hurting. You've got a big heart, and you don't often let it loose in the world. It's awful when that happens."

Shawn nodded, grateful for the understanding and lack of advice. She patted Bree's knee. "We'd better get out there. Hopefully it'll be a quick look and then we'll head back to the plane to go home."

Bree shuddered. "I'd rather stay here forever than get back on a plane. Even drugged, I don't think I'll ever like flying."

Shawn nodded. "But you did it. And now you know you can do it again if you want to go somewhere. It doesn't have to hold you back anymore. That must feel good."

Bree stopped tucking her pants into her boots and looked up. "You're right. And if nothing else comes from this trip, that's a huge thing right there."

Her big smile made Shawn smile in return. She might not have Kelly, but she had Bree, and that friendship was worth more than she could ever quantify.

Outside, the group was gathering around the sleds. Dave had the drone in hand, and when everyone was ready to go, he set it off ahead of him on the front sled. The fresh powder sparkled in the sunlight, and the sound of the sleds sweeping over the crisp, white landscape made Shawn smile despite herself.

When they got to the tents, only one was still standing, though it sagged heavily with the snow on top. The other was only visible thanks to the corners sticking out beneath the white blanket covering it. Everyone went to work using small hand shovels as well as the larger snow shovels the sled team had with them, and it didn't take long to uncover everything and get the tents back into position, though the poles were bent, and the tents looked a little worse for wear.

While they'd been working, Dave had been flying the drone, and Pam and Rena had been watching the footage on the computer. They set it up on the table in the tent so everyone could see.

"The crevasse is still open." Pam pointed to the area they'd been digging in. "As far as I can tell though, the ice quakes broke it open a little further. It's deeper than it was by probably another twenty feet at least." She drew a few crosses on the screen. "I'm not positive, but these look like snow bridges over new crevasses. If that's the case, then heading to the dig site is going to be dangerous."

"I take it a snow bridge isn't as sturdy as it sounds." Bree scanned the computer image, leaning close.

"It's not a great term, that's for sure. A snow bridge is just a covering of snow over the crevasse so that you can't see it. Step on it, and down you go." Chay stood with her legs wide, her arms crossed, her jaw set. "I don't think it's a good idea."

The tent flap opened, and Grandpa Morris and Grace came in. "Glad to see you all made it through the first storm of the season." Grace looked around and smiled at the tense group.

Grandpa Morris lowered his thick hood. "We wanted to make sure you were okay. Are you going back out?"

Shawn thought it was interesting that his first thought wasn't for the dig or the artifacts, but rather for the safety of people he didn't know. Strangers who were on his land. It spoke to his character, and she decided she liked him.

"We were just about to figure that out. Which way did you come in?" Kelly asked, motioning toward the computer screen.

Grace stepped forward and took the e-pencil. "We came from this direction, making our way using snowshoes from here." She drew a long, thin line. "So we crossed over a large section that would take you to your site, and it was solid. That doesn't mean it will be closer to the divide itself, obviously."

Kelly looked at Chay. "Last chance."

Chay shook her head. "If you want to, but I'm not convinced, Kel."

Kelly looked at the rest of the group, her gaze finally stopping on Shawn. "What do the rest of you think?"

Shawn shrugged. She wasn't in a position to give any input, and she wasn't about to pretend she knew better than Chay. No one else spoke up either.

"Okay...show of hands. Who wants to go?"

Rena, Gianna, Dave, and Pam all raised their hands. Chay, Bree, and Shawn stayed motionless.

"To be clear, I don't have an opinion one way or another," Bree said, glancing at Shawn. "And I don't think Shawn does either. We have to depend on the knowledge of the group." She winked at Chay. "And I feel some need to support my fiancée."

Chay choked on the sip of water she was taking.

"Okay. Vote says we go. Like the other day, we rope together and take it slow and steady. If the site itself doesn't look like it will hold us, then we come back."

"Another storm is coming in tomorrow." Grandpa Morris looked closely at the items in the trays and gently stroked a few. "And then there will be more after that. This is likely your last chance to see anything else and to get these items back where they belong."

Grace moved to his side, and they spoke quietly together while the rest of the team went outside. Shawn wondered what they were talking about. Were they awed by what had been uncovered? Would they change their minds? No, she thought. She was sure she'd been right about that before. When Grandpa Morris looked at her over his shoulder, it was like he knew she'd been thinking about them.

"Wisdom has to be balanced with respect. We don't always know what we want or need until we're presented with a choice." His smile was small, his eyes serious. He turned away and continued to look at the finds.

Shawn walked out, puzzled at the enigmatic wording. Was the message meant for her? Or for someone else in the team? He'd been looking at her, certainly. But the vague wording didn't help her feeling of being out of place and out of sorts.

Stymied, she focused instead on various ropes and carabiners attaching her to the others. She picked up her two packs and strapped them on and noticed Chay helping Bree with hers. She was being gentle, and her smile seemed to make Bree glow. Shawn turned away to find Kelly watching her from the front of the line. Her expression was inscrutable, and Shawn simply gazed back, uncertain what to say or do.

Kelly turned away first, looking down the line at the team. "Okay. Let's go. If anyone sees anything at all they're not sure about, say something. Better to have it be nothing than to get dragged down to our deaths to die of hypothermia at the bottom of a crevasse. My corpse won't be nearly as sexy."

There was some nervous laughter that broke the tension, and the group set out, slowly making their way toward the dig site. The snow was deep, and although the snowshoes made it easier, it was still hard work. Sweat slid down Shawn's back and made her temples itch under the helmet. She wouldn't miss this bit of field work when she was back at her desk, that was certain.

Everyone was out of breath by the time they reached the dig site. Bags were dropped unceremoniously into the snow, and Bree sat down heavily. "I'm not made for this," she said, rolling her shoulders.

Chay patted her head as she walked past. "I know exactly what you were made for." She grinned when Bree half-heartedly threw a snowball at her butt.

Shawn mentally shook her head. How could they be so free and easy with one another? If only it were that simple with Kelly. The easy-going nature of the moment changed when they began placing the anchors for the abseiling lines. Chay took a hand shovel and crawled close to the crevasse. She began tapping along the lip, sending pockets of snow down into the narrow valley below until she was satisfied.

"Okay. I've cleared a section, but be aware of where your lines are as you drop in. Going in after this much snow is risky."

Much as they had before, the group separated into teams, with three lowered into the crevasse. Gianna, Pam, and Kelly went first. Dave continued to fly the drone along the crevasse to gather more details, while Chay, Shawn, and Rena fed the ropes over the edge. Bree knelt near the edge, anchored to the ice, and watched the group below.

"This is incredible!" Kelly called from down below. "The crack shifted more ice, and I can see a few animal skulls as well as what looks like more weaponry."

Shawn nodded. This was what they'd come for, and it was good they had one more chance at it. She heard Bree and Chay chattering about the finds, pontificating on their origins and possible time frames, but she wasn't interested. There was something off. Something felt strange, but she couldn't put a name to it. There was a sort of tension held in the air itself, like it was waiting to exhale. Remembering Chay's admonishment from before, she turned.

"Do you feel that?" she asked, interrupting the conversation.

Chay stopped talking abruptly and listened. There was nothing but the sound of ice tools chipping away below. She looked at Shawn. "Explain."

Shawn gritted her teeth at the peremptory tone. "I don't know. There's something in the air. Like, just before a rubber band snaps."

Chay studied her for a moment and then grabbed the rope. "Up and out! Now!" she yelled.

Startled at Chay's sudden reaction, Shawn gripped her rope and pulled up the slack as Pam began climbing out. Beside her, Chay and Rena were doing the same. When Shawn saw Pam's head crest the lip she held the line and went forward to help her out. Gianna was up next, with Rena handing her out.

And then the quake struck.

They flattened themselves to the snow, and Shawn felt the lip give way beneath her thighs. The others around her managed to scramble forward, and Shawn's arms jerked as more of the ice came loose.

"Kelly!" Chay's scream echoed above the sound of the snow slamming into the ground from the mountains around them.

Shawn looked over her shoulder into the crevasse. Kelly swung from her line like a limp rag doll, her head lolling. Blood was smeared on the ice wall in front of her and covered one side of her face. She looked away from that horrifying site to see Chay's arms shaking as she held onto the anchor, her crampons dug into the snow as she took the brunt of Kelly's weight, the ice still shaking beneath them.

Shawn let go of her ice axe, grabbed the rope, and flung herself into the crevasse.

"What the fuck!" Chay's yell was clear. "Grab Shawn's rope!"

Shawn felt the tug as someone yanked on the rope, but she continued to abseil down the ice wall, moving swiftly toward Kelly's swinging body. If Chay's grip failed or if the snow gave way under her, Kelly would fall to her death.

And Shawn wasn't about to watch that happen.

She waited as Kelly swung one way and then the other, then shifted forward to grab her when she came close. The movement slammed them both into the ice wall, knocking the wind from Shawn. But she kept her grip and managed to wrap her arm around Kelly's waist. She grabbed the vertical line they'd put in on the first day, the one meant to be used only in an emergency.

"Kelly. Kelly, baby, come on. We need you to wake up." She held Kelly's limp body to her and noted the way one arm looked wrong. It was bent funny. Even if she woke up, she wouldn't be able to climb out. Quickly, she tied the emergency loop Chay had taught her and used her rope and carabiner to attach Kelly's rig to hers. If they went down, they'd go together. So be it.

That same hissing, cracking noise started again, and she braced them hard against the ice.

This time, there was a roaring sound like a jet plane about to land on their heads.

"Avalanche!"

She wasn't sure who yelled it, but at that moment, she wished with all her might that she believed in God. She held tight, her eyes shut against the onslaught of ice and snow. The rope tethering her to the land above dropped once again, and she and Kelly fell another ten feet before Shawn slammed the spikes on her shoes into the ice to stop their descent, still holding onto the vertical line they'd nailed into the ice on their first day, which had come loose except for the anchors at the beginning and end. It wouldn't hold for long.

The wait for silence took an eternity.

"Kelly! Shawn!" Chay's head popped over the edge far above them. "Are you okay?"

"No. Kelly's unconscious, and I think her arm is broken. I've put a belay loop from her rope to mine so we're attached." Shawn stayed as still as possible as ice continued to crumble around them. "The avalanche?"

"On the mountainside opposite. Everyone up here is okay. We just need—"

The ice broke away like a sheet of paper sliding from a pack.

Shawn and Kelly went cascading down, the line yanking and jerking them but hardly slowing their descent. All Shawn could do was hold Kelly to her and try to keep them from bashing into the ice wall. Grabbing her line to try and stop them would likely just break her hand, and she was going to need both hands to get them out of this.

The rope jerked hard, making her grunt as it snapped them upward, pulling on what felt like every bone in her body.

Chay's head came over the edge, this time further down the crevasse. "Still with us?" she shouted.

"Yeah." Breathless, she couldn't say much else. Her arms were starting to ache. "Next step?"

"Shawn, you're nearly at the bottom. We're going to lower you the last few feet so you can get Kelly into a recovery position. Then we'll figure out how to get you out of there."

"Right." Shawn would be glad to set Kelly down and look at her injuries.

"Okay. Ready? Release from the wall. We're going to lower your rope. Yell when your feet touch the ground."

Shawn felt her rope go slack and tentatively released her grip on the wall, letting her feet swing free while holding Kelly's body to her own. Fear slithered through her, oily and nauseating, but she focused instead on the feel of Kelly's soft hair against her cheek. "I've got you," she whispered.

Her toes hit ice. "We're down!" She waited until her feet were firmly in place and then knelt to lower Kelly to the ice floor. The blue walls reflected off her skin, and while it might have been beautiful in other circumstances, in this one, it made her look deathly. Shawn ripped off her glove and felt for her pulse, which was strong and steady against her fingertips. After whispering a silent thanks, she yelled up.

"She's still unconscious but her pulse is good."

"Okay. Give us a minute to work things out."

Shawn moved to Kelly's side and looked at her arm. From the elbow down, the arm was twisted sideways. There didn't appear to be any blood, but she had on several layers of clothing. "Chay!" she called, looking up.

Almost immediately, Chay looked over the edge, even further down this time.

"Her arm is broken. Do I need to take off her jacket to make sure the bone hasn't come through?"

Chay grimaced. "Fuck me backwards. If you can unzip it and reach in to check for any wetness, that would be better than letting the cold in. We're already going to have to worry about hypothermia."

Nodding, Shawn went to her knees and moved as gently and carefully as she could. She reached in and felt her way along Kelly's arm, and her hand came away dry. "No blood."

"Okay. We're going to lower a couple of thermal blankets. Get her wrapped up as well as you can without moving her too much. What about the head wound?"

Shawn gently brushed the blood-soaked hair from Kelly's cheek. "It looks like she may have slammed her helmet into the wall, and it cut her. The bleeding has stopped." She looked up as a shadow came over her and then stood to reach out for the blankets coming down. After unhooking them, she moved quickly, trying to be careful of Kelly's arm and glad she wasn't conscious because it would probably have hurt like the devil.

She sat beside her and waited, her hand resting on Kelly's shoulder. "Kelly? Baby, come on. You have so many more adventures to go on. So many more things to see. You said you want to be invited to a dig in Egypt. You have to be awake and well for that." She swallowed and blinked back tears. "Please, baby.

Please come back."

As though in answer, Kelly's eyelids flickered, and she groaned. "Shit," she whispered. She started to shift.

"Hey now. Wait. Stay still for a second, okay?" Shawn pressed her shoulder down and moved so Kelly could see her without turning her head.

"What happened?" Kelly asked, and it looked like it was hard for her to focus.

"An ice quake. The others got out, but it looks like you hit your head and knocked yourself out." Shawn caressed her cheek. "Can you take stock and tell me what hurts?"

"My fucking head feels like I smashed it against an ice wall." She gave a wry smile. "And...and my arm. Jesus Christ." Suddenly she shifted sideways and vomited, her broken arm hanging limply behind her.

Shawn held her hair back, then helped her lay flat again. "Yeah. It's definitely broken." She scooped up some snow from the wall and held it to Kelly's mouth so she could rinse.

"Did we fall all the way to the bottom? It's a miracle we're not dead." Kelly's eyes closed, her face pinched with pain. Then her eyes opened again. "Wait. You weren't digging. You were up top."

"Hey, you're awake. Trust you to take a nap and leave the rest of us sweating." Chay's relief was obvious in her tone.

"I don't think this is optimal," Kelly called up. "You could work a little harder, if you don't mind."

"Here's the thing." Chay was joined by Pam. "We've got a problem."

"More than a problem." Pam shifted away from the edge a little as ice showered down the side. "This crevasse has become so unstable we can't lower anyone for a rescue. The rope ladders are down there with you as well, thanks to the walls giving way. We shouldn't even be this near to the lip really."

Shawn went cold deep inside. "You're saying there's no way to get us out of here?"

"There's no way to get you out *here*. A helicopter couldn't land, and the vibrations from having it hover could very well cause the walls to crumble further, burying you." Pam motioned to the drone. "Grace and Grandpa Morris told us about an ice cave tunnel they know of in the area, and the drone showed us not only where it is, but that it's likely a tunnel connecting to a cave not far from where we are now. That area on the other side appears more stable and isn't as deep, so we could get you out there."

Shawn looked at Kelly, who'd managed to sit upright, her arm hanging loosely at her side. "I'm not sure we can walk very far."

Kelly closed her eyes. "It doesn't sound like we have a choice unless we want to die at the bottom of a crack of ice together." With a deep sigh, she reopened her eyes.

"We can track you pretty much all the way, except when you enter the cave and the tunnel. We'll be able to see you on either side of it." The positivity in Pam's tone sounded forced.

"How far are we talking, Pam?" Shawn asked and noticed the hesitation before she answered.

"About eight miles, give or take."

Walking eight miles in a regular situation wouldn't be a problem. Walking eight miles on slippery ice, in crampons, with someone with a head injury and a broken arm was going to be rough going. It was also already afternoon, and they wouldn't have a lot of daylight left.

"We'd better get going then." Kelly started to stand, and Shawn quickly stood to help her.

She held on as Kelly swayed and then stood still.

"Chay, I need you to throw me something to stabilize Kelly's arm."

"Coming down."

Shawn held Kelly with one hand while she grabbed the yellow medical box with the other. Inside there was a splint and an Ace bandage. She held them up. "This is going to be really awful. I'm sorry."

Kelly nodded and leaned against the ice wall. "Is there anything I can bite down on?"

Shawn found another bandage and held it out. Kelly put it between her teeth and then gave a short nod. Shawn took a deep breath and placed the plastic splint on the backside of her arm, then wrapped the bandage around it, tight enough to hold it in place but not so tight it would make it even worse. Kelly's muted sounds of pain tore at her heart, and she wished she could make it stop. When she was done, she thumbed at the icy tears on her cheeks. "All done."

Kelly nodded, her hand shaking as she took the bandage from her lips and dropped it into Shawn's hand. "Thank you. Kind of."

Shawn folded the thermal blankets, then hooked them and the medical box to her back with her ropes, like a backpack. She looked up to see Chay watching them. She looked over her shoulder and accepted something from someone. "I'm sending a radio down, along with a bag full of rations and other random shit you might need. The sled team have given us the other radio so we can keep in touch with you throughout, okay?"

Shawn took Kelly's good hand. "Ready?"

Kelly already looked exhausted, but she gave Shawn a small smile. "Let's go on an adventure."

They began their walk along the ice, vast opaque walls reaching up on either side of them, casting an eerie blue glow along the path ahead. As Shawn held tightly to Kelly's hand, she could only hope that they made it before Kelly went into shock or had permanent damage to her arm. She'd saved her from dropping to her death, but could they move fast enough for her to get Kelly to the help she needed?

CHAPTER SEVENTEEN

EVERYTHING HURT. FROM THE top of her pounding skull to the tips of her frozen toes, Kelly's body was a mess of pain. And although she didn't want to say it out loud and worry Shawn even more, confusion and dizziness were growing. There was no question she had a concussion. At least this way they didn't have to worry about her falling asleep and not waking up though. They kept moving as the sky began to darken, and Shawn turned on her head torch. Movement was slow and careful, and the few times that Kelly slipped, Shawn was at her side to catch her. They spoke little, and Kelly was grateful since she couldn't seem to hold onto words long enough to get them out anyway.

Shawn lifted the radio from the loop on her belt. "Chay?"

The radio crackled. "Go ahead."

"We're at the mouth of the cave system." Shawn looked up. "Can you see us?"

"No. The crevasse has narrowed, but we can't get close enough to the edge to look down because of the snow bridges. We kept track of you with the drone for as long as we could, but the light isn't good enough now. We're going to go ahead with the sled dog teams and make camp on the other side of the cave system. We'll set off the beacon where we know a chopper can land. Radio from inside if you can, but otherwise, we'll wait for you on the other side. How's Kelly?"

Shawn looked at her, scanning clinically. "Bad, I think. She hasn't said so, but I'd bet she's got a concussion. She's pale and shaking. I think we'll need to stop soon."

"Copy. Get into the cave and undercover and wrap up in those thermal blankets. Use body heat too. Hold her hands and feet the way I did with Gianna's to get the blood flowing. Hold your own too."

Kelly could hear the worry in Chay's tone, even though she was trying to keep it direct and professional. The thought of being able to stop and rest almost made her cry.

Shawn hooked the radio back to her belt. "We're nearly there, okay? Just keep going."

Kelly nodded and, trembling so hard it hurt, followed Shawn into the ice cave. For a brief moment, she was distracted from her pain by the beauty around her. Blue waves of ice moved in sensual lines around them, creating a dome overhead. It was almost like being under a frozen river.

"Wow," Shawn said, scanning the area. "Let's use that wall. There's real stone to sit on, so we won't be directly on the ice."

Kelly stumbled forward, and Shawn grabbed her good arm to steady her. At the designated place, she slumped to her knees. It was all she could do to remain upright.

Shawn opened her bag and methodically began laying things out. First, a small tarp to sit on as a little protection from the cold. Then she moved Kelly on top of it and draped a blanket around her. She took out the small camping stove and dumped some snow in it to boil water, then moved to Kelly's feet. Kelly whimpered when Shawn removed one of her boots and began to warm her feet, simply holding them tightly between her gloves, and the feeling of warmth set off the nerves, making them hurt even more. But Shawn didn't let up even when Kelly half-heartedly tried to pull her foot away, and soon the pain dulled, and she let her shoulders drop a little.

"Tell me about your childhood. What is it like going to school in England?" Shawn asked as she replaced Kelly's sock with a dry one from her bag and then put her boot back on. She moved to the other foot and began the process over again.

Kelly's teeth chattered, but she forced the words out. "It's rather different from what you have here. We wear uniforms and still have religion in the schools. That said, it's been a while since I was in knee socks."

"What's your best memory?" Shawn continued warming Kelly's other foot until she could flex her toes without pain, then she repeated the dry sock and shoe process. "Your hand."

Kelly held her hand out and watched as though from a distance as Shawn gently tugged off her glove. "I punched a boy in primary school. He was throwing rocks at a bird. I kept telling him to stop, but he wouldn't. So I hit him."

"Did you get in trouble?" Shawn asked, tucking Kelly's hand beneath her armpit.

"They called my mum. She said I'd warned the boy, and it should be the boy in trouble, not me. She always stood up for me that way." Her mum and dad...would she see them again? She'd put off calling them and now she might die in a snowy ditch. If she wasn't worried that her tears would freeze on her cheeks, she'd cry.

"I can imagine you sticking up for a poor little bird." Shawn tucked the blanket around her and then moved to get them a hot drink. She made cups of strong coffee with instant granules and powdered milk.

Kelly wondered if anything had ever tasted so good. "Thank you." Her lip trembled. "Thank you for coming in after me."

Shawn nodded and continued to pull things from the pack. She unwrapped some beef jerky and handed it to Kelly. "Eat this, please. It'll help keep you awake while I make us some food."

Kelly did as she was asked, though it seemed to take monumental effort to chew, let alone to keep her eyes open. The smell of the rice concoction was good when Shawn poured the hot water into the foil pouches. When they were ready, Shawn handed one to Kelly and set the other on the ice, then she undid the thermal blanket from around Kelly and sat beside her before pulling it tight over them both. Kelly snuggled in close, her arm throbbing in time with the pounding in her head.

"Hey." Shawn gently nudged her and took the food pouch from her hand, which she'd nearly dropped. "Come on. Eat this for me." She held the bamboo spoon to Kelly's lips, and she was too exhausted to protest at being fed. Gratefully, she swallowed the pain pills Shawn gave her with a bottle of water.

She ate most of the meal before she shook her head and turned away. "No more. Thanks."

Shawn nodded and scarfed down her own portion as well as the remnants of Kelly's. She set them aside and then leaned back against the wall. "This is really beautiful, isn't it?"

Kelly nodded, her eyes drifting shut. "Ice caves are little miracles, I think."

"Go ahead and sleep. I'll wake you up in a little while to make sure you're still alive." Shawn shifted so that Kelly could rest her head against her shoulder. "We'll get out of this. I promise."

"I'll hold you to that. I know you don't say things you don't mean." Kelly finally stopped fighting her exhaustion and let herself sink into Shawn's strong, comforting embrace.

It felt like it had only been about two minutes when Shawn gently shook her awake. "Kelly, can you open your eyes for me?"

Kelly groaned. She thought she'd hurt before. But now her entire body felt like the glacier had landed on top of it. "I don't want to. Probably ever again."

"Don't say something like that in a situation like this." Shawn's tone was sharp. "Go back to sleep. I'll wake you again in a few hours."

Kelly didn't need to be told twice. She slept almost instantly, once again aware of Shawn's body against hers. Shawn woke her another two times in the night, and she fell asleep again right away.

"Kelly," Shawn said softly. "Babe, I need to move."

Kelly felt the tears gather in her eyes. The pain in her head and neck was sickening, as was the pain in her arm. "Okay. Is everything all right?" she asked, slowly shifting away from Shawn's warmth and instantly regretting it.

"It's fine. I just need to pee." Shawn gave her a quick smile. "Back in a minute." Stiff and slow, she rose and then stretched before heading further into the cave system and out of sight.

Kelly couldn't help but giggle a little as the sound of Shawn having a wee echoed off the cave walls around them.

Shawn came back, shaking her head. "How's that for romance?" She smiled and squatted in front of Kelly. "Need to go?"

Kelly sighed. "I do, but..." She tilted her head toward her arm and felt the fire of embarrassment heat her cheeks.

"Good thing we've already slept together, or it might be really awkward." Shawn stood and held out her hand. "Come on. I'm pretty sure there are rules about being shy during a crisis."

"I can't believe you just asserted something you can't prove." Kelly grasped her hand and stood, gasping at the pain that shot through her.

Shawn held her close until she could breathe regularly again, and then led the way toward an offshoot of the tunnel. She unzipped Kelly's pants and pulled everything down, though she seemed to keep her gaze averted. She tucked some toilet paper in the top of Kelly's top. "I'll be just over there. Shout when you're done."

It took a long moment before Kelly could relax enough to let go, but the relief was instant. Balancing without the use of one arm was harder than she'd anticipated, and this time the tears fell when the feeling of being helpless hit her.

Shawn's arms were around her in an instant. "It's okay. We're going to get through this. I'm here."

Kelly put her head against Shawn's shoulder and sobbed as Shawn redressed her. "If you hadn't come down... Shawn, we could die down here, but I'm so glad you're with me. And that's so selfish. I'm so sorry."

Shawn continued to hold her close as she led the way back to their little makeshift camp. "There's nothing to apologize for. But we should get going. I think we have a long way to go, and I want to get you help as soon as we can."

Kelly watched numbly as Shawn carefully repacked everything, making sure not to leave any trace behind. She tried the radio but got nothing but silence, and their eyes met briefly before she tucked it away. They were on their own down here, below the frozen earth. Then she moved to Kelly and looked at her analytically.

"Are you trying to figure me out?" Kelly asked with a tired smile.

"Well, that too. But no. I want to work this out." Shawn moved carefully around her, twisting the thermal blanket and clipping it in places until Kelly was walking in a cocoon of warmth, with only her one good arm out so she could balance herself. "Take it slow so you don't lose your footing. If you need to stop, just say so."

"Thank you."

They started walking, and Kelly let the sound of their boots on the ice lull her into a kind of moving meditation, helping to drown out the pain.

"Step on a crack, break your mother's back," Shawn sang softly as she stepped over thin veins of ice.

"That's morbid," Kelly murmured behind her.

"You don't have that children's rhyme in England?" Shawn asked, looking over her shoulder.

"Certainly not." Kelly looked at where she was stepping but looking down like that made her head pound.

"So what do you have?"

"I can't think of one, but definitely not anything so maternally malevolent." Kelly laughed a little. "But then children's rhymes and fairy tales are often dark, aren't they?"

"Almost always. I heard an author once say that the point of them isn't to tell kids monsters don't exist, but rather that they do exist, and they can be overcome. I've always liked that." Shawn slowed and touched a thick stalactite. "This is like being in a fantasy world." She glanced over her shoulder. "With a princess."

Kelly's laugh wasn't far from a sob. Shawn's sweet, gentle nature almost made it worse because she felt like she could break down if she needed to. Someone like Chay would just say, "Come on, build a bridge and get over it," and it might have made it easier to grit her teeth and keep going. "A broken princess wrapped in a thermal cocoon and wearing a beanie and climbing boots. Not exactly the Disney version, is it?"

"I think Disney would be so lucky." Shawn frowned and faced her. Her gaze went from eye to eye the way it often did.

"Why do you do that?" Kelly asked and sagged against the wall.

"What?"

"Look from eye to eye that way instead of just in both at once? I've never seen anyone do it before."

Shawn shrugged and leaned against the wall next to her. "Honestly? I don't know. For some reason, I find looking into both eyes difficult. Like, I can't really see the person that way? I don't know. I know other people don't do it. But I can't help myself. Sometimes I feel like I see something different in different eyes." She sighed. "Just another weirdness."

"I think it's wonderful." Kelly closed her eyes and was glad for the darkness that eased the headache a little. "I like that you interact with the world differently."

"That must be some head wound."

Kelly's eyes opened again when Shawn's bare hand touched her cheek and then her forehead. Her brows furrowed, and she looked more alert. "I think you've got a fever."

"I'm probably just warm from the blanket." She looked away just in case Shawn could see the lie in one or the other of her eyes. The cold felt bone-deep and achy in a way she knew full well wasn't good.

"Come on. We need to keep moving." Shawn started to walk, but Kelly stopped her.

"I should go first." At Shawn's look of confusion, she tilted her head slightly toward her bad arm. "If there's a pitfall ahead, like a well or a deeper crevasse or something, and you fall in, I won't be able to help you. If I go down, at least we have one fully able-bodied person."

Shawn blew out a breath. "I was hoping to keep either of us from falling into anything."

Kelly slipped past and shuffled forward. "Better this way."

They walked on, surrounded by magnificent blue ice offset by the occasional boulder or bit of earth that seemed out of place. "You said you were trying to figure me out. What is it you want to understand?" she asked, needing a distraction.

"Why you run from relationships." Shawn's tone wasn't judgmental, just curious.

"What makes you think that I do?" They stopped as a hissing sounded through the cavern. Kelly's skin crawled. An ice quake down here could easily bury them. It passed, and they began walking again.

"I've been thinking about it since you said you don't want anything serious with me. Not because it's me. But that you don't have anything serious with anyone you meet up with. You've said yourself that you have a lot of casual flings but never anything real. At our age, that seems strange. Plenty of people travel a lot for work and still have lasting relationships. So I was wondering what it is that makes it so you don't want one."

A philosophical conversation like this one would have been something Kelly relished any other time. Right now, it was hard enough to keep one foot going in front of the other. So she kept her response simple. "Not everyone wants someone waiting for them at home. Not everyone wants roots they can't escape from."

Shawn was silent at that, and Kelly didn't have the words or energy to say more. But it did get her thinking. Was she afraid?

"What's so wrong with having roots? I like having a home to go to, and places I know, and people I recognize. I think homo sapiens are animals who like stable locations and regular mates."

Kelly laugh-grunted. "I think you'll find that there have been plenty of homo sapiens who are also nomadic and prefer to live on the move, and who also take relationships more fluidly."

Shawn pondered that for a while longer, and Kelly knew she

had made her point. They were simply coming at existence from different angles.

"Do you ever miss having someone to talk to at night? To tell about your day, and to talk over the things in your mind?" Shawn's voice was a little tighter now. "I do. My exes weren't right for me, but there were times when it was nice to simply have someone who wanted you around."

This time it was Kelly's turn to walk in silence as she pondered a question that deserved an honest answer. "Yes. Sometimes it would be nice to come home and have a cup of tea with someone and discuss normal things like whether or not the clothes would dry on the line or what absurd thing the Prime Minister said that day. It would be nice to wake up and know the person would still be around tomorrow or next week." The ache in her chest now wasn't from the injuries. "But ultimately, people want you to want what they do. They don't like when you say you're going away for three months on a dig. Jealousy is a witch's tit that most relationships eventually suckle on when you're apart for long stretches of time."

Shawn's laugh echoed off the ice. "That's an interesting image."

Kelly smiled a little. "I love seeing the world and don't want to stop seeing it because someone at home feels like they can't let me go. I'd need to be with someone so secure that they could handle long stretches by themselves and not grow resentful. As of yet, I haven't met a woman who fits that criteria."

"Have you given anyone a chance to prove that they meet the criteria?" Shawn asked after a moment's pause.

Kelly stopped when a shiver so hard shook her body and made her dizzy. They were in a narrower part of the system, and when Shawn moved to steady her, they ended up body to body. Kelly let her head fall to Shawn's shoulder and leaned into her one-armed embrace. At this angle, she couldn't fully hold her without touching her bad arm. They stayed that way for a while, and then Shawn kissed her head.

"Let me go ahead a little and see if there's a place to sit down and eat something. I'll be right back."

Reluctantly, Kelly let go of her and rested her head against the wall instead. The cold felt good against her skull. She wasn't sure how long it had been before Shawn came back.

"This opens out into a huge cavern. You're going to love it, and you're not going to believe what's there." The excitement in Shawn's voice got Kelly to open her eyes. "Not much further and you can rest, okay?"

Kelly nodded tiredly and pushed away from the wall. They set off, this time with Shawn going ahead since she'd already done it once. As she'd said, the tunnel opened into an enormous cavern where the blues and whites swam together and climbed high above their heads, mixing with gray rock that made up part of the walls.

"Over here. Look." Shawn led the way to a far wall.

It took a moment for Kelly to grasp what she was seeing, and when she did, her knees went weak. Behind the ice wall, almost like looking through a misty window, was a structure. "Is that the remnants of a building?"

"Yes!" Shawn was practically vibrating. "I know I shouldn't make an assumption like that without excavation and testing, but those corners are clearly manmade, and those stones have been fit together in a way that isn't natural." She knelt and wiped at the ice like she would a window, but it made no difference.

Kelly wobbled as her vision went blurry. "Shawn, I—"

Shawn caught her as her knees gave way and she collapsed, darkness rushing in.

***

Kelly murmured at how good the gentle caress felt in her hair. She didn't want it to stop and when she shifted to feel it even more, the pain ripped through her and she decided she didn't want to wake up, thank you very much.

"Are we out yet?" she asked, keeping her eyes closed.

"Not yet, beautiful."

Telling herself to stop being a wimp, she opened her eyes and looked up into Shawn's caring ones. Her head was cradled in Shawn's lap. "I'm never excavating in the cold again. Only tropical locations that never get snow."

"Wise decision." Shawn touched her cheek. "Can you sit up? I want to look at your hands and feet and get some food and water in you."

With Shawn's help, Kelly managed to rise and then scoot back so she was propped against the wall opposite the one with the amazing find in it. That would give her something to focus on.

"Have you taken pictures yet?" she asked, her throat sore and her voice hoarse.

"I was a little busy making sure you didn't crack your head on the ice again." Shawn grinned a little as she looked up from where she was unpacking their gear. "You've been out longer than you should, I'm guessing, and I was getting worried about how I was going to carry you out of here. I'm strong, but you're tall. I'd have to drag you along on my back like a cloak."

Kelly laughed at the visual. "I have a feeling that wouldn't be fun for either of us."

"No, I'd much rather be behind you that way." Shawn gave her a smile that warmed her a little, but in the wrong area.

As Shawn got their food and hot drinks ready, Kelly studied the faint outline of what she could see. "How the hell did a building get trapped in ice this low down?"

Shawn glanced over her shoulder at it. "If I had to guess, I'd say it was probably up higher before the last ice age. Then it froze, and when things began to thaw, it was brought down with snow melt and avalanches. It might even prove your long chronology theory. But who knows? That's a wild hypothesis." She looked back at Kelly with a wide smile. "What isn't a wild hypothesis is the cave art up top, on the left."

Kelly looked so quickly it made her nauseous and she had to close her eyes for a second. When she reopened them and moved more slowly, she searched until she saw the red ochre drawings high up. Too high for them to see properly. "The ice must have been higher back then. Can you make out what they are?"

Shawn got the hot water into the food pouches and brought Kelly a cup of coffee. "My phone has a really good camera. I'll get photos of everything before we leave. Right now, I need to take care of you."

While Kelly sipped the blessedly hot coffee, Shawn took off her boots and began the routine of warming her feet, but Kelly could see by her expression that she was worried.

"Am I going to be missing some digits when this is over?" she asked lightly, trying not to show her fear.

"If you do, I'm sure people more clever than I am will give you fun nicknames. People like to do that." Shawn continued her gentle warming. "I wish I knew how much further we had to go, but down here, I have no sense of direction or pace."

Kelly didn't either, and Shawn's response about her toes wasn't reassuring, fun nicknames aside. "Have you checked the radio?"

Shawn stopped for a second to grab the radio. Nothing but silence greeted her call. She set it aside and continued working on Kelly's feet before she moved to her hand.

"I should check your other hand too, if you can handle me moving your arm a little."

Kelly shook her head. "If you check it, I couldn't handle you warming it, so I'd rather you leave it, if it's all the same."

Shawn didn't look convinced but handed Kelly her food. "Okay. Let's eat."

Kelly watched as Shawn ate quickly. "Chay said you needed to take care of yourself too. I'm sorry I can't rub your feet for you. And eating food all mixed together in a pouch must make you itch."

"I'll take a raincheck on the foot rub. And the food isn't so bad. I'm too hungry to really taste it anyway." Shawn, finished eating, worked off her boots and grunted as she began warming her feet between her hands. She put on dry socks from her pack and nodded. "That's better."

Kelly managed to eat her full portion and then rested against the wall. "Any idea what time it is?"

Shawn looked at her watch. "Just after midday. If we keep going, there's a chance we'll be out by nightfall, maybe."

"I can't get moving yet. Maybe get some photos until I get my mojo back?" Kelly wanted to sleep for the next month, but she'd have to settle for a small respite so they didn't both freeze to death.

Shawn stood and took out her phone. She began taking photos and then switched to video. "We're in an ice cave below the Broken Swan glacier crevasse we were excavating. In this enormous cavern, which I'd estimate to be approximately sixty feet wide and a hundred feet high, we've found what appears to be the remains of an ancient building." She videoed from different angles, going high and low. "We've also found these cave drawings, which are too high to view up close."

Kelly watched as Shawn continued to video and dictate, moving slowly. As desperately as she wanted to sleep, watching Shawn's excitement reminded her of her own first finds when they'd come across wonderful things in unexpected places. And here, below the earth, they were likely the first humans in centuries to see these things. They'd also likely be the last, until climate change melted all the ice entirely.

She closed her eyes, Shawn's husky, smooth voice making her feel warm and safe. It was only when she felt Shawn shaking her that she realized she'd fallen asleep.

"Babe? Babe, come on." Shawn's worried expression made Kelly come awake fully.

"What's wrong?"

Shawn's head dropped and she let out a whoosh of breath. "I thought you were just sleeping, but it was too hard to wake you up. We need to keep going."

Kelly understood what Shawn wasn't saying. Hypothermia was setting in, along with probably other problems related to her injuries. If they held still, she wasn't going to make it out.

She was too exhausted to cry.

Shawn gathered their things once again and got Kelly upright. With one last lingering look, they left the ancient area behind and entered another long tunnel. Kelly shuffled forward, her stupor growing until she saw only white and was using every fiber of her being to keep moving.

"Look!"

Bemused at the sudden sound, Kelly forced her eyes up from the ground. She gave a soft, strangled sob at the opening ahead. She kept her eyes on it, feeling almost like she was falling toward it.

It wasn't the end. It was a snow bridge over a moulin, a simple circular opening high above that their rescue team probably wouldn't even have seen. A little waterfall fell from the opening into a shallow pool that glinted off the walls. She sank to her knees and had a feeling she wouldn't get off them again. She was going to die. The only good part about it was that she would be in Shawn's arms when she did.

CHAPTER EIGHTEEN

SHAWN HAD NEVER FELT so helpless or lost in her entire life. When Kelly collapsed, Shawn had caught her just in time to keep her from hitting the ground. Her lips were blue, and her skin had gone pasty pale. Shawn had tried the radio again, hoping that the hole above them would allow for a signal, but there was nothing but silence yet again.

Forcing herself to stay calm and think rationally, she unpacked their gear and laid down the tarp, then carefully lifted Kelly onto it. Then she pulled out their blankets and lay beside her, snuggling up to her as closely as possible to share her body heat. She tucked Kelly's good hand inside her jacket and put her legs over her feet. It was awkward and uncomfortable, but the more of her own heat she could share, the better. As she lay there, she tried to come up with alternatives. Maybe she could create a kind of sled from the tarp after all. She might have to if Kelly either didn't wake or couldn't walk any further.

When she started to go numb herself, she unhooked herself from Kelly and tucked the blankets in around her once more. She was shivering even in her unconscious state, but she was also burning with fever. Shawn prepared some food and poured water into a cup.

"Kelly?" She shook her gently and tapped her face. When she didn't get a response, she got a small piece of ice from against one wall and held it to her forehead. It melted quickly, and Kelly's eyes fluttered open. "Welcome back. I need you to sit up and try to eat and drink, okay?"

Kelly's nod was miniscule but there, and Shawn helped her

edge up in the thermal blanket cocoon and held the bottle to her lips. Her sips were small at first, and then she worked one arm loose and took the bottle herself. She drained half and sat back.

"That's nice," she murmured, and her eyes drifted shut again.

"Hey. Don't go back to sleep. Take these." Shawn handed her some more pain pills, hoping they'd help with not just the pain she was clearly in, but also with the fever. "And now eat this." She positioned the bag of food on Kelly's knees so she could eat with one hand at her own pace.

"Shawn," she said after a few mouthfuls. "You may need to leave me behind."

Shawn swiveled to look at her, incredulous. "What are you talking about?"

Tears slid down Kelly's cheeks. "If you stay with me, we could both die of hypothermia. If you leave me behind, you'll make it out."

Shawn squatted in front of her. "That's true. It's logical. It also isn't going to happen. We're both going to get out of here even if I do have to wear you like a cloak. Or if I have to pull you along behind me like I'm a sled dog." She wiped away Kelly's tears. "Save your energy and don't argue with me."

"But—"

"Nope." Shawn held up a spoonful of food and pushed it into her mouth. "I don't want to hear any more of that nonsense. We can't be that far away now. We didn't get as far as I thought we might, or maybe the tunnel is longer than the drone showed, but we're going to be there by tomorrow." She cupped Kelly's cheek, the unnatural warmth felt even through her glove. "Just hang on, babe. We'll make it."

Kelly nodded and sighed like the weight of the world was pressing on her, which it probably was if she was worried about Shawn's life expectancy too.

"I'm coming in." Unable to do anything more, she sat up behind Kelly like a chair, giving her something warm to lean against instead of the ice wall. She wrapped herself around her as best she could without jarring her arm.

Kelly drifted off again, her breathing shallow but regular. Shawn, left alone with her thoughts, tried to think about the artifacts they'd found and what it meant for science. A strange light caught her eye, and she blinked as the cave walls seemed to move. When she looked up, her breath caught.

"Kelly. Baby, wake up. Look."

Kelly slowly came to. "What's wrong?" she mumbled.

"Nothing. Look up."

Kelly tilted her head and gasped softly.

Through the hole high above them, the night sky danced with color. The aurora borealis greens and blues moved over their little peephole to the sky, sending light into their icy sanctuary and turning it into a magical palace. For about half an hour, they were treated to a sublime show that felt less like a natural phenomenon and more like a promise that things were going to be okay.

"If you were up to it, I'd dance with you right now. The music of the spheres and the light show would be enough to hold you in my arms. In fact, I compared you to a sunbeam in a cave not so long ago. You're even more like this though. Magic in so many ways."

Kelly's tears fell onto Shawn's jacket, and she sniffled. "I like that."

The shimmering blues and greens died away, leaving them in the dark cave. "Rest. When you wake up, we'll get moving again, okay?"

Kelly let her bodyweight fall against Shawn. "I know you should leave me behind," she whispered, "but I'm so glad you're here. I don't..." She sobbed softly. "I don't want to die alone."

Shawn's heart lurched. "You're not going to die, and you need to stop thinking like that. I don't know about the truthfulness or scientific aspects of positive thinking on physical health, but if there's anything to it, then we need it right now. I'm not going to have found you just to lose you this way."

She wasn't sure if Kelly heard her, given that her breathing had slowed once more and she seemed to be out again. *This way.* It was a slip of the tongue, but one that held truth. When they got out of here, she was going to lose Kelly at some point. After a hospital stay, she might or might not come back to Oklahoma to finish the Brazil job. If she didn't, then Shawn would lose her sooner than later.

And what then? She sure as heck wouldn't be doing any more expeditions into the frozen sections of the world. Would she do any expeditions at all? At this point, she couldn't say. She had all the time in the world to think, but all she could think about was getting Kelly out of here.

She managed to set the alarm on her watch so they didn't fall asleep and not wake up ever again, and then drifted off. Three hours later, she felt sick and numb when it woke her, but she knew they had to get moving if they were going to move at all. It took too long to wake Kelly, but she managed to get her upright and moving after she hurriedly packed their stuff.

"Not much further, beautiful. Just keep going." Shawn started to sing silly songs, letting the echoes of her voice provide a chorus, just to keep Kelly going.

Kelly didn't say anything. She simply shuffled forward, the effort clearly taking everything she had left.

Shawn startled from her singing and looked up when an icy breeze caressed her face. "Oh my God. Kelly, we made it."

Kelly didn't seem to hear her. She just kept moving forward, getting slower and less steady.

Shawn grabbed the radio. "Anyone there?"

"We're here!"

Shawn's knees went weak, and she touched the wall to steady herself. She'd never been so glad to hear Chay's voice, and she heard Bree's exclamation in the background too. "I hope you're ready to get us out of here. I don't think we've got much left."

"We're ready and waiting. The chopper is here to take Kelly to a hospital. How are you holding up?"

Shawn couldn't answer that question because she didn't know.

She couldn't afford to check in with her body at this point, because she had a feeling it wouldn't be great news. "You're going to need a way to get Kelly out without her help. She's barely upright as it is."

There was a moment's silence. "Okay. We're going to lower a stretcher along with a rescuer from the chopper. They'll lift her out with the chopper. It's going to get blowy down there. How far are you from the exit?"

Shawn's chest vibrated with hope. "I can see your lights. We should be out there in the next five minutes, I think."

"Copy. We'll be ready for you. Shawn, do you need a stretcher too, or can we haul you out?"

"You can haul me out, but I admit I don't have a lot of arm strength, and I'm not sure I can grip a rope." Even now, after all this, she hated admitting to any weakness. Chay probably would have carried Kelly out action-star style.

"No problem. We've got the gear and people to get you out of there. See you in a minute."

"Chay, Kelly's got a severe fever and she's not talking. She's in bad shape. The medical folks should know." Shawn still wasn't sure Kelly was aware of what was going on. She hadn't given any indication that she'd heard Shawn talking or felt the wind on her face.

"Okay, Shawn. They heard you, and they're ready." Chay sounded less elated now than she had when she'd heard Shawn's first call.

"Shawn?" Bree's voice came over the radio. "If you can't use your hands and you don't have any strength, you need to tell us how you really are. Facts, please."

Shawn smiled a little at how well Bree knew her and how to get through to her. "No fever, no broken bones. Extreme fatigue and probably hypothermia. Hands and feet are no longer painful and can't actually be felt at all. Mild confusion but not speech impaired."

Once again, there was a moment of silence. "Okay, Shawn. You're going with Kelly in the chopper. They'll get her out first and then take you up as well."

As much as she didn't like the idea of being in a helicopter, at least she knew the sky was brilliant and clear. Otherwise, they wouldn't have been treated to the dancing lights in the sky.

And then, suddenly they were out in the open. The cave exited into a long, narrow crevasse. Cheers erupted above them, and she looked up to see Chay and Bree standing at the edge, lights all around them, with several others she couldn't make out in the shadows.

Kelly stumbled to a stop and looked up, seemingly confused. And then she slowly crumpled to the ground, as though the very last of her energy was gone now that she'd made it out.

Shawn held her close. "We're ready," she called up. "Get us out of here."

Within moments the rhythmic thump of the helicopter blades starting rang through night and snow began to blow up top. Soon Shawn could see it up above them, and then there was a rescuer being lowered. Shawn watched as they came closer, her eyes narrowed against the blowing snow and ice.

"Hey there. Good to see you. You've had some very worried people up there." The woman's voice was the only indication of gender given her full face covering and heavy clothing. She knelt next to Kelly, who didn't even look at her.

"She's got a broken arm and concussion. She's been running a fever." Shawn squatted beside her even though her muscles protested the movement.

"Okay. We'll get both of you up and out of here." The rescuer gave a thumbs-up to the helicopter and the stretcher began to lower.

Shawn wanted it to go faster. Now that they were out of the tunnel system, she just wanted it over. The bed landed, and together she and the rescuer got Kelly into it. The moment she lay down, her eyes closed. But her hand didn't let go of Shawn's.

"Don't leave me," she whispered, tears rolling down her cheeks and then flying into the wind.

"I'm not leaving you. We have to go up separately, but I'll be right there with you. I promise." Shawn kissed her burning forehead, and Kelly's hand fell limp.

The rescuer finished zipping Kelly into what looked like a giant red sleeping bag, and then gave a thumbs-up to the pilot as well as shouting into a radio, and the stretcher began to lift slowly.

Shawn watched, her stomach turning as Kelly flew away from her, out of her reach, away from her care. The people on the helicopter took the stretcher onto the big metal beast, and she disappeared from sight.

"Okay, our turn!" The rescuer turned to her and held up a big red thing that looked like a children's pool toy. "We wrap this around your back and under your arms. I'll loop you up to the lines and to myself. Hold on to me and we'll do what's called a double lift into the air."

Shawn nodded her understanding and let the rescuer fit the things onto her, and now her own energy seemed to run out too. They were waiting for the lines to come down from the chopper when Shawn heard an exclamation from above just as the ground began to shake.

She and the rescuer hit the ground, covering their heads as snow and ice rained down, and the walls beside them seemed to shake. All she could think was that she was glad Kelly was already gone, so she wouldn't see Shawn die at the last minute. Tears of frustration finally fell. After all that, this was going to be it.

Startled, she jerked when the rescuer dragged her to her feet and attached them together at various points. "Time to go!" She grabbed the line, hooked them in, and they almost immediately started to rise.

Shawn dangled there in the darkness and saw her expedition group already mounting the dog sleds. Behind them, dawn was cresting over the mountains, painting pink streaks over the white peaks. Sound receded as did the light, and Shawn gave in to her exhaustion.

***

The incessant beeping would have been irritating if it weren't for the fact that the rhythm was also somehow soothing. The antiseptic smell that filtered in made Shawn wince, and she slowly came around. Her first real thought was that she was warm, and it felt so, so good. The second was that there was something on her face and something attached to her arm, neither of which she liked. But opening her eyes was taking a monumental effort.

A rustling sound let her know someone was in the room with her, and she mumbled something, though she wasn't sure what.

"Oh, thank God. Sitting here in silence has been driving me crazy."

The bed shifted, and Shawn forced her eyes open, and the light immediately sent a bolt of pain into her head. Bree sat beside her and gently smoothed the hair from Shawn's forehead.

Shawn said something again and then realized the oxygen mask over her face was muffling her. She tried to raise her arm to take it off but found it attached to a blood pressure machine as well as some kind of intravenous drip.

"Let me," Bree said and gently pulled the mask down. "Better?" Shawn nodded. "Water?"

Bree held the straw to her lips, and nothing had ever tasted so good. She let her head fall back. "Kelly?"

Before she could answer a nurse came in. "Nice of you to rejoin the living." He buzzed around her, checking numbers and the IV and then shining a light into her eyes. "I'll let the doc know you're awake, and she'll come see you soon. In the meantime, I'll get some food brought up so we can slowly rebuild your strength. No sudden movements, okay? You had a close call."

And then he was gone, leaving Shawn a little bewildered. She looked at Bree. "How close?" It was only then that she really saw how haggard Bree looked. There were bags under her eyes and her hair, usually just right, stuck out at odd angles. Shawn started to sit up. "Are you okay? Were you hurt?"

Bree lightly pushed Shawn's shoulder to get her to lie back down. "I'm fine. It was crazy, and you've been here for two days. They told me to go to a hotel, but I refused to leave you. I wanted to be here when you woke up, so you knew you weren't alone."

Shawn gripped her hand tightly. "Thank you. When I was down there, I promised myself I'd tell you how much I appreciate you if I made it out. Thank you for being my best friend."

Bree smiled and wiped away a stray tear. "It's a pleasure. But let's not do this again."

Shawn shook her head. "Kelly?"

Bree's smile faded. "She was in bad shape. They're not sure how you managed to get her to keep going. Another half hour and she wouldn't have made it. Her lungs and heart were at breaking point."

Shawn's stomach churned. "And? Is she okay?"

"I don't know." Bree made a vague motion toward the door. "When you both got here, they took you off the chopper and brought you in, but Kelly's condition was serious enough that they needed to get her to a critical care unit, and this hospital doesn't have one. So they took her away. I've tried to reach Chay a few times, but I haven't had any answer. I assume she's with her." She held up Shawn's phone. "It's all charged up when you're ready for some distraction."

Shawn tried to capture some of her spinning thoughts. "How bad was I when I got here?"

"You were severely hypothermic. They used rewarming oxygen and some kind of IV drugs. They said it was good you were so healthy and strong, but they had to move slowly because you could have a heart attack." Bree's words were factual, but the worry in her eyes told Shawn how hard it had been on her.

"If that was a worry with me and I was still on my feet, then

Kelly..." Shawn couldn't actually find the words to complete the sentence. "I have to know what's going on."

"Right now, you have to rest." The doctor, a woman with gray hair tied back in a loose ponytail, came in with a clipboard under her arm as she pulled on gloves. "I'm not authorized to tell you about another patient, but I can tell you she's alive and in good hands."

Knowing Kelly was alive was at least something, and Shawn relaxed back into the bed to let the doctor check her out.

"You changing your socks a lot helped make sure you kept your toes, but you may have a little nerve damage. It might go away, it might not. We'll have to wait and see." She listened to Shawn's heart, moving the little metal circle around. "I can't rule out an arrythmia either. You put your body through it out there, and it's going to take some time and attention to make sure there's no damage. We're going to keep you here for a few days to monitor your heart in particular." She stepped back and looked at Bree. "And maybe you can convince your friend here to go get some rest. She refused to leave your side from the moment she got here."

Shawn nodded her thanks and the doctor left. "Will you try Chay again?"

Bree nodded and made the call. She was about to hang up at the fifth ring when Chay answered, her voice hoarse. "Hey."

"Hey. Shawn has just woken up and is asking about Kelly. I'm putting you on speaker."

"How are you, Shawn?" she asked.

"Worried about Kelly." Shawn wanted to reach through the phone and shake her.

The answering silence didn't bode well. "She's in a coma. She hasn't woken up since they got her in the chopper. Her heart gave out, and they had to use a defibrillator during the flight. She's stable right now, but they aren't sure how much damage she sustained, and she's on a ventilator. They said it was a miracle she made it at all."

Shawn gripped the bedsheet with one hand and her hair with the other. "Do...I mean...what now?" She wasn't even sure what to ask.

"We wait. I've called Jack, her boss, and he's called her parents. I don't know what's being decided on their end."

"And you?" Bree asked gently. "I can't imagine how you're feeling."

"Fuck. I mean, fuck, you know? How did it go so wrong?" Chay sounded broken, defeated. "I wish you were here."

Bree's hand shook as she took the conversation off speaker and held it to her ear. "I wish you were here. Maybe we just both wish we were together." She held up her finger and left the room, going into the hall to finish her call.

Shawn let the tears fall. Kelly was in a coma, and they didn't know if she'd survive. Knowing she'd lose her to London and her travels was one thing. Knowing she was in a hospital bed on a ventilator and Shawn couldn't get to her was another thing altogether. Could she have done anything differently? Warmed her better, moved them through the cave system more quickly, given her more hot drinks? She'd done all she could think to do, but maybe it hadn't been enough.

She looked away when Bree came back in and sat on the bed. Guilt was swallowing her whole.

"If you hadn't gone down there to be with her, she would have died." Bree's voice was soft and kind but firm. "We couldn't have rescued her from that crevasse. The area was too unstable for the helicopter to have lowered a stretcher and gotten her out safely. She would have died with us up above, watching." She shuddered and took Shawn's hand. "You walked her out the only way possible. You're the reason she has any chance at all, and you couldn't have done anything differently."

Shawn shook her head. "You don't know that. Chay would have known what to do. Maybe Kelly would be okay."

Bree squeezed her hand. "But Chay wasn't down there with

her. She isn't the one who jumped into an icy ravine the very first moment it became clear that Kelly was in trouble. If you had other training, might you have done something different? Maybe. But we both know what good maybe is."

Shawn tried to let her words sink in. "I'll think about that. Do you want to go be with Chay?"

She shook her head. "No. I'm staying here with you. I'll see Chay again one day but for now, we're both looking after the people we love." She stood and stretched. "That said, I'm going to take the doctor's orders and go to a hotel to sleep for a while now that I know you're back in the land of the living. What do you want me to bring back?"

Shawn turned her phone over and over in her hands. Somehow, bothering to look at it felt like a betrayal, as she wouldn't be thinking of Kelly. An absurd thought, perhaps, but true, nonetheless. "A book, maybe."

Bree nodded and picked up her bag. "Okay. I'll be back in a few hours. Rest, and if Chay gives me any more updates, I'll text you." She kissed Shawn's cheek. "I'll be glad to get home. And don't ever scare me that way again."

Shawn nodded her agreement and then Bree left, and it was silent except for the beeping that indicated she was still alive. But then, Kelly would have beeping machines too, and her life was hanging in the balance. She'd held her hand, promised not to leave her. She could still see her lying there, pale, nearly unconscious, and so afraid. Through no fault of her own, Shawn had inadvertently broken that promise. Now, she had no idea if she'd ever see her again.

CHAPTER NINETEEN

THERE WAS A BOULDER on Kelly's chest that rose and fell with every breath. Something tight gripped one arm and something pinched the other. It was too warm and the thing on her face reeked of wet plastic. There was a gross sucking sound and the more she concentrated on it, the more she began to panic at the feeling of not being able to swallow. Her eyes flew open, and she raised her hands to jerk at whatever was in her mouth. Panic welled and strange guttural sounds making their way out of her.

"Relax. Relax, baby. We're here. Hold on, your mum is getting a nurse."

She focused on her dad's face and his big, strong hand resting on her arm. She knew her eyes were wide, and she shook her head, trying to dislodge the intruder in her body.

"It was helping you breathe, sweetheart. Try to relax. Concentrate on things that soothe you. Think of a nice cuppa and some fish and chips with a side of mushy peas, eh?"

Tears welled and fell. What was happening? Hospital. It was a hospital. There was beeping. Whitish walls with pukey green stripes. Her dad was beside her. Her mum had gone to get the doctor. She'd been...where? Where had she been that had led her to this hospital bed?

A doctor came in with a couple nurses, and her mum following quickly behind.

"Good to see you awake." She looked down at Kelly, her hand on the rail. "We're going to take the ventilator out. I'll be honest, it's going to be unpleasant. But once it's out, you'll feel a million times better. Just try to stay calm, okay?"

Kelly felt like she was choking as the tube slid from her throat, and she knew she'd never want that experience again. But the doctor was right. Once it was out, the anxiety slowly began to recede. Someone cleaned up her face and then gave her an ice cube to suck on, which felt heavenly in her dry, sore mouth.

Ice...something about ice. The memory was slippery and eased out of her grasp.

"So. Let's talk." The doctor shined a light in her eyes and listened to her chest. "Do you remember the accident?"

Kelly shook her head. She tried to speak but it hurt too much.

"That's okay. It's not unusual when you've been in a coma. In all likelihood, you'll remember in bits and pieces over the next few days."

A coma? She looked at her parents, who looked back at her, their expressions hard to read.

"It would be better if you were allowed to remember on your own, instead of people feeding you the information, so that your brain begins restoring those connections. I've asked your parents to ask leading questions but not provide any actual answers. That may get frustrating, but I don't think it will last long. You're clearly a fighter." The doctor sat down beside her bed. "You sustained a severe concussion as well as a neck injury, fracturing your T1 vertebrae. You had severe hypothermia, which had to be treated by putting warm air into your lungs as well as with other measures. The fact that you didn't lose any fingers or toes is astounding, especially since you couldn't use your left hand thanks to you fracturing both the ulna and radial bones in your forearm. We had to insert pins to hold the fragments together, and you'll have that cast on for another five weeks or so. I understand you walked nearly eight miles in that condition. As I say, you're a fighter."

"What happens now?" her mum asked as she came to Kelly's side and took her hand.

"Now we monitor her heart and lungs and make sure there's no damage. We get her upright and moving to get blood flowing naturally and to make sure there's no nerve damage. With any luck, you'll be able to go home by the end of the week." The doctor stood. "I'll be in every day to check on your progress. Just take it nice and slow, and let your body and brain come back on their own."

Kelly wanted to say that wasn't good enough, that she wanted to know what had happened and why. She wanted to go home now. Not at the end of the week. And when was that, anyway?

She looked at the cup of ice chips and then at her mum, who pressed one to her mouth and ran it over her dry, sore lips.

"You have no idea how scared we've been." Her dad took the seat the doctor had vacated. "You've scared us plenty with some of your adventures over the years, but this definitely takes the biscuit."

She smiled a little at the old saying and then let her eyes close. She was safe, warm, and her parents were beside her. She was also more exhausted than she could ever remember being. She drifted off again, nebulous memories fading to mist.

Cold. It's so cold. But warm, strong arms wrapped around her and the cold receded for a moment, the pain diminishing as she looked at the lights dancing across the sky...

"Shawn," she gasped, sitting up, sweat beading on her forehead. "Where's Shawn?" Wildly, she looked around the room as though she might materialize.

"Hey. Calm down." Jack pushed his considerable bulk out of the chair he'd been draped over. "Shawn is fine. It's you we're worried about."

Kelly's pulse pounded hard in her temples. "But where is she?" Her throat hurt, and her voice was hoarse. Shaking, she picked up a cup of water, sloshing most of it on herself before Jack gently took it away and held the straw to her lips.

"She's back in Oklahoma. A couple days in the hospital in Anchorage was all she needed. But believe me when I say she's a pain in the ass. She texts me every couple hours to see how you're doing. I had to talk her out of coming over until you'd actually woken up. Having her underfoot while you were still out might have driven us all crazy."

Kelly lay back, taking that in. "I'm in London?"

Jack nodded and lowered himself back into the chair that looked too small for him. "You started out in Mt. Edgecumbe Medical Center because they have a level one trauma unit, which is what you needed since you were damn near clinically dead by the time they got you there. Once you were stable, I pulled a couple strings to get you transferred home. UK care is better by virtue of it being free, and I thought you'd want your parents nearby when you finally rejoined us." His brow furrowed. "Do you remember what happened?"

Kelly rested against the mountain of pillows and thought. "There was an accident in the crevasse. I...I hit my head. When I came to, Shawn was in the crevasse with me. I think...was there an ice quake?" She saw Jack nod from the corner of her eye. "And we had to go through a tunnel to get out." The journey came crashing back. The pain, the exhaustion, the desperation, and most of all, the absolute knowledge that she was going to die. "I told her to leave me there, Jack," she whispered, remembering the look of horror in Shawn's expression. "I told her that we shouldn't both die, and that she should go without me."

He grunted. "I imagine that will haunt her dreams for the rest of her life. Nice one, Kel." When she shot him a glare, he laughed. "Seriously though. The docs say she saved your life as well as all your digits by taking care of you the way she did." He waved his fingers at her.

"But she's okay?" More than anything in the world she wanted to see Shawn's handsome face right now.

"She's fine. Her hypothermia wasn't as significant." His eyebrows raised. "Aside from the fact that she literally saved your life, is there a reason you're asking about her?"

Kelly sighed and looked away. "I'm not sure. I have some stuff to think about. I had a lot of dreams while I was in the coma." She swallowed the bile that rose at those words. "Dreams about Shawn and some of the things we talked about."

He nodded and stood. "Your parents went home for some rest, but they said they'll be back around tea time. I'll head out and give you some space."

"Jack, will you tell Shawn..." What? Thank you was what you said when you got flowers or a nice meal. Not when someone kept you from dying alone in an icy pit. "Tell her I miss her."

His eyes narrowed, but he just nodded. "Yup. Will do. You're not allowed to use your phone in here, but if they move you around, maybe you could use that brutal charm of yours to get them to take you to a cell area." He paused at the door, his expression turning serious. "I'm sorry, Kelly. If I'd have known how dangerous this would be, I'd never have asked you—"

"Shut up, you pillock." Kelly closed her eyes, unable to deal with anyone else's guilt. "I went on a dig and shit went sideways. That happens." She rolled her head and looked at him. "And we found some incredible things, didn't we?" She hated that it was a question rather than a statement, but she couldn't quite remember. But she had an inkling there was more, something really spectacular, that she couldn't put her finger on.

"Truly fantastic. Some of the items didn't go back in the ice because of the instability of the area, so the tribe took them for safekeeping. They'll replace them ceremonially when they feel it's best." His grin widened. "The 3-D prints we'll make of them for the museum will get you funding for years."

She nodded, pleased that at least some part of it had gone well. "I think I'll just join the Stonehenge team for a while. Work above ground in a place without quakes, or ice, or animals that could eat you."

"Rest up." His tone was gentle, and the door shut softly.

Alone, she let her thoughts wander. Free of the pain she knew would hit if it weren't for the painkillers, she breathed herself into a meditative state she'd learned to use on a dig in Thailand.

The ground shook, and her rope jerked. She'd had an artifact in her hand and had nearly dropped it. Unbalanced, she'd swung sideways and crashed into the ice, breaking her impact with her forearm, which she'd felt snap just before her head had cracked into the wall too. Nausea and darkness.

Then Shawn, looking down at her, scared, intense, comforting. The pain had been awful and yet, she'd been calmed by having Shawn at her side. They'd set off into the cave and tunnel system, and it had gotten harder to breathe, harder to keep moving. But Shawn had talked to her and kept her focused as well as hydrated and fed.

And then... "For fuck's sake." She sat up and looked around for her phone, but it wasn't there, just as Jack had said. She lay back. Surely if Shawn had told Jack about the building and cave art he would've said something? Why would Shawn hold that information back?

Then it all went misty. She was paradoxically numb and in pain, certain she was going to die and equally certain that if she just kept moving, maybe she'd make it after all. There was Shawn's voice in the background, urging her on, singing little tunes...and then nothing. She didn't remember making it out of the cave or the helicopter ride, and it sounded like maybe that's because she was actually and literally dead on her feet.

Tears rolled down her cheeks. She hadn't been able to say goodbye. Or thank you. Or any of the other things she'd felt but been unable to find words for as she'd fallen deeper into a stupor.

Emotionally spent, she tried her best to get comfortable with the cast and wires still attached and drifted to sleep. This time it was Shawn's arms around her and whispers of encouragement in her ear that lulled her into the mists of the dream world.

***

"I promise, I'll only be a minute. Really. You're beautiful and sweet. I love your smile. Yup, I promise. Cross my honest little heart."

Kelly couldn't help but smile a little at the voice that woke her. "One day that won't work, you know. You'll get old and wrinkly, and they'll just think you're a pain in the arse."

Chay pulled a seat noisily to Kelly's side. "That day will never come. I'll always be hot and adorable." She rested her chin on the bed rail. "How you doing, babe?"

Kelly reached for her water before speaking. The soreness was lessening, but it still hurt to talk. "I was dead and now I'm not, so it seems that complaining about anything is rather ungrateful. You?"

Chay tilted her head a little. "I like your way of thinking. I'm good too. I was pretty pissed off when Jack had you transferred here and I couldn't come with you, but I'll only slug him once for it."

"Help me sit up, would you?" Kelly shifted, and Chay hit the raise button so she could see her without it hurting her neck. "Thanks. So you were at the hospital with me?"

"Yeah. They dropped Shawn at one hospital because her injuries weren't severe, but then you got all squirrely and decided you were above breathing, and they took off to another hospital. Bree stayed with Shawn, and I caught a lift to the one you were at." She pointed to herself. "I was the one who called your parents and Jack, thank you very much. Just call me hero." She gave a mock bow.

"I'll call you something but probably not that." Kelly grinned, and Chay smiled back. "Thank you for staying with me and making the calls."

Chay's expression turned somber. "It killed me not to be the one down there with you. But since I was the one you were roped to, and then there was the rest of the team, and with you down—"

"Christ. There's enough guilt going around to make us all religious. You did what you needed to do, Chay. You got the others to safety," she paused, "I assume, unless you're not telling me other people are dead?" She gave a soft breath of relief when Chay shook her head, a half-smile on her lips. "And I'm guessing you were there when we made it out the other side of the tunnel. Like I said to Jack—things went sideways. No one is to blame." She searched Chay's expression. "Is Shawn really okay?"

Chay took a deep breath. "Yeah. She's really okay. Damn, Kel. You should have seen her. I wish we had recorded it. The moment she looked over the lip and saw you injured...fucking hell. She roped up and jumped in using nothing but an anchor. She went straight to you and kept you from hitting the ground. Like she had nothing on her mind but getting to you and damn her own safety to hell." She crossed her arms and stretched out her legs. "It was impressive."

Kelly could picture Shawn doing just that, but the thought that she'd put herself in that kind of danger made her breath hitch. "I wouldn't have made it without her. I was ready to give up, but she wouldn't let me."

Chay's jaw clenched. "I'd have kicked your ass if you'd let yourself die down there. I never would have forgiven myself."

"How is Bree? It must have scared the life out of her as well."

"You know how trauma and disaster bring out the truth of people? I think that's what it did with Bree. She was way pissed off at Shawn for going down, but then she was all facts and plans. It helped keep me from going crazy waiting for you guys to come out. I even considered going in after you from the other side, but she convinced me that more people to rescue would be a bad idea. And she was right, obviously. The flight home was mostly stress-free, at least with regard to the being in the air bit, and she seems to have realized she has to put some distance between her and her catastrophizing mother. It was pretty amazing to watch the transformation."

"What's wrong with your face?" Kelly asked, peering at her. "It's gone all...dopey. The way you see characters look in romantic films when they get all dreamy about someone." She put her good hand to her mouth in mock astonishment. "Has the indomitable bachelor gone and fallen in love?"

Chay grinned and flicked some of Kelly's water at her face. "So what if I have? Jealous?"

"As if. She can have you." She softened her gaze. "I'm happy for you. Does she feel the same?"

"Yeah. That time we spent in the cabin together was something special, and I've talked to her every day since we left Alaska. I didn't think I could fall for someone, but..." She shrugged. "What about you? After that day, it seemed like there was tension between you that wasn't the sexy-time kind."

"What are you going to do about the distance between you? Hell, do you even have a home base anymore?" Dodging her question with an important one of her own seemed like the best way forward.

Chay's expression told her she knew exactly what Kelly was doing. "I sold my apartment in New York a few years ago. Between digs, I stay in rentals. Oklahoma wasn't ever on my list of places to stay, but hell, why not? Bree said she'll come on the occasional no-snow dig with me, and I'll spend my downtime with her. Plenty of couples do it." She narrowed her eyes and leaned forward. "Don't tell me that's the excuse you're using?"

"It's not an excuse. It's a valid..." She sighed. "Yeah. That's one thing. And it's dumb, because Shawn can fly to London and I can fly there, and if we really want it, we can make it work."

"So what is it really?" Chay picked at Kelly's food tray and eventually plucked up the green Jell-O. "I can't believe they still serve this." She opened it and started eating it anyway. "I mean, you've had me, and I know I'm a hard act to follow."

Kelly rolled her eyes. "Believe me, your act has been followed repeatedly and well." She watched as Chay ate the Jell-O, looking at it suspiciously all the while. "I don't want to be with someone who will resent me for doing what I love to do. And Shawn has her own way of doing things. My wanderlust doesn't exactly match up with her desire to eat lunch at twelve thirty every day."

Chay nodded slowly. "Yeah, I can see that it would cause some issues. Still, pretty lame as excuses go." She set down the empty Jell-O carton and gave a cheeky grin to the nurse who popped in and gave her a stern look. "I was just leaving."

The nurse shook her head, her cheeks turning pink when Chay winked at her.

"I'd better go. Visiting is just for family or people on your celebrity list. I won't be offended that you left me off it, since you didn't know I'd be here." She stood and kissed Kelly's cheek. "Give some real thought to what you want, Kel. Life is precious, and if you didn't learn that we need to grab hold of what little happiness we can get in this life while you were down there in the boxing ring with Dani Death, then I don't know what to tell you."

Kelly grabbed her hand. "Thanks for coming. I can't believe you flew here just to check on me."

Chay backed toward the door. "I wanted a pint and a pickled egg. Nothing to do with you." She winked and blew her a kiss. "I'll come back before I head to the States."

After she left, Kelly let her thoughts wander once more. Damn it, she'd forgotten to ask Chay about the find she and Shawn had made in the cave. Oh well. There'd be time. The thought of Chay finally falling in love made her smile. And for someone she'd called a math nerd. But then, Kelly had liked Bree from the start. She was smart, funny, cute, and full of beautiful positive energy.

Shawn was all those things too. Plus she was handsome, strong, capable, kind, caring, and didn't waste time on drama. She was all the things Kelly wanted in a partner. And when she thought of the person she most wanted at her side right now, there was no question. But what the hell was she going to do about it from a hospital bed with months of recovery ahead of her? And what if Shawn had taken to heart Kelly's constant refrain about not wanting a real relationship?

She flicked at her cast in frustration. If nearly dying hadn't taken Shawn away from her, then time and distance certainly wouldn't.

CHAPTER TWENTY

SHAWN SHIFTED IN THE uncomfortable chair for the tenth time in the last half hour. Plato's Republic had long ago lost its allure, as she couldn't properly concentrate on the language and arguments with all the noises and people moving about. The one on the significance of the soul after death had created enough arguments in her head to keep her occupied for a while anyway. Not that she wanted to think any more about death. Ever again, really.

"Hey, superhero." Kelly's raspy voice was the best sound ever.

Shawn jumped up and went to stand awkwardly by the bed. "I've thought of all the things to say, and now I can't think of any of them." She reached out to touch Kelly's hand, then pulled away, unsure it would be welcome. "How are you?"

"I'm alive, thanks to you." Kelly held out her hand and squeezed it lightly when Shawn took it. "I'm surprised to see you here. When did you arrive?"

Shawn looked at her watch. "Four hours and seven minutes ago. I've been here for two hours and thirteen minutes. It took me fifty-eight minutes to get through immigration and to get my baggage. Then your parents and Chay insisted on taking me to lunch, even though I just wanted to get to the hospital. I told them that, but they didn't listen."

Kelly frowned and hit the button to raise her bed. Shawn wanted to caress her face, kiss her lips, and take away anything causing her discomfort. But as of yet, she wasn't sure it was her place.

"My parents and Chay picked you up from the airport?" Kelly took a sip of water and grimaced, setting it back down. "I can't wait to get a good cup of coffee."

Shawn finally sat down, feeling strange standing over her. "After I got the news that you were awake, I called Chay and told her I was coming, and she had your parents put me on the visitor list. She also said it was about time, even though I wasn't cleared to fly just yet, and I wasn't sure if you'd want to see me." She took a breath. "Bree couldn't come. She needed to get things going at the office. She said to tell you she loves you and hopes she'll get to see you again soon." Shawn shrugged and shook her head. "I don't know how she can love you, but I promised I'd say it."

"Good to know." Kelly gave her a wry smile.

Shawn thought about it and winced. "I mean, I know how she could love you. You're very loveable. I just mean, she hasn't spent that much time with you, or slept with you, so I don't know how she's already arrived at love." She groaned and ran her hands through her freshly cut hair. "This isn't at all the way I wanted this to go."

"No? How did you imagine it going? Want to start again?" Kelly's smile was sweet and soft, and she looked so beautiful with her hair mussed and her tired eyes.

Shawn took a deep breath and clasped her hands in her lap. "I know what you said about not wanting a real relationship and not wanting to be with someone who would tie you down. And I respect it. That said, I need to tell you how I feel, or I'll regret it. Will you hear me out?" She swallowed nervously and waited for Kelly to nod. This had been so much easier when she'd rehearsed it on the eleven-hour flight.

"Okay. I think you're remarkable. That day in the cabin meant everything to me. I know it was just a day. But the other days, where we went out together and had fun and laughed and got to just be, they were amazing days too. When we were in that cave, I was so afraid I was going to lose you." She paused to take a shaky breath, and let Kelly pry her hands loose to hold one. "I really thought you were going to die in my arms, and the thought of living in a world without you was incomprehensible. Before I knew you existed, my world was organized and stable. Living without you was fine because I didn't know you. But then, I got to know you, and a world without you wouldn't have been okay. It wouldn't have been right. Or bearable. I was going to get you out of that cave no matter what."

"And you did—"

"Wait. Please let me get this out. If I don't, I'm not sure I'll be brave enough to try again." Again, she waited for Kelly's nod before she continued. "I thought, if you died in that cave, that I still wouldn't leave you. I'd lay there with you right to the end."

Kelly's eyes went wide, and her hand trembled in Shawn's.

"We got out, and they took you away. And then they said you were in a coma, and you might not make it. What was I going to do without you? I couldn't think. I couldn't function. I felt like someone was trying to yank my heart from my chest every second I didn't know you were okay. Then Chay texted me to say you'd woken up and were out of the woods. Though that expression makes little sense, as the woods are often a perfectly nice place to be."

Kelly squeezed her hand, as though to keep her from going off on a tangent.

"I promised myself that I'd come to you if you woke up. And now you're awake." Shawn's stomach turned and tumbled as she fought to keep talking, to shake off the fear of the ultimate rejection. "I love you, Kelly. Not the way Bree loves you, or the way Chay loves you. Because she does, you know. She told me so when she threatened to throw me back in a ravine if I hurt you. But how could I hurt you when I've come to tell you that I love you, and I want to be with you, and I know it's soon and it's fast, but why would that matter when you feel like home to me? And if you'll give us a chance, I swear to you that I'll be the kind of partner you deserve." She took a deep, ragged breath, the words finally out. "But if you still feel the way you did before, then I'll go away, and I won't bother you again. I'll just be glad that you're still in the world making it a more beautiful, wonderful place."

She finally looked up when Kelly didn't say anything. Tears ran down her cheeks.

"Shoot. I'm sorry. I won't–" She tried to pull her hand away, but Kelly held firm.

"I love you too." Kelly's smile grew, and she began to laugh. "I love you too, and before you start to wonder, no, it isn't because you saved me from certain death or because you made a beautiful speech that I want to remember for the rest of my life. It's because you're the only woman on earth I want at my side to share things with. I knew I was glad it was you with me in that cave, and when I could remember what happened, it was you I wanted here at my side. I was stubborn and scared, and I realize now I don't need to be."

Shawn was glad she was sitting down because if she hadn't been, her legs would have given out in relief *and* disbelief. "You love me too?"

"I do. And we'll figure out the logistics somehow. For now, I hope it's enough that we love each other."

Shawn jumped up and placed kisses all over Kelly's face. "It's definitely enough."

***

Shawn finished her final set of sit-ups and drank from her water bottle. Her phone rang from the other room, and she figured she'd get it now that her workout was over. She'd taken Kelly's assertion about it being a leash to heart, and although she still used it as her tether to the world, she'd turned off the notifications so she only checked it when she wanted to. Interestingly, her anxiety and mental health overall were a lot better.

"Did you do it? What did she say? Are you okay?" Bree's rapid-fire questions were as enthusiastic as always.

"I did. She loves me too. I'm better than I've ever been." Shawn flopped backward onto the plush hotel bed. Kelly's parents had offered their guest room, but Shawn wasn't comfortable staying with strangers who were already worried about their daughter. They didn't need her new lover awkwardly underfoot too.

"And did you discuss how you're going to make it work?" Bree was shuffling papers from the sound of it.

"No, not yet. She's still exhausted and needs time to recover. After we talked, I just held her hand until she went back to sleep." Shawn bit her lip, the question on her mind hard to ask. "Do you think you could run the department for a while without me?"

"Obviously. You've taught me everything you know. You're going to stay and help her recover?"

"That's what I'm hoping. I've got plenty of time off accrued. At least I can get her all settled and see how I can help. After that, I guess we'll see." Would Kelly's parents resent the intrusion? Again, she'd have to wait and see.

"That's fine with me. Chay says she's coming back over the weekend, and she's going to stay with me for a little while. I'll be running my own department and have a hottie in my bed. Who knew a little expedition would change my life this way?" Kelly laughed, open and loud.

"A little expedition?" Feels like an understatement." Her phone buzzed with another call, a number she didn't recognize. "I'll talk to you tomorrow." She accepted the other call.

"Hi, Shawn. This is Jack, Kelly's boss. We spoke before you left for the Alaska expedition."

"I remember." Shawn wasn't sure what else to say to someone else's boss.

"I was wondering if you would have lunch with me today. I'd like to discuss a work opportunity with you."

Shawn frowned and looked out the window. From here, she could see the roof of the hospital, and it made her feel a little closer to Kelly. "Okay. Where and when?"

"There's a café not far from your hotel called Olives and Oregano. Within walking distance. In an hour?"

Shawn checked her watch. "That's fine, but I only have an hour. I want to be in Kelly's room as soon as visiting hours open."

"Understood. I'll text you a photo of myself, so you know who you're looking for."

Shawn hung up and waited for the photo, which came in right away. He was probably in his forties, with a receding hairline and a large frame. He also had a big smile and held a sign that said, "Welcome to the UK." It made her smile and eased her anxiety at meeting someone new who was also close to Kelly.

She took her time getting ready, wanting to look good when she showed up at the hospital again, and then walked to the café. The roads were narrow and the buildings high, but she found she didn't mind. She would never have thought of walking anywhere in Oklahoma but here, it seemed pretty common as lots of people were walking in various directions. When she entered the café, it wasn't terribly busy, but Jack waved like she wouldn't be able to see him. She walked over to the table by the window, noticing the brushed wood décor and the simple, bohemian-type tables and decided she liked it.

Jack rose and held out his hand, and she shook it. "Thanks for meeting me."

She gave him a quick smile. "Kelly really likes you."

"We have a fantastic brother-sister type relationship. We rib each other relentlessly, but I think she's one of the finest archeologists I've ever worked with."

"I can see why." Shawn could easily picture Kelly's excitement when they'd begun recovering artifacts.

"I've been told you have little patience for small talk, so I'll just dive right in, if that's okay?" He sipped his drink and waited for her to order a bottle of water, then smiled. "As you know, I tapped you for the Alaska job. You and Bree, because of the damn fine work you set up in Oklahoma. Your reputation is stellar and well-earned."

Shawn didn't say anything. That was all true.

"Right. Moving on. You created something special in Oklahoma.

Something unusual and useful to the field of archeology in general. We've got some money here in London to develop something new, and I think you'd be the right person to bring it to life. I'd like you to replicate what you've done in Oklahoma. Build your own unit. Hire your own team. I'd be there to give any help you needed, but it would be entirely in your hands."

Astounded at the offer, Shawn wasn't sure what to say. "But I'd have to move."

He tilted his head. "Well, yes. You'd need to live here while you got set up. We'd get you a work visa."

"What about my department back home?" She knew the answer. She'd already put it into play.

"I understand Bree was an incredible asset and your second-in-command. Could she handle it as interim director?"

Shawn nodded and spun a fork in slow circles on the table. "I have a cat."

"Um. Okay. Well, we'll arrange for the cat to come with you."

She wasn't sure why she'd mentioned the cat. It had just come out. "Does Kelly know about this offer?"

"No." He leaned back and smiled as though he understood something she didn't. "It wouldn't have been professional to tell her before making you the offer, and I understand you're a stickler for things being done correctly."

Was that reputation a good thing? He was offering her a huge job, so it must be. "I need to think about it. I never make decisions like this without working it through."

"Nor would I expect you to. Here's the information, including salary, holiday time, things like that, as well as what we're offering as a relocation package. If you decide to tell Kelly, then I imagine she can help you with finding a place suitable to your needs." He shrugged. "That's it. That's my spiel. Any questions?"

There would undoubtedly be many of them later but right now, she couldn't think of any. "When do you need my answer?"

"Well, the sooner the better, obviously, but if you could let me know by the end of next week, that would be great. In the meantime, if you have any questions, want a tour of the facility where you'd be working, or just need the names of some really great take-aways, give me a call." He stood and held out his hand. "And please make sure that if Kelly needs anything at all, she calls me."

Shawn shook his hand. "Thank you. Really. I'm a little overwhelmed."

His laugh filled the small café. "I imagine you are. I felt the same when they offered me the position here. Happy to share my experience if you decide you want to talk it through."

She watched him leave and then checked her watch. She still had some time on her hands before she could see Kelly. A good walk might help her clear her mind, not that she'd ever considered that option before. First though, she got a coffee to go for Kelly, so she could finally have something decent. She headed out into the damp, chilly air and watched for a moment as some electricians strung lights between lampposts, probably in preparation for the holiday season, which felt like it was fast approaching given the wintery weather. She wandered the streets near the hospital, noticing architecture and how it felt being there. There was a tiny park with a few benches on some grass, and she stopped on one to consider what had happened. Her phone buzzed in her pocket, and she answered without looking at the screen.

"Hello."

"Your mother's dead. Her kidneys gave out and other shit happened because of it. If you'd gone for the test, maybe this wouldn't have happened. But we'll never know, will we? You'd better get your ass to her funeral on Tuesday, or I'll send your brothers over to drag you there."

Her father hung up without her saying a word.

Mom's dead.

She stared at her phone, the words ringing in her head. But she felt...nothing. What should she feel? Loss, grief, anger. *Something.* But she felt less than she would if she'd been told the milk she liked was out of stock. It was a fact devoid of emotional attachment. Right now, anyway. Maybe it would hit her harder later.

She got up and headed toward the hospital. By the time she got to Kelly's floor, she should be able to go right in. As she made her way through it, down stark halls and people in hospital gowns, her thoughts went to her mom. Had she suffered? They hadn't called to say she was even in the hospital, let alone about to die. Had the family gathered around her? Probably. They'd likely been praying and saying things like, "When it's your time, it's your time," while complaining loudly about Shawn not doing her duty.

"Shawn?" Kelly's mom touched her arm, pulling her from her thoughts.

"Hi. Sorry. I was thinking about something." She gave her a quick smile. Kelly was the spitting image of her mom. Long, lustrous hair, a trim physique and an open, kind face that made Shawn momentarily think of telling her the news. But she'd long since learned not to overshare, that people were put off by it.

"Anything we can help with? After all you've done, we'll be there for you come hell or high water." She hooked her arm through Shawn's, and they walked together towards Kelly's room.

"I don't think so but thank you. It's been a morning full of surprises." Her heart leapt when she saw Kelly sitting up in bed, laughing with her dad. She was so achingly beautiful. What would she think of Shawn's news? Would she be put off by Shawn's inability to feel anything at the death of her mother? Would she be glad that Shawn might be staying in London, or would it feel like pressure? What if she wasn't ready for them to have that kind of proximity?

"I know that look." Kelly held out her hand and beckoned Shawn over. "What's bouncing around that big brain of yours?"

"So many things. How are you feeling?" Shawn pressed Kelly's hand to her face, needing the contact.

"A lot better actually. I felt dire last night, but I feel like a new person today." She still sounded a little hoarse, but her color was better and her eyes even brighter. "I can't wait to get out of here." She looked at the coffee cup in Shawn's hand. "Please tell me that's for me."

Shawn had forgotten she was carrying it. "Yes, of course. I asked the nurse yesterday. You can have small amounts of caffeine, but not too much so it doesn't mess with your brain. So you've only got a little one, but I thought it would be better than nothing."

Kelly sighed in appreciation after taking a sip. "You're a god among women, my love."

Shawn flushed when Kelly's parents looked at one another. "She loves me. She told me so yesterday." Why? Why did she say that out loud?

Kelly laughed, and her parents followed suit.

"It's about time." Kelly's dad slapped her on the back. "And I think she's made a damn fine choice." He turned to Kelly's mom. "Let's go get ourselves a cup of tea and let them talk for a minute, shall we?" He winked at Shawn as they left. "No funny business while we're gone."

Shawn felt her face heat. "God, no. Not here."

Kelly laughed and squeezed her hand. "He's winding you up, love. Teasing you."

Shawn let out a breath and sat down. "Are you okay to talk for a minute?"

"Of course. Is something wrong?" Kelly's smile dimmed.

"No. Yes. I don't know." Shawn ran her hand through her hair. "Jack offered me a job and my mom died."

Kelly blinked rapidly for a second. "Okay. Let's start with the big one first. Your mom died? When?"

"I don't know, actually. My dad called just before I came to see you to say she's gone, and he wants me at the funeral. I don't know why. Probably so they have someone to poop on the whole time." That was exactly why, she realized. It had nothing to do with familial love or affection at a time of need. "I've always been the scapegoat, and because I didn't get tested and wasn't there at the end, they blame me."

"Your kidneys don't suddenly give out, Shawn. She has to have been sick for a very long time. You know that, right?"

Shawn nodded, but it was a relief to hear it out loud. "I know."

"And how are you feeling?" Kelly shifted as though trying to look at her more closely.

"About that?" She pressed her lips tight, then spilled it. "Nothing. I hope you don't think I'm a monster. You know emotion and I aren't huge friends. But I don't feel anything at all. It's like hearing about someone you kind of knew once upon a time. I mean, it didn't even occur to me to tell them I was in the hospital, and Bree is my emergency contact. She knew not to call them." She finally met Kelly's gaze. "Do you love me less because of it?"

Kelly's gaze was soft and sweet. "Love, your family aren't nice people, to put it mildly. They hurt you deeply, and it doesn't sound like they care about that. The fact that you're not grieving your mother's death isn't surprising. You might, one day, or you might not. Either way, that wouldn't stop me loving you."

Shawn blew out a breath. "Thank you."

"And the other thing? What's this about Jack offering you a job?"

Shawn was able to smile now as a feeling of excitement began to well up. "He wants me to replicate the system I built in Oklahoma here in London." She searched Kelly's eyes, hoping to see and understand how she'd feel about the news. "I'd have to move here."

Kelly's eyes grew big and then her smile widened as she began to laugh. "Yes! The Universe heard my request for help to keep you at my side." She paused, looking suspicious. "You're going to take it, aren't you?"

Shawn nodded slowly. "I think so. It feels like an impossible change, but I like the idea of being here with you while you recover, and I enjoyed the challenge of building the department in Oklahoma. It would be more challenging in a culture and city I don't know, and that appeals to me...strangely. Obviously I still want things to be stable, and I'll have to adjust to a new routine, but I can do that." She ran her thumb over Kelly's knuckles. "And it would give us time to be together without worrying about dying."

Kelly tapped the bedrail in frustration. "Put this down, would you?"

Shawn complied and wrapped her arms around Kelly when she shifted to hug her.

"This is incredible news, and Jack is one of my new favorite people on earth. Mum and Dad will be happy to hear it too. I've been complaining about the fact that planes don't go fast enough for me to see you all the time."

Shawn leaned back to look at her. "You've been talking to your parents about me?"

"And anyone else who will listen." Kelly rested her head against Shawn's chest. "I meant to ask you. Why didn't you tell anyone about what we found in the ice cave? Jack would be wetting himself."

Shawn grimaced. "That's not a nice image. I didn't want to tell anyone without talking to you about it first. We found it together, so we should tell people together. Is that okay?" Once again she was reminded of her ineptness when it came to peopling.

"It's so you to think about that. Thank you." She tapped Shawn's pocket. "Send him a video now, and let's see how he reacts."

Shawn did as requested and within seconds, her phone was buzzing. She smiled as she put it on speaker phone.

"Unfuckingbelievable!" he shouted. "How did you not tell me this before? Do you have more?"

"Lots more." Shawn laid her hand against Kelly's soft hair as she rested her head on Shawn's chest again. "We found it about halfway through the cave system. I'm hoping I took enough to develop some solid reproductions and analysis."

"Fucking hell. If I didn't already know I'd made the right decision in trying to poach you from America, I sure as hell know it now. Send me everything you've got!" He hung up without saying more.

"I think we've just made his day." Kelly smiled but didn't lift her head.

"What we could see was only a fragment of what was probably under there. But it's better than nothing, right?" Shawn stepped back and eased Kelly back into bed when it seemed like she'd slumped a little.

"Hey, fragments make up a whole picture eventually." Kelly didn't let go of her hand, though she did settle into the pillows.

Shawn cupped Kelly's cheek, wondering how her chest could feel so full without bursting. "I feel like I was fragments of a picture before you. Now the picture is becoming complete." She laughed softly. "That sounds cheesy, doesn't it?"

Kelly nuzzled against Shawn's palm. "It sounds perfect. Fragments of a heart that we've put together to create something special."

They talked about the job offer, and Shawn showed her the file Jack had given her. Kelly made notes on it, telling her to negotiate for some things that Shawn wouldn't have thought of. She'd have to talk to Bree about the new position, but she knew full well it wouldn't be an issue and that Bree would be happy for her. Not being around her family anymore held an undeniable appeal too.

Kelly's parents came in, and they shared the news. Her parents were immediately on board and suggesting places she needed to see and where to go. The warmth of acceptance and kindness enveloped her, and she knew deep down that this was where she was meant to be. Together, they'd build a life where they could be themselves in every way, helping each other grow and continue the adventures that suited them both. Love would be the biggest adventure, and Shawn couldn't wait to get started.

EPILOGUE

"To the left. A little more. Too much. An inch, maybe. That's good." Shawn turned away from the people moving the table to look at the florists.

"Babe." Kelly stepped in front of her, blocking her view. She cupped her cheeks and kissed her lightly. "Let these people do their job while you help me in the foyer." In truth, Kelly didn't need help. But she was fairly certain more than one of the crew setting up outside were going to quit if Shawn became any more specific with what she wanted.

"It needs to be perfect." Shawn wrapped her arms around Kelly's waist. "Don't think I don't know what you're doing."

"Then let me do it. Come on." She took Shawn's hand and led her inside. "As long as you and I are there, it's going to be perfect."

"Well, and Bree and Chay."

"If they aren't there, it won't be nearly as perfect. That's true." Kelly laughed. "Have you been upstairs to see how Bree is doing?"

Shawn shook her head vehemently. "This is where our butch-femme roles come in handy. You go deal with the stressed-out bride. I'll deal with the too calm other bride."

Kelly kissed her and pulled her close by her tux lapels. "Pay close attention to how it's done so we can outdo them when it's our turn."

Shawn kissed her back and ran her finger over Kelly's engagement ring. "I didn't know it was a competition."

"Silly goose. It's always a competition." Kelly winked and put a little more sway into her hips as she headed upstairs, knowing full well how much Shawn liked the slinky, rose-colored dress Bree had chosen for her maid of honor. She could swear she heard Shawn whimper a little behind her.

She opened the door to Bree's room. "Haven't eloped or run off then?"

Bree looked at her with such a stricken expression that Kelly's stomach dropped. "What's wrong? What is it?"

"Does my lipstick look orange? I feel like it looks orange and is washing me out. And my heels hurt my feet almost as soon as I put them on." Bree went to touch her hair and then clearly thought better of it. "I think I'm going to vomit."

Kelly laughed and pressed Bree into a chair. "Breathe. Feel the carpet under your feet. Smell the gorgeous roses of your bouquet. Listen to the breeze blowing the windchimes outside."

Slowly, Bree's breathing settled. "Thank you," she whispered. "I admit, I'm feeling a little overwhelmed and alone."

Kelly's heart ached for her. Bree's mother had wanted to come but simply couldn't overcome her fears. Over the last year, Bree had moved beyond those fears thanks to Chay and therapy, and they no longer ran her life. But that meant the wedding in London didn't include anyone on the bride's side of the aisle. It would be the same for Shawn, who had sent a final message to her family to tell them not to contact her ever again, and the unburdening had clearly healed some old wounds.

London had become a de facto base for all of them. Bree and Chay had often come over to visit, and Bree had worked beside Shawn occasionally as she'd set up the new department, which was already in global demand.

Kelly had gladly stepped in to help with wedding plans, and they'd done most of it together when she'd returned from her dig in Egypt. She'd flown home more regularly than she would have done in the past—now she had a woman she adored waiting for her and friends who made it even more fun.

"Five minutes," someone called from the other side of the door.

Bree's eyes widened, and Kelly took her hands.

"You look stunning. You're ready for this. And fuck the heels. Go barefoot so you can concentrate completely on the woman you're about to tie yourself to for all eternity."

Bree giggled, and her shoulders relaxed. "That isn't very proper."

"Who would see? Your dress covers your feet, and you're shorter than Chay no matter what. This is your day. Own it." Kelly had already planned on wearing flats for her big day with Shawn, but now she thought she might go barefoot too. Shawn was still self-conscious about being shorter than Kelly.

"You ready?" Kelly pulled Bree to her feet.

Bree hugged her tightly. "Thank you for being so wonderful. Shawn is happier than I've ever seen her. I miss her so much back home, but knowing she's happy is amazing. And you're the sister I never had."

Kelly hugged her back. "Enough of the mushy stuff. Come on."

They headed down the hotel stairs to the doors leading into the event room. She kissed Bree's cheek, then started the walk down the aisle toward Chay and Shawn, who stood at the front, already waiting.

Her heart felt like it could burst when she looked into Shawn's eyes and saw the love shining from them. She looked so handsome in her tux. Kelly couldn't wait to be making this walk in Bree's position. For now, she smiled at Chay, who'd become the kind of friend you only had once in a lifetime. Their little unit, forged under the worst circumstances, had become inseparable.

She stepped to the side and only looked away from Shawn when the music changed and Bree walked down the aisle, her train trailing behind her, her toes occasionally peeking out from beneath the satin gown. Chay laughed softly, clearly having noticed, and Shawn grinned too.

The ceremony was beautiful and brief. Neither of them had wanted someone droning on, and when they kissed and Bree raised her bouquet in victory, Kelly wondered how it was possible to be this happy. She'd come to realize that she'd only been content before, floating through life without any tether. Now, life was as beautiful as the borealis she and Shawn had watched through the peephole in the ice.

Later, after the photos and speeches, she rested her head against Shawn's as they danced.

"I love you, Kelly," Shawn whispered against her hair. "You look amazing, in case I didn't make it clear already."

Kelly leaned away to look into her eyes. "Oh, the way you looked at me let me know that, I assure you. And you'd better already be thinking of ways to get me out of this dress."

Shawn grinned, and her grip tightened a little. "I think I'll keep you in it first. Then take you out of it later for more."

"Promises make me happy." She twirled as Shawn turned her and pulled her back into her arms.

"I promise—"

"No." Kelly put her finger to Shawn's lips. "Save the beautiful words for our own wedding day."

Shawn bit the tip of Kelly's finger. "Whatever you say, boss."

They danced the night away, surrounded by love and laughter. London had become the place they lived, but their home was wherever they were, and Kelly couldn't think of a better location than that.

THE END

Thank you for reading *Fragments of the Heart*. If you enjoyed Kelly and Shawn's sweet romance, it'd be wonderful if you would take a moment to put a review on Amazon! And if this is your first book of mine, maybe you'd like to try my first romance novel, *Where the Heart Leads*. It's a celebrity romance, single mom story with hot chemistry.

Happy reading.
Ally

Other Great Butterworth Books

Here You Are by Jo Fletcher
Can they unlock their hearts to find the true happiness they both deserve?
Available on Amazon (ASIN B0CBN935ZB)

Stunted Heart by Helena Harte
A stunt rider who lives in the fast lane. An ER doctor who can't take chances. A passion that could turn their worlds upside down.
Available on Amazon (ASIN B0C78GSWBV)

Dark Haven by Brey Willows
Even vampires get tired of playing with their food...
Available on Amazon (ASIN B0C5P1HJXC)

Green for Love by E.V. Bancroft
All's fair in love and eco-war.
Available from Amazon (ASIN B0C28F7PX5)

Call of Love by Lee Haven
Separated by fear. Reunited by fate. Will they get a second chance at life and love?
Available from Amazon (ASIN B09CLK91N5)

Where the Heart Leads by Ally McGuire
A writer. A celebrity. And a secret that could break their hearts.
Available on Amazon (ASIN B0BWFX5W9L)

Stolen Ambition by Robyn Nyx
Daughters of two worlds collide in a dangerous game of ambition and love.
Available on Amazon (ASIN B0BS1PRSCN)

Cabin Fever by Addison M Conley
She goes for the money, but will she stay for something deeper?
Available on Amazon (ASIN B0BQWY45GH)

Zamira Saliev: A Dept. 6 Operation by Valden Bush
They're both running from their pasts. Together, they might make a new future.
Available from Amazon (ASIN B0BHJKHK6S)

What's Your Story?

Global Wordsmiths, CIC, provides an all-encompassing service for all writers, ranging from basic proofreading and cover design to development editing, typesetting, and eBook services. A major part of our work is charity and community focused, delivering writing projects to under-served and under-represented groups across Nottinghamshire, giving voice to the voiceless and visibility to the unseen.

To learn more about what we offer, visit: www.globalwords.co.uk

A selection of books by Global Words Press:
Desire, Love, Identity: with the National Justice Museum
Aventuras en México: Farmilo Primary School
Times Past: with The Workhouse, National Trust
Young at Heart with AGE UK
In Different Shoes: Stories of Trans Lives

Self-published authors working with Global Wordsmiths:
Steve Bailey
Ravenna Castle
Jackie D
CJ DeBarra
Dee Griffiths
Iona Kane
Maggie McIntyre
Emma Nichols
Dani Lovelady Ryan
Erin Zak

Made in the USA
Middletown, DE
09 September 2024

60628378R00156